lbert Camus was born in Algeria in 1913. The works that established his
ternational reputation include *The Rebel*, *The Myth of Sisyphus*, *The Out-
der*, *The Plague* and *The Fall*. His last novel, *The First Man*, unfinished at
ne time his death, appeared for the first time in 1994 and was an instant
b stseller. Camus died in a road accident in 1960.

R bin Buss has translated several works for Penguin, including a selection
of writings by Sartre and the forthcoming new Penguin edition of Henri
Ba busse's *Under Fire*. He has also written books on the French and Italian
ci ema.

Tony Judt teaches at New York University. He is the author of *Past Imperfect:
French Intellectuals 1944–1956* and *The Burden of Responsibility: Blum,
Camus, Aron and the French Twentieth Century*.

ALBERT CAMUS

The Plague

Translated by Robin Buss
with an Introduction by Tony Judt

PENGUIN BOOKS

PENGUIN BOOKS

Published by the Penguin Group
Penguin Books Ltd, 80 Strand, London WC2R ORL, England
Penguin Putnam Inc., 375 Hudson Street, New York, New York 10014, USA
Penguin Books Australia Ltd, 250 Camberwell Road, Camberwell, Victoria 3124, Australia
Penguin Books Canada Ltd, 10 Alcorn Avenue, Toronto, Ontario, Canada M4V 3B2
Penguin Books India (P) Ltd, 11, Community Centre, Panchsheel Park, New Delhi – 110 017, India
Penguin Books (NZ) Ltd, Cnr Rosedale and Airborne Roads, Albany, Auckland, New Zealand
Penguin Books (South Africa) (Pty) Ltd, 24 Sturdee Avenue, Rosebank 2196, South Africa

Penguin Books Ltd, Registered Offices: 80 Strand, London WC2R ORL, England

www.penguin.com

La Peste first published 1947
This translation first published by Allen Lane The Penguin Press 2001
Published in Penguin Classics 2002
1

Copyright © Gallimard (Paris) 1947
Translation copyright © Robin Buss, 2001
Introduction copyright © Tony Judt, 2001
All rights reserved

The moral right of the translator and of the author of the introduction has been asserted

Printed in England by Clays Ltd, St Ives plc

Contents

Introduction

The Plague is Albert Camus's most successful novel. It was published in 1947, when Camus was thirty-three, and was an immediate triumph. Within a year it had been translated into nine languages, with many more to come. It has never been out of print and was established as a classic of world literature even before its author's untimely death in a car accident in January 1960. More ambitious than *L'Etranger*, the first novel that established his reputation, and more accessible than his later writings, *The Plague* is the book by which Camus is known to millions of readers. He might have found this odd – *The Rebel*, published four years later, was his personal favourite among his books – but then authors are not perhaps well-placed to judge.

The Plague was a long time in the writing, like much of Camus's best work. He started gathering material for it in January 1941, when he arrived in Oran, the Algerian coastal town where the story is set. He continued working on the manuscript in Le Chambon-sur-Lignon, a mountain village in central France where he went to recuperate from one of his periodic bouts of tuberculosis in the summer of 1942. But Camus was soon swept into the Resistance and it was not until the liberation of France that he was able to return his attention to the book. By then, however, the obscure Algerian novelist had become a national figure: a hero of the intellectual Resistance, editor of *Combat* (a daily paper born in clandestinity and hugely influential in the post-war years) and an icon to a new generation of French men and women hungry for ideas and idols.

Camus seemed to fit the role to perfection. Handsome and charming, a charismatic advocate of radical social and political change, he held unparalleled sway over millions of his countrymen. In the words of Raymond Aron, readers of Camus's editorials had 'formed the habit of getting their daily thought from him'.[1] There were other intellectuals in post-war Paris who were destined to play major roles in years to come: Aron himself, Simone de Beauvoir and of course Jean-Paul Sartre. But Camus was different. Born in Algeria in 1913, he was younger than his left-bank friends, most of whom were already forty years old when the war ended. He was more exotic, coming as he did from distant Algiers rather than from the hothouse milieu of Parisian schools and colleges; and there was something special about him. One contemporary observer caught it well: 'I was struck by his face, so human and sensitive. There is in this man such an obvious integrity that it imposes respect almost immediately; quite simply, he is not like other men.'[2]

Camus's public standing guaranteed his book's success. But its timing had something to do with it too. By the time the book appeared, the French were beginning to forget the discomforts and compromises of four years of German occupation. Marshal Philippe Pétain, the head of state who initiated and incarnated the policy of collaboration with the victorious Nazis, had been tried and imprisoned. Other collaborating politicians had been executed or else banished from public life. The myth of a glorious national resistance was carefully cultivated by politicians of all colours, from Charles de Gaulle to the Communists; uncomfortable private memories were soothingly displaced by the airbrushed official version, in which France had been liberated from its oppressors by the joint efforts of domestic resisters and Free French troops led from London by de Gaulle.

In this context, Albert Camus's allegory of the wartime occupation of France reopened a painful chapter in the recent French past, but in an indirect and ostensibly apolitical key. It thus avoided arousing partisan hackles, except at the extremes of Left and Right, and took up sensitive topics without provoking a refusal to listen. Had the novel appeared in 1945, the angry, partisan mood of revenge would have drowned its moderate reflections on justice and responsibility. Had it been delayed until the 1950s its subject-matter would probably have been overtaken by new alignments born of the Cold War.

Whether *The Plague* should be read, as it surely was read, as a simple allegory of France's wartime trauma is a subject to which I shall return. What is beyond doubt is that it was an intensely personal book. Camus put something of himself – his emotions, his memories and his sense of place – into all his published work; that is one of the ways in which he stood apart from other intellectuals of his generation and it accounts for his universal and lasting appeal. But even by his standards *The Plague* is strikingly introspective and revealing. Oran was a town he knew well and cordially disliked, in contrast to his much-loved home town of Algiers. He found it boring and materialistic and his memories of it were further shaped by the fact that his tuberculosis took a turn for the worse during his stay there. As a result he was forbidden to swim – one of his greatest pleasures – and was constrained to sit around for weeks on end in the stifling, oppressive heat that provides the backdrop to the story.

This involuntary deprivation of everything that Camus most loved about his Algerian birthplace – the sand, the sea, physical exercise and the Mediterranean sense of ease and liberty that he always contrasted with the gloom and grey of the north – was compounded when he was sent to the French countryside to convalesce. The Massif Central of France is tranquil and bracing, and the remote village where Camus arrived in August 1942 might be thought the ideal setting for a writer. But twelve weeks later, in November, the Allies landed in North Africa. The Germans responded by occupying the whole of southern France (hitherto governed from the spa town of Vichy by Pétain's puppet government) and Algeria was cut off from the continent. Camus was thenceforth separated not just from his homeland but also from his mother and his wife, and would not see them again until the Germans had been defeated.[3]

Illness, exile and separation were thus present in Camus's life as in his novel, and his reflections upon them form a vital counterpoint to the allegory. Because of his acute first-hand experience, Camus's descriptions of the plague and of the pain of loneliness are exceptionally vivid and heartfelt. It is indicative of his own depth of feeling that the narrator remarks early in the story that 'the first thing that the plague brought to our fellow-citizens was exile' (p. 56), and that 'being separated from a loved one . . . [was] the greatest agony of that long period of exile' (p. 53).

This in turn provides, for Camus and the reader alike, a link to his earlier novel: for disease, separation and exile are conditions that come upon us unexpectedly and unbidden. They are an illustration of what Camus meant by the 'absurdity' of the human condition and the seemingly chance nature of human undertakings. It is not by accident that he has Grand, for no apparent reason, report a conversation overheard in a tobacconist concerning 'a young company employee who had killed an Arab on a beach' (p. 43). This, of course, is an allusion to Meurseault's seminal act of random violence in *L'Etranger*, and in Camus's mind it is connected to the ravages of pestilence in *The Plague* by more than just their common Algerian setting.

But Camus did more than insert into his story vignettes and emotions drawn from his writings and his personal situation. He put himself very directly into the characters of the novel, using three of them in particular to represent and illuminate his distinctive moral perspective. Rambert, the young journalist cut off from his wife in Paris, is initially desperate to escape the quarantine town. His obsession with his personal suffering makes him indifferent to the larger tragedy, from which he feels quite detached − he is not, after all, a citizen of Oran, but was caught there by the vagaries of chance. It is on the very eve of his getaway that he realizes how, despite himself, he has become part of the community and shares its fate; ignoring the risk and in the face of his earlier, selfish needs, he remains in Oran and joins the 'health teams'. From a purely private resistance against misfortune he has graduated to the solidarity of a collective resistance against the common scourge.

Camus's identification with Dr Rieux echoes his shifting mood in these years. Rieux is a man who, faced with suffering and a common crisis, does what he must and becomes a leader and an example not out of heroic courage or careful reasoning but rather from a sort of necessary optimism. By the late 1940s Camus was exhausted and depressed by the burden of expectations placed on him as a public intellectual: as he confided to his notebooks, 'everyone wants the man who is still searching to have reached his conclusions'.[4] From the existentialist philosopher (a tag that Camus always disliked) people awaited a polished worldview; but Camus had none to offer.[5] As he expressed it through Rieux, he was 'weary of the world in which he lived'; all he could offer with any certainty was 'some feeling for his fellow men and was determined for his part to reject any injustice and any compromise' (p. 12).

Dr Rieux does the right thing just because he sees clearly what needs doing. In Tarrou, Camus invested a more developed exposition of his moral thinking. Tarrou, like Camus, is in his mid-thirties; he left home, by his own account, in disgust at his father's advocacy of the death penalty – a subject of intense concern to Camus and on which he wrote widely in the post-war years.[6] Tarrou has reflected painfully upon his past life and commitments, and his confession to Rieux is at the heart of the novel's moral message: 'I thought I was struggling against the plague. I learned that I had indirectly supported the deaths of thousands of men, that I had even caused their deaths by approving the actions and principles that inevitably led to them' (p. 193).

This passage can be read as Camus's own rueful reflections upon his passage through the Communist Party in Algeria during the 1930s. But Tarrou's conclusions go beyond the admission of political error: 'we are all in the plague . . . All I know is that one must do one's best not to be a plague victim . . . And this is why I have decided to reject everything that, directly or indirectly, makes people die or justifies others in making them die' (p. 194–5). This is the authentic voice of Albert Camus and it sketches out the position he would take towards ideological dogma, political or judicial murder and all forms of ethical irresponsibility for the rest of his life – a stance that would later cost him dearly in friends and even influence in the polarized world of the Parisian intelligentsia.

Tarrou/Camus's apologia for his refusals and his commitments returns us to the status of *The Plague*. It is a novel that succeeds at various levels as any great novel must, but it is above all and unmistakably a moral tale. Camus was much taken with *Moby Dick* and, like Melville, he was not embarrassed to endow his story with symbols and metaphors. But Melville had the luxury of moving freely back and forth from the narrative of a whale hunt to a fable of human obsession; between

Camus's Oran and the dilemma of human choice there lay the reality of life in Vichy France between 1940 and 1944. Readers of *The Plague*, today as in 1947, are therefore not wrong to approach it as an allegory of the occupation years.

In part this is because Camus makes clear that this is a story about 'us'. Most of the story is told in the third person. But strategically dispersed through the text is the occasional 'we', and the 'we' in question – at least for Camus's primary audience – is the French in 1947. The 'calamity' that has befallen the citizens of fictionalized Oran is the one that came upon France in 1940, with the military defeat, the abandonment of the Republic and the establishment of the regime of Vichy under German tutelage. Camus's account of the coming of the rats echoed a widespread view of the divided condition of France itself in 1940: 'It was as though the very soil on which our houses were built was purging itself of an excess of bile, that it was letting boils and abscesses rise to the surface, which up to then had been devouring it inside' (p. 15). Many in France, at first, shared Father Paneloux's initial reaction: '"my brethren, you have deserved it"' (p. 73).

For a long time people don't realize what is happening and life seems to go on – 'In appearance, nothing had changed' (p. 49), 'The town was inhabited by people asleep on their feet' (p. 141). Later, when the plague has passed, amnesia sets in – 'they denied that we [*sic*] had been that benumbed people' (p. 229). All this and much more – the black market, the failure of administrators to call things by their name and assume the moral leadership of the nation – so well described the recent French past that Camus's intentions could hardly be misread.

Nevertheless, most of Camus's targets resist easy labels, and the allegory runs quite against the grain of the polarized moral rhetoric in use after the war. Cottard, who accepts the plague as too strong to combat and who thinks the health teams are a waste of time, is clearly someone who 'collaborates' in the fate of the town. He thrives in the new situation and has everything to lose from a return to the 'old ways'. But he is sympathetically drawn, and Tarrou and the others continue to frequent him and even discuss with him their actions. All they ask, in Tarrou's words, is that he 'try not to spread the microbe knowingly' (p. 122).

At the end Cottard is brutally beaten by the newly liberated citizenry – a reminder of the violent punishments meted out at the Liberation to presumed collaborators, often by men and women whose enthusiasm for violent revenge helped them and others forget their own wartime compromises. Camus's insight into the anger and resentment born of genuine suffering and guilty memory introduces a nuance of empathy that was rare among his contemporaries and it lifts his story clear of the conventions of the time.

The same insights (and integrity – Camus was writing from personal experience) shape his representation of the resisters themselves. It is not by chance that Grand, the mousy, downtrodden unaspiring clerk, is presented as the embodiment of the real, unheroic resistance. For Camus, as for Rieux, resistance was not about heroism at all – or, if it was, then it was the heroism of goodness. 'It may seem a ridiculous idea, but the only way to fight the plague is with decency' (p. 125). Joining the health teams was not in itself an act of great significance – rather, 'not doing it would have been incredible at the time' (p. 101). This point is made over and over again in the novel, as though Camus were worried lest it be missed: 'when you see the suffering it brings,' Rieux remarks at one point, 'you have to be mad, blind or a coward to resign yourself to the plague' (p. 96).

Camus, like the narrator, refuses to 'become an over-eloquent eulogist of a determination and heroism to which he attaches only a moderate degree of importance' (p. 101). This has to be understood in context. There was of course tremendous courage and sacrifice in the French resistance; many men and women died for the cause. But Camus was uncomfortable with the smug myth of heroism that had grown up in post-war France, and he abhorred the tone of moral superiority with which self-styled former Resisters (including some of his famous fellow intellectuals) looked down upon those who did nothing. In Camus's view it was inertia, or ignorance, which accounted for people's failure to act. The Cottards of the world were the exception; most people are better than you think – as Tarrou puts it, 'You just need to give them the opportunity' (p. 115).[7]

In consequence, some of Camus's intellectual contemporaries did not particularly care for *The Plague*. They expected a more 'engaged' sort of writing from him and they found the book's ambiguities and the tone of disabused tolerance and moderation politically incorrect. Simone de Beauvoir especially disapproved strongly of Camus's use of a natural pestilence as a substitute for (she thought) Fascism – it relieves men of their political responsibilities, she insisted, and runs away from History and real political problems.[8] Even today this criticism sometimes surfaces among academic students of Camus: he lets Fascism and Vichy off the hook, they charge, by deploying the metaphor of a 'nonideological and nonhuman plague'.[9]

Such commentaries are doubly revealing. In the first place they show just how much Camus's apparently straightforward story was open to misunderstanding. The allegory may have been tied to Vichy France but the 'plague' transcends political labels. It was not Fascism that Camus was aiming at – an easy target, after all, especially in 1947 – but dogma, conformity, compliance and cowardice in all their intersecting public forms. Tarrou, after all, is no Fascist; but he insists that in earlier days, when he complied with doctrines that authorized the suffering of others for higher goals, he too was a carrier of the plague even as he fought it.

Secondly, the charge that Camus was too ambiguous in his judgements, too unpolitical in his metaphors, illuminates not his weaknesses but his strengths. This is something that we are perhaps better placed to understand now than were *The Plague*'s first readers. Thanks to Primo Levi and Vaclav Havel we have become familiar with the 'grey zone'. We understand better that in conditions of extremity there are rarely to be found comfortingly simple categories of good and evil, guilty and innocent. We know more about the choices and compromises faced by men and women in hard times, and we are no longer so quick to judge those who accommodate themselves to impossible situations. Men may do the right thing from a mixture of motives and may with equal ease do terrible deeds with the best of intentions – or no intentions at all.

It does not follow from this that the plagues that humankind brings down upon itself are 'natural' or unavoidable. But assigning responsibility for them – and thus preventing them in the future – may not be an easy matter. And with Hannah Arendt we have been introduced to a further complication: the notion of the 'banality of evil' (a formulation that Camus himself would probably have taken care to avoid), the idea that unspeakable crimes can be committed by very unremarkable men with clear consciences.[10]

These are now commonplaces of moral and historical debate. But Albert Camus came to them first, in his own words, with an originality of perspective and intuition that eluded almost all his contemporaries. That is what they found so disconcerting in his writing. Camus was a moralist who unhesitatingly distinguished good from evil but abstained from condemning human frailty. He was a student of the 'absurd' who refused to give in to necessity.[11] He was a public man of action, who insisted that all truly important questions came down to individual acts of kindness and goodness. And, like Tarrou, he was a believer in absolute truths who accepted the limits of the possible: 'Other men will make history . . . All I say is that on this earth there are pestilences and there are victims – and as far as possible one must refuse to be on the side of the pestilence' (p. 195)

Thus *The Plague* teaches no lessons. Camus was a *moraliste* but he was no moralizer. He claimed to have taken great care to try and avoid writing a tract, and to the extent that his novel offers little comfort to political polemicists of any school he can be said to have succeeded. But for that very reason it has not merely outlived its origins as an allegory of occupied France but has transcended its era. Looking back on the grim record of the twentieth century we can see more clearly now that Albert Camus had identified the central moral dilemmas of the age. Like Hannah Arendt, he saw that 'the problem of evil will be the fundamental question of post-war intellectual life in Europe – as death became the fundamental question after the last war'.[12]

Fifty years after its first appearance, in an age of post-totalitarian satisfaction with our condition and prospects, when intellectuals pronounce the End of History and politicians proffer globalization as a universal palliative, the closing sentence of Camus's great novel rings truer than ever, a firebell in the night of complacency and forgetting: '[Rieux] knew that . . . the plague bacillus never dies or vanishes entirely

... it can remain dormant for dozens of years in furniture or clothing ... it waits patiently in bedrooms, cellars, trunks, handkerchiefs and old papers, and ... perhaps the day will come when, for the instruction or misfortune of mankind, the plague will rouse its rats and send them to die in some well-contented city.'

Notes

1. Raymond Aron, *Aron's Memoires* (Paris, Julliard, 1983), p. 208.

2. Julien Green, *Journal*, 20 February 1948, quoted in Olivier Todd, *Albert Camus: Une vie* (Paris, Gallimard, 1996), pp. 419–20.

3. The literary editor Jean Paulhan, meeting Camus in Paris in January 1943, noted how he 'suffered' from his inability to return to Algiers, to 'his wife and his climate'. Jean Paulhan to Raymond Guérin, 6 January 1943, in Paulhan, *Choix de lettres, 1937–1945* (Paris, Gallimard, 1992), p. 298.

4. Albert Camus, *Essais*, ed. Roger Quilliot (Paris, Gallimard, 1965), p. 861.

5. 'I am not a philosopher and I never claimed to be one', in 'Entretien sur la révolte', *Gazette des lettres*, 15 February 1952.

6. In his posthumous autobiographical novel, *Le Premier homme* (Paris, Gallimard, 1995), Camus writes of his own father coming home after watching a public execution and vomiting.

7. It is worth noting here that it was in Le Chambon-sur-Lignon, the very same mountain village where Camus was convalescing in 1942–3, that the local Protestant community united behind their pastor to save the lives of a large number of Jews who took refuge among the remote inaccessible farms and hamlets. This uncommon act of collective courage, sadly rare in those years, offers a historical counterpoint to Camus's narrative of moral choice – and a confirmation of his intuitions about human decency. See Philip Hallie, *Lest Innocent Blood Be Shed: The Story of the Village of Le Chambon and How Goodness Happened There* (New York, Harper & Row, 1979).

8. Simone de Beauvoir, *La Force des choses* (Paris, Gallimard, 1963), p. 144.

9. Susan Dunn, *The Death of Louis XVI: Regicide and the French Political Imagination* (Princeton University Press, 1994), p. 150.

10. See Hannah Arendt, *Eichmann in Jerusalem: A Report on the Banality of Evil* (Harmondsworth, Penguin, 1994). The point is well-illustrated in Christopher Browning's study of mass murder on the Eastern Front in World War Two:

Ordinary Men: Reserve Police Battalion 101 and the Final Solution in Poland (New York, Harper, 1992).

11. In an early review (1938) of Jean-Paul Sartre's *La Nausée*, written long before they met, Camus observed: 'The mistake of a certain sort of writing is to believe that because life is wretched it is tragic . . . To announce the absurdity of existence cannot be an objective, merely a starting point.' See 'L'Enigme' in Camus, *Essais*, pp. 859–67.

12. Hannah Arendt, 'Nightmare and Flight', *Partisan Review* 12, ii (1945), reprinted in *Essays in Understanding: 1930–1954*, ed. Jerome Kohn (New York, Harcourt Brace, 1994), p. 133.

The Plague

Part I

It is as reasonable to represent one kind of imprisonment by another, as it is to represent anything that really exists by that which exists not.

DANIEL DEFOE

The peculiar events that are the subject of this history occurred in 194–, in Oran. The general opinion was that they were misplaced there, since they deviated somewhat from the ordinary. At first sight, indeed, Oran is an ordinary town, nothing more than a French Prefecture* on the coast of Algeria.

It has to be said that the town itself is ugly. Its appearance is calm and it takes some time to appreciate what makes it different from so many other trading ports all over the world. How can one convey, for example, the idea of a town without pigeons, without trees or gardens, where you hear no beating of wings or rustling of leaves, in short, a neutral place? The change of season can only be detected in the sky. Spring declares itself solely in the quality of the air or the little baskets of flowers that street-sellers bring in from the suburbs; this is a spring that is sold in the market-place. In summer the sun burns the dried-out houses and covers their walls with grey powder; at such times one can no longer live except behind closed shutters. In autumn, on the contrary, there are inundations of mud. Fine weather arrives only with winter.

A convenient way of getting to know a town is to find out how people work there, how they love and how they die. In our little town, perhaps because of the climate, all these things are done together, with the same frenzied and abstracted air. That is to say that people are bored and that they make an effort to adopt certain habits. Our fellow-citizens work a good deal, but always in order to make money. They are especially

* Prefecture: the chief town in a *département*. In these days, Algeria was administratively part of France [translator's note].

interested in trade and first of all, as they say, they are engaged in doing business. Naturally, they also enjoy simple pleasures: they love women, the cinema and sea bathing. But they very sensibly keep these activities for Saturday evening and Sunday, while trying on other days of the week to earn a lot of money. In the evenings, when they leave their offices, they gather at a set time in cafés, they walk along the same boulevard or else they come out on their balconies. The desires of the youngest among them are short and violent, while the lives of their elders are limited to clubs for players of *boules*, dinners of friendly associations or groups where they bet heavily on the turn of a card.

You will say no doubt that this is not peculiar to our town and that, when it comes down to it, people today are all like that. Of course, there is nothing more normal nowadays than to see people work from morning to evening, then choose to waste the time they have left for living at cards, in a café or in idle chatter. But there are towns and countries where people do occasionally have an inkling of something else. On the whole, it does not change their lives; but they did have this inkling, and that is positive in itself. Oran, on the other hand, appears to be a town without inklings, that is to say, an entirely modern town. As a result it is not necessary to describe in detail how people here love one another. Men and women either consume each other rapidly in what is called the act of love, or else enter into a long-lasting, shared routine. Often there is no middle between these two extremes. That, too, is original. In Oran, as elsewhere, for want of time and thought, people have to love one another without knowing it.

Something more distinctive about our town is how difficult it can be to die there. 'Difficult' is not actually the right word; it is more a question of discomfort. It is never pleasant being ill, but there are towns and countries which support you in sickness and where one can, as it were, let oneself go. A sick person needs tenderness, he quite naturally likes to lean on something. But in Oran, the extreme climate, the amount of business going on, the insignificance of the surroundings, the speed with which night falls and the quality of pleasure, all demand good health. A sick person is very lonely here. So just think of one who is about to die, trapped behind hundreds of walls sizzling with heat, while at the same time there are all those people, on the telephone or in cafés, talking of drafts, of bills of lading and of discounts. You will understand what could be disagreeable about death, even a modern one, when it happens in such a dry place.

Even so this meagre information may give a sufficient idea of our town. In any event, one should not exaggerate. It is important to stress the ordinariness of the town and its life. But one easily passes the time away when one has a routine. To the very extent that our town encourages routine, one might say that all is for the best. Admittedly, seen like that, life is not too exciting. At least disorder is unknown among us. And our people, open, likeable and energetic, have always elicited a fair degree of respect from travellers. This town, which has nothing picturesque about it, no vegetation and no soul, comes eventually to seem restful; in short, induces sleep. But it is only fair to add that it is situated in an unrivalled countryside, in the midst of a bare plain surrounded by luminous hills, at the edge of a perfectly formed bay. One can only regret that it was built with its back turned to the bay and that, as a result, it is impossible to see the sea. You always have to go and look for it.

By now, it will be easy to accept that nothing could lead the people of our town to expect the events that took place in the spring of that year and which, as we later understood, were like the forerunners of the series of grave happenings that this history intends to describe. To some people these facts will seem quite natural; to others, on the contrary, improbable. But a chronicler cannot, after all, take account of such contradictions. His task is merely to say: 'This happened', when he knows that it did indeed happen, that it affected the life of a whole society and that there are consequently thousands of witnesses who will weigh up in their hearts the truth of what he is saying.

Moreover, the narrator, whose identity will be revealed in due course, would not have any claim to authority in an enterprise of this kind if chance had not made it possible for him to gather a considerable number of testimonies and if force of circumstance had not involved him in everything that he describes. This is what entitles him to act as a historian. Of course a historian, even if he is an amateur, always has documents. The narrator of this history has his documents: first of all, his own testimony, then that of others since, by virtue of his role in this story, he came to collect the confidences of all the characters in it; and, finally, he has written texts which he happened to acquire. He intends to borrow from them when he sees fit and to use them as he wishes. He intends . . . But perhaps it is time to have done with preliminaries and caveats, and turn to the story itself. The narrative of the early days must be given in some detail.

On the morning of April 16, Dr Bernard Rieux emerged from his consulting-room and came across a dead rat in the middle of the landing. At the time he pushed the animal aside without paying attention to it and went down the stairs. But once he was in the street it occurred to him that the rat should not have been there and he turned back to inform the concierge. Old M. Michel's reaction made him still more aware of the incongruity of his discovery. To him the presence of this dead rat had seemed merely odd, while for the concierge it was an outrage. In fact, the man was adamant: there were no rats in the house. However much the doctor assured him that there was one on the first-floor landing, probably dead, M. Michel's conviction was firm. There were no rats in the house, so this one must have been brought in from outside. In short, it was a practical joke.

That same evening Bernard Rieux was standing in the corridor of the building, looking for his keys before going up to his flat, when he saw a large rat emerge hesitantly from the dark depths of the corridor, its fur damp. The creature stopped, seemed to be trying to get its balance, stopped again, spun round and round with a faint cry and eventually fell, blood spurting from its half-open lips. The doctor looked at it for a moment, then went upstairs.

He was not thinking about the rat. That spilled blood brought him back to the subject preoccupying him at the time. His wife, who had been ill for the past year, was due to leave the next day for a sanatorium in the mountains. He found her lying in bed in their room, as he had asked her to do. She was gathering strength for the journey. She smiled.

'I'm feeling fine,' she said.

The doctor looked at the face that was turned towards him in the light of the bedside lamp. To Rieux, despite its thirty years and the marks of illness, this face was still that of a young woman, perhaps because of the smile that dispelled all the rest.

'Sleep if you can,' he said. 'The nurse will come at eleven and I'll take you to the twelve o'clock train.'

He kissed her slightly moist forehead. The smile followed him to the door.

The next day, April 17, at eight o'clock, the concierge stopped the doctor as he went past and accused some jokers of having put three dead rats in the middle of the corridor. They must have been caught with large traps because they were covered in blood. The concierge had stayed for some time on the doorstep, holding the rats by their paws and waiting for the culprits to give themselves away with a sarcastic remark. He had been disappointed.

'Oh, I'll get them in the end,' said M. Michel.

Rieux was intrigued and decided to start his rounds in the outer districts where the poorest of his patients lived. Here the rubbish was collected much later in the day and his car, driving along the straight, dusty roads of this area, brushed against boxes of rubbish lying on the edge of the pavement. In one street he drove down in this way the doctor counted a dozen rats, tipped out on the dirty rags and vegetable peelings.

He found his first patient in bed in a room overlooking the street which served both as bedroom and dining-room. The man was an old Spaniard with a tough, heavily lined face. In front of him on the blanket he had two saucepans full of chick-peas. When the doctor came in, the sick man, half-seated in the bed, leant back in an attempt to get his breath, gasping with the shingly rasping of an old asthmatic. His wife brought a basin.

'Well, doctor,' he said, while Rieux was injecting him. 'They're coming out: have you seen?'

'Yes,' said the wife. 'Our neighbour picked up three of them.'

The old man rubbed his hands.

'They're coming out. You can see them in all the dustbins. It's the hunger.'

Rieux was soon to find that the whole district was talking about the rats. When he had finished his visits he went home.

'There's a telegram for you upstairs,' said M. Michel.

The doctor asked if he had seen any more rats.

'Oh no,' the concierge answered. 'You see, I'm keeping a lookout. The pigs don't dare.'

The telegram was to tell Rieux that his mother was arriving the next day. She would be looking after her son's house while his sick wife was away. When the doctor came in the nurse was still there and he found his wife out of bed, wearing a suit and with makeup disguising her pallor. He smiled:

'Good,' he said. 'Very good.'

A short while later, at the station, he was settling her into the sleeping-car. She looked around the compartment.

'Isn't this too expensive for us?'

'A necessary expense,' Rieux said.

'What is this business about the rats?'

'I don't know. It's peculiar, but it will pass.'

Then, very quickly, he asked her to forgive him: he should have been looking after her and he had neglected her a lot. She shook her head, as though telling him to be quiet. But he added:

'Everything will be better when you come back. We'll start again.'

'Yes,' she said, her eyes shining. 'We'll start again.'

A moment later she turned away from him and stared out of the window. People were pushing and shoving each other on the platform. They could hear the hissing of the steam-engine. He called his wife by her first name and when she looked round he saw that her face was bathed in tears.

'No,' he said softly.

Her smile, slightly strained, returned beneath the tears. She sighed deeply and said:

'Go now, everything will be all right.'

He hugged her and then, on the platform, outside the window, could see nothing except her smile.

'Please,' he said. 'Take care of yourself.'

But she could not have heard him.

On the station platform near the exit Rieux ran into M. Othon, the examining magistrate, holding his little boy by the hand. The doctor asked if he was going somewhere. M. Othon, tall and dark, half-resembling what used once to be called a 'man of the world', and half an undertaker, replied in a friendly, but brisk manner:

'I'm waiting for Madame Othon who has been away paying her respects to my family.'

The engine whistled.

'Rats . . . ,' said the judge.

Rieux made a movement towards the train, then turned to leave the platform.

'Yes,' he said. 'It's nothing.'

The only thing he recorded in that moment was a station guard walking past with a packing-case full of dead rats under his arm.

On the afternoon of the same day, as he was starting his surgery, Rieux had a visit from a young man, a journalist who, he was told, had called already to see him that morning. His name was Raymond Rambert. Short, with stocky shoulders, a determined face and clear, intelligent eyes, Rambert wore sporty clothes and seemed at ease with the world. He came straight to the point. He was doing an investigation for a large Parisian newspaper about the living conditions of the Arabs and wanted information about their state of health. Rieux told him that their health was not good; but before going further, he wanted to know if the journalist could tell the truth.

'Certainly,' the other man said.

'I mean, can you make an unqualified indictment?'

'Unqualified? No, I have to say I can't. But surely there wouldn't be any grounds for unqualified criticism?'

Rieux gently answered that a total condemnation would indeed be groundless, but that he had asked the question merely because he wanted to know if Rambert's report could be made unreservedly or not.

'I can only countenance a report without reservations, so I shall not be giving you any information to contribute to yours.'

'You're talking the language of Saint Just,' the journalist said with a smile.

Without raising his voice Rieux said that he knew nothing about that, but that it was the language of a man weary of the world in which he lived, yet who still had some feeling for his fellow men and was determined for his part to reject any injustice and any compromise. Rambert, hunching his shoulders, looked at the doctor.

'I think I understand,' he said at last, getting up.

The doctor accompanied him to the door.

'Thank you for taking it like that.'

Rambert seemed irritated.

'Yes,' he said. 'I understand. Forgive me for bothering you.'

The doctor shook his hand and told him that there was an intriguing report to be written about the number of dead rats that were turning up in the town at the moment.

'Ah!' Rambert exclaimed. 'Now that does interest me.'

At five in the evening, as he was going out on a new round of house calls, the doctor passed a man on the stairs; he was young, despite his heavy build and large, pock-marked face with thick eyebrows. The doctor had met him once or twice in the flat of the Spanish dancers who lived on the top floor of the block. Jean Tarrou was earnestly smoking a cigarette, watching the last throes of a rat giving up the ghost on a stair at his feet. He looked up at the doctor with a calm, slightly insistent look in his grey eyes, said good evening and added that the appearance of these rats was a peculiar thing.

'Yes,' Rieux answered. 'But it's starting to become annoying.'

'In a sense, doctor, but only in a sense. We've never seen anything like it, that's all. But I find it interesting, yes, decidedly interesting.'

Tarrou ran a hand through his hair to push it back, took another look at the rat which was now motionless, then smiled at Rieux:

'But, when it comes down to it, doctor, it's chiefly a matter for the concierge.'

As it happened the doctor found the concierge at the entrance to the house, leaning against the wall near the front door, with an expression of weariness on his normally florid face.

'Yes, I know,' old Michel told Rieux when the latter mentioned the new discovery. 'They're turning up in twos and threes now. But it's the same in other buildings.'

He seemed worried and despondent. He was rubbing his neck in a mechanical way. Rieux asked how he felt. The concierge answered that, of course, he couldn't say he was ill, but that, even so, he was not feeling quite himself. In his view, it was a matter of morale. These rats had been a shock for him and everything would be much better once they had gone.

The next morning, however, April 18, the doctor was bringing his mother home from the station and found M. Michel looking even more poorly: from the cellar to the attic, there were a dozen rats lying on the stairs. The dustbins in the neighbouring houses were full of them. The doctor's mother was not surprised when he told her.

'Things like that happen.'

She was a little, silver-haired woman, with soft, dark eyes.

'I'm glad to see you again, Bernard,' she said. 'The rats can't change that.'

He agreed; it was true that with her everything always seemed easy.

Even so, Rieux phoned the district rodent control service, where he knew the director. Had he heard about these rats which were emerging in large numbers and dying in the open? Yes, Mercier, the director, had been informed; they had even discovered more than fifty of them in his own offices, which were not far from the port. Yet he wondered how serious it was. Rieux could not give an opinion on that, but he thought the rodent control service should do something.

'We can,' Mercier said. 'With an order. If you really think it's worthwhile, I'll try to get one.'

'I think you should,' said Rieux.

His cleaner had just told him that they had picked up several hundred dead rats in the large factory where her husband worked.

In any event, it was around this time that our townspeople started to become concerned. Indeed, from the 18th onwards, factories and warehouses began to produce hundreds of bodies of dead rats. In some cases, people were obliged to finish the creatures off, if they were taking too long to die. But, from the outskirts to the centre of the town, wherever Dr Rieux happened to go and wherever our fellow-citizens gathered, piles of rats were waiting, in the dustbins or in long rows in the gutters. That was the day the evening papers picked up the matter, asking if the civic authorities intended to do something, or not, and what emergency measures had they planned to protect the public from this disgusting infestation. The authorities had not considered or planned anything at all, but started by holding a council meeting to discuss it. An order was given to the rodent control service to collect the dead rats every morning at dawn. When the collection was over, two of the service's vans should take the animals to the waste incineration plant to have them burnt.

Despite this, in the days that followed the situation got worse. The number of rodents picked up continued to increase and the harvest was greater morning by morning. After the fourth day the rats started to emerge in groups to die. They came up from basements and cubby-holes, cellars and drains, in long swaying lines; they staggered in the light, collapsed and died, right next to people. At night, in corridors and side-streets, one could clearly hear the tiny squeaks as they expired. In the morning, on the outskirts of town, you would find them stretched out in the gutter with a little floret of blood on their pointed muzzles, some blown up and rotting, others stiff, with their whiskers still standing up. In the town itself you found them in small heaps, on landings or in the courtyards of houses. They also came to die, one by one, in council offices, in schoolyards, sometimes on the terraces of cafés. Our fellow-citizens were amazed to come across them in the busiest parts of town. The parade-ground, the boulevards and the sea-front promenade were contaminated by them at intervals. Cleared of its dead animals at dawn, the town got them back through the day in increasing numbers.

More than one person walking at night along the pavement would experience the feeling of the elastic bulk of a still fresh corpse under his feet. It was as though the very soil on which our houses were built was purging itself of an excess of bile, that it was letting boils and abscesses rise to the surface, which up to then had been devouring it inside. Just imagine the amazement of our little town which had been so quiet until then, ravaged in a few days, like a healthy man whose thick blood had suddenly rebelled against him!

Things got to the point where Infodoc (the agency for information and documentation, 'all you need to know on any subject') announced in its free radio news programme that 6,231 rats had been collected and burned in a single day, the 25th. This figure, which gave a clear meaning to the daily spectacle that everyone in town had in front of their eyes, disconcerted them even more. Up to then people had merely complained about a rather disgusting accident. Now they saw that there was something threatening in this phenomenon, the extent and origin of which was not yet clear to them. Only the asthmatic old Spaniard kept rubbing his hands and repeating, with senile delight: 'They're coming out, they're coming out!'

However, on April 28 Infodoc announced a collection of around eight thousand rats and anxiety reached its peak in the town. People called for radical measures, accusing the authorities of inaction, and some families who had seaside homes were already talking about escaping to them. But the following day the agency announced that the phenomenon had abruptly stopped and that the rodent control service had gathered only an insignificant number of dead rats. The town heaved a sigh of relief.

Yet it was on that same day, at twelve, that Dr Rieux, pulling up in his car in front of his block of flats, saw the concierge at the end of the street, walking along painfully, his head bent forward, his arms and legs akimbo, like a puppet. The old man was holding on to the arm of a priest whom the doctor recognized. This was Father Paneloux, a learned, militant Jesuit who was very highly regarded in our town, even among those who cared little for anything to do with religion. He waited for them to join him. Old Michel's eyes were shining and he whistled as he breathed. He had not been feeling very well and decided to get some fresh air, but sharp pains in his neck, his armpits and his groin obliged him to turn back and ask for Father Paneloux's help.

'There are swellings,' he said. 'It was a struggle for me.'

Leaning out of the car window the doctor ran his finger over the base of the neck that Michel offered him: a sort of wooden knot had appeared there.

'Go to bed, take your temperature and I'll come to see you this afternoon.'

When the concierge had gone Rieux asked Father Paneloux what he thought about the business of the rats.

'Oh, it must be an epidemic,' the priest said; and his eyes were smiling behind his glasses.

After lunch Rieux was re-reading the telegram from the sanatorium announcing his wife's arrival, when the telephone rang. It was a call from one of his former patients, who was on the staff of the Hôtel de Ville. For a long time he had suffered from a narrowing of the aorta and, since he was poor, Rieux treated him for nothing.

'Yes,' he said. 'You remember me. But I'm calling about someone else. Come quickly, something has happened at my neighbour's.'

He was out of breath. Rieux thought about the concierge and decided to go and see him afterwards. A few minutes later he was going through the door of a low-built house on the Rue Faidherbe, on the edge of town. Halfway up the cold, stinking stairway he crossed Joseph Grand, the civil servant, coming down to meet him. He was a man of about fifty, with a yellow moustache, tall, bent, with narrow shoulders and thin limbs.

'He's better,' he said as he reached Rieux. 'But I thought he was done for.'

He blew his nose. On the second (and top) floor, on the left-hand door, Rieux read the words 'Come in, I'm hanged' in red chalk.

They went in. The rope was hanging from the ceiling light above a chair, lying on its side, with the table pushed into a corner; but the rope was hanging in the void.

'I got him down in time,' Grand said, still seeming to have trouble finding his words, even though he was speaking in very simple terms. 'I just happened to be going out and I heard a noise. When I saw the writing . . . what can I say? I thought it was a joke. But he gave an odd kind of groan, you could even say quite a sinister one.'

He scratched his head.

'Doing that must be painful, I should think. Of course, I went in.'

They had pushed open a door and were at the entrance to a bright, but poorly furnished room. A little round man was lying on a brass bedstead. He was breathing heavily and looked at them with bloodshot eyes. The doctor stopped. In the pauses between the man's breaths he thought he could hear rats squeaking, but nothing was moving anywhere in the room. Rieux went over to the bed. The man had not fallen from high enough or too suddenly, and his spine had taken the blow. Of course there was some asphyxia. He would need an X-ray. The doctor gave him an injection of camphorated oil and told him that he would be fine in a few days.

'Thank you, doctor,' the man said in a choked voice.

Rieux asked Grand if he had reported the matter to the police and the civil servant looked uncomfortable.

'No,' he said. 'Well, no . . . I thought that the most urgent thing . . .'

'Of course,' Rieux said, interrupting him. 'I'll do it then.'

But at that moment the sick man stirred and sat up on the bed, protesting that he was well and that there was no need.

'Don't worry,' said Rieux. 'It's nothing much and I have to make a statement.'

'Oh!' the other man said, and lay back. He started to weep, with little sobs. Grand, who had been twirling his moustache for a while, went across to him.

'Come now, Monsieur Cottard,' he said. 'You must understand. They might say that the doctor was responsible. I mean, suppose you took it into your head to try again.'

But Cottard, between his sobs, said that he would not try again, that it had just been a moment of panic and that all he wanted was to be left in peace. Rieux wrote out a prescription.

'Very well,' he said. 'Let's leave it and I'll come back in two or three days. But don't do anything stupid.'

Outside on the landing he told Grand that he was obliged to make a report, but that he would ask the police commissioner not to start his enquiry for a couple of days.

'He shouldn't be left alone tonight. Does he have any family?'

'None that I know of. But I can stay with him myself.'

He shook his head.

'Mind you, he's another that I can't really say I know. But we must help one another.'

Automatically, Rieux looked into the dark corners of the corridors and asked Grand if the rats had entirely vanished from the area. The civil servant had no idea. Certainly people had spoken a good deal about the business, but he paid very little attention to rumours in the neighbourhood.

'I have other concerns,' he said.

Rieux was already shaking his hand. He was in a hurry to see the concierge before writing to his wife.

The vendors of the evening papers were shouting that the invasion of rats had ended. But Rieux found his patient lying half out of bed, one hand on his belly and the other around his neck, convulsively vomiting reddish bile into a rubbish bin. After long efforts the concierge lay back on the bed, gasping for breath. His temperature was 38·5, the lymph nodes on his neck and his limbs had swollen and two blackish patches were spreading on his sides. He was now complaining of internal pains.

'It's burning,' he said. 'The swine is burning me.'

His clogged throat made him stumble over his words and his head was aching so much that there were tears in the bulging eyes that he turned towards the doctor. His wife looked anxiously at Rieux, who said nothing.

'Doctor,' she asked. 'What is it?'

'It could be anything. So far, we can't be sure. Until this evening, diet and purgatives. He must drink a lot.'

Indeed, the concierge was consumed with thirst.

Once he got home Rieux telephoned his colleague Dr Richard, one of the leading doctors in the town.

'No,' Richard said. 'I haven't seen anything out of the ordinary.'

'Not high temperature with local inflammation?'

'Well, yes, as it happens: two cases with very enlarged lymph nodes.'

'Abnormally so?'

'Huh!' said Richard. 'You know . . . What's normal?'

That evening the concierge was delirious and, with his temperature at 40 degrees, was complaining about the rats. Rieux tried a fixation abscess. As the turpentine burned him, the concierge screamed: 'Oh, the swine!' The lymph nodes had swollen even more and were hard and wooden to the touch. His wife was in a terrible state.

'Keep an eye on him,' said the doctor. 'And call me if you need.'

The following day, April 30, an already warm breeze was blowing beneath a damp blue sky. It brought a scent of flowers from the most distant suburbs. The sounds of morning in the streets seemed livelier and merrier than usual. Throughout our little town, freed from the dull sense of foreboding which it had endured for a week, this was a day of rebirth. Even Rieux, reassured by a letter from his wife, went down to see the concierge in a light-hearted mood. And that morning, indeed, the man's temperature had fallen to 38 degrees. Though weak, the patient was smiling in his bed.

'He's improving, doctor, isn't he?' said his wife.

'It's a bit too soon to say.'

But at noon the patient's temperature suddenly rose to 40 degrees, he was constantly delirious and vomiting again. The lymph nodes in his neck were painful to the touch and the concierge seemed to want to keep his head as far as possible away from his body. His wife was sitting at the end of the bed with her hands on the blanket, gently holding the sick man's feet. She looked at Rieux.

'Listen,' he said. 'We'll have to isolate him and try some emergency treatment. I'll phone the hospital and we'll get him there by ambulance.'

Two hours later, in the ambulance, the doctor and the wife were leaning over the patient. Broken words emerged from his mouth, which was covered in a fungoid growth. 'The rats!' he said. Greenish, with waxy lips, leaden eyelids and short, panting breath, tormented by his lymph nodes and pressed against the back of the stretcher bed as though he wanted to close it around him or as if something rising from the depths of the earth were constantly calling him, the concierge was stifling beneath some invisible weight. His wife wept.

'Is there no hope then, doctor?'

'He is dead,' Rieux said.

You might say that the death of the concierge marked the end of this period full of troubling signs, and the start of another, comparatively more difficult, in which the original sense of surprise gradually gave way to panic. Our fellow-citizens, as they now realized, had never thought that our little town might be a place particularly chosen as one where rats die in the sun and concierges perish from peculiar illnesses. From this point of view, indeed, they were mistaken and discovered that they had to adjust their ideas. If it had all stopped there, old habits would no doubt have regained the upper hand. But others of our fellow-citizens, who were not concierges or poor people, were to follow M. Michel down that same path. This was where fear began – and with it, serious reflection.

However, before describing these new events in detail, the narrator feels that it would be helpful to give the views of another witness of the period which has just been described. Jean Tarrou, whom we have already met at the start of this account, had settled in Oran a few weeks earlier and had since been living in a large hotel in the centre. Apparently, he was well enough off to live on a private income. But even though the town had gradually become accustomed to him, no one could tell where he came from or why he was there. People ran into him in all the public places around town. Since the start of spring, he had been seen a lot on the beach, often swimming with obvious pleasure. Pleasant, always smiling, he seemed to enjoy all normal pleasures without being enslaved by them. As a matter of fact, the only habit he was known to have was that he regularly spent time with the Spanish dancers and musicians, of whom there are quite a few in our town.

In any case, his notebooks also constitute a sort of chronicle of that difficult period – though this is a very particular type of chronicle in that it seems to adopt a deliberate policy of insignificance. At first sight you might think that Tarrou had gone out of his way to view people and things through the large end of the telescope. In short, in the midst of this general confusion, he determined to become the historian of that which has no history. Of course one may deplore this bias and suspect that it derives from some dryness of heart. But the fact remains that, as a chronicle of the time, these notebooks can give us a mass of minor details which are none the less important. Indeed, their very oddity will prevent us from being too hasty in passing judgement on this interesting character.

The first notes that Jean Tarrou made date from his arrival in Oran. From the very start they exhibit a curious satisfaction at finding himself in a town that is so intrinsically ugly. Here we find a detailed description of the two bronze lions on the Hôtel de Ville, and charitable reflections on the absence of trees, the unprepossessing houses and the ridiculous layout of the town. Tarrou also includes conversations overheard in trams or on the street, with no comment except a little later, in the case of one such exchange about a certain Camps. Tarrou had heard two tram conductors talking:

'You knew Camps, didn't you,' one of them said.

'Camps? A tall fellow with a black moustache?'

'That's the one. He was on points.'

'Yes, of course I did.'

'Well, he's dead.'

'Oh! When was that?'

'After the business with the rats.'

'Well, well. What was wrong with him?'

'I don't know; a temperature. And then, he wasn't strong. He had abscesses under his arms. He couldn't fight it off.'

'Even so, he seemed like anyone else.'

'No, he had a weak chest. And he played music for the choir. It wears you out, always blowing down a tube.'

'Ah, well,' the second man said. 'When you're ill, you shouldn't blow down a tube.'

After this brief dialogue Tarrou wondered why Camps had joined the choir when it was so obviously not in his interest, and what were the fundamental reasons that drove him to risk his life to take part in its Sunday marches.

Next, Tarrou seems to have been favourably impressed by a scene that was often played out on the balcony opposite his window. His room looked out over a small side-street where cats would sleep in the shade of the walls. But every day after lunch, at a time when the whole town was drowsing in the heat, a little old man would appear on the balcony on the other side of the street. With well-combed white hair, stern and upright in clothes of military cut, he would call to the cats with a 'puss, puss' that was at once soft and distant. Pale with sleep, the cats raised their eyes without at first bothering to move. The man would then tear up little pieces of paper above the street, and the creatures, attracted by this shower of white butterflies, came out into the middle of the road, raising enquiring paws towards the last pieces of paper. At this the little old man would spit on the cats, firmly and accurately. When one of his gobs of saliva hit the target he would laugh.

Finally, Tarrou seemed to have been entirely taken with the commercial character of a town whose appearance, life and even pleasures seemed to be dictated by considerations of trade. This peculiarity – that is the term he uses in his notebooks – was one that Tarrou approved of – one of his passages praising it even ends with the exclamation: 'At last!' These are the only places where the traveller's notes, in this period, seem to have something personal about them. However, it is hard to assess the meaning and the seriousness of such remarks. So after describing how the discovery of a dead rat had caused the cashier at the hotel to make a mistake in his bill, Tarrou added, in writing that was less clear than usual: 'Question: how can one manage not to lose time? Answer: experience it at its full length. Means: spend days in the dentist's waiting-room on an uncomfortable chair; live on one's balcony on a Sunday afternoon; listen to lectures in a language that one does not understand, choose the most roundabout and least convenient routes on the railway (and, naturally, travel standing up); queue at the box-office for theatres and so on and not take one's seat; etc.' But immediately after these extravagances of language or thought, the notebooks launch into a detailed description of the trams in our town, their gondola shape, their indeterminate colour and their customary dirty appearance, ending these observations with the expression: 'It's remarkable' – which explains nothing.

In any event, here is what Tarrou has to say about the business of the rats:

'Today, the little old man opposite is very put out. There are no more cats. They have vanished, excited by the dead rats that are being found in great numbers in the streets. In my opinion, it's not a matter of the cats eating the dead rats. I remember that mine hated them. Even so, they must be running around the cellars and the little old man is very put out. His hair is untidy and he seems less hale and hearty. You can see he is worried. After a while, he went back inside, but he did spit, once, into thin air.

'In town, a tram was stopped today because they found a dead rat on it; no one knew where it came from. Two or three women got off. The rat was thrown out and the tram drove away.

'In the hotel, the night porter, who is a reliable sort, told me that he was expecting something bad to come of all these rats. "When the rats leave the ship . . ." I replied that this was true in the case of ships, but that it had never been proved bad where towns were concerned. But he remains convinced. I asked him what misfortune he thought we should expect. He didn't know, since misfortune is impossible to predict – though he wouldn't be surprised if an earthquake were to fit the bill. I agreed that it was possible and he asked me if I were not worried.

' "The only thing I'm interested in," I said, "is to find inner peace."
'He understood that perfectly.

'There is a rather interesting family in the hotel restaurant. The father is a tall, thin man, dressed in black, with a stiff collar. The crown of his head is bald and he has two tufts of grey hair on either side. His hard little round eyes, his slender nose and his straight mouth make him look like a well-trained owl. He is always the first to arrive at the door of the restaurant and stands back so that his wife can pass; she is as tiny as a black mouse, and walks in with a little boy and a little girl at her heels, dressed like performing dogs. Once the man has reached his table, he waits for his wife to sit down, then does so himself before the two poodles are allowed to perch on their chairs. He addresses his wife and children using the formal *vous*, and delivers himself of politely cutting remarks to the first and summary orders to his heirs:

'"Nicole, you are behaving in a supremely unpleasant manner."

'The little girl is about to burst into tears. That's what he wants.

'This morning the boy was very excited by the business of the rats. He wanted to say something during the meal.

'"We don't talk about rats at table, Philippe. From now on, I forbid you to mention the word."

'"Your father is right," said the black mouse.

'The two poodles stuck their noses into their bowls and the owl thanked her with a nod that gave little away.

'Despite this good example, people around town are talking a great deal about the business of the rats. The newspaper has taken it up. The local news pages, usually very diverse, are now entirely occupied by a campaign against the town authorities: "Are our town dignitaries aware of the danger that may arise from the rotting corpses of these rodents?" The manager of the hotel cannot talk about anything else. But this is partly because he is angry about it. It seems unimaginable to him that rats should be discovered in the lift of a respectable hotel. To console him, I said: "But everybody has the same thing."

'"Exactly," he replied. "Now we are like everybody."

'He was the one who mentioned to me about the first cases of that unusual infection that people are starting to worry about. One of his chambermaids has it.

'"But it surely can't be catching," he insisted.

'I told him that it was all the same to me.

'"Ah, I see! Monsieur is like me, a fatalist."

'I had said nothing of the sort and in any case, I am not a fatalist. I told him as much . . .'

From here on Tarrou's notebooks start to give rather more details about this unknown illness which was already causing concern among the public. Noting that the little old man had finally got his cats back after the disappearance of the rats, and was patiently adjusting his aim,

Tarrou added that one could already mention a dozen cases of this infection, in most of which it had proved fatal.

Finally, for the record, one may copy Tarrou's portrait of Dr Rieux. As far as the narrator can judge, it is quite accurate:

'Appears thirty-five years old. Medium height. Broad shouldered. Almost rectangular face. Dark, straight eyes, but protruding jaw. His strong nose is regular. Black hair, cut very short. The mouth is a bow with full lips, almost always tight shut. He looks rather like a Sicilian peasant with his bronzed skin, his black body hair and his clothes, which suit him, but are always in dark colours.

'He walks fast. He steps off the pavement without altering his pace, but two times out of three goes up onto the opposite pavement with a little jump. He is absent-minded when driving and often leaves his car's indicators up even after he has taken a bend. Never wears a hat. Looks as if he knows what is going on.'

Tarrou's figures were correct. Dr Rieux knew what was up. Once the concierge's body had been put in isolation, he telephoned Richard to ask him about these inguinal infections.

'I don't understand it,' Richard replied. 'Two deaths, one in forty-eight hours, the other in three days. I left the second of these one morning giving every appearance of being on the mend.'

'Let me know if you have any other cases,' said Rieux.

He called a few other doctors; and enquiring in this way he uncovered about twenty similar cases in a few days. Almost all had been fatal. So he asked Richard, the president of the Association of Doctors in Oran, if new patients could be isolated.

'There's nothing I can do,' Richard said. 'The measure would have to be taken by the Prefect. In any case, who told you there was any risk of infection?'

'Nothing tells me that there is, but the symptoms are disturbing.'

However, Richard felt that 'he was not qualified'. All he could do was to mention it to the authorities.

But even as they spoke, the weather was deteriorating. Great mists covered the sky the day after the death of the concierge. Brief but torrential rain storms swept across the town and these sudden showers were followed by thundery heat. Even the sea had lost its deep blue colour and, beneath the misty sky, took on the sheen of silver or iron, making it painful to look at. The humid heat of this spring made you long for the blazing sunshine of summer. A dull torpor lay over the town, crouching like a snail on its plateau, with only a small area fronting the sea. Amid its long roughcast walls, in the streets with their dusty windows and the dirty yellow trams, one felt something of a prisoner of the sky. Only Rieux's old patient overcame his asthma and enjoyed the weather.

'It bakes you,' he said. 'That's good for the tubes.'

It was indeed baking, but neither more nor less than a fever. The whole town had a high temperature: that, at least, was the feeling that haunted Dr Rieux on the morning when he went to the Rue Faidherbe to take part in the enquiry into Cottard's attempted suicide. But he thought this feeling was unreasonable. He attributed it to irritation and to all the things he had on his mind, deciding that he must quickly try to sort out his head.

When he arrived the commissioner was not yet there. Grand was waiting for him on the landing and they decided first of all to go into his place and leave the door open. The town official lived in a two-room flat, very sparsely furnished. All one could see was a white wooden shelf with two or three dictionaries on it and a blackboard on which one could still read the half-effaced inscription 'paths of flowers'. According to Grand, Cottard had had a good night. But that morning, he had woken up with a headache, unable to do anything. Grand himself seemed tired and nervous, pacing up and down, opening and closing a large folder on the table, full of handwritten pages.

Meanwhile, he was telling the doctor that he knew Cottard very little, but that he imagined he must have some small personal income. Cottard was an odd person. For a long time they had said nothing to one another apart from a greeting on the stairs.

'I've only had two conversations with him. A few days ago I dropped a box of chalks on the stairs when I was bringing it home. There were red chalks and blue ones. At that moment Cottard came out onto the landing and helped me to pick them up. He asked what I used these different coloured chalks for.'

So Grand explained that he was trying to revise a bit of Latin: since he left school he had forgotten much of it.

'Yes,' he told the doctor. 'People have assured me that it is useful for understanding French words.'

So he would write Latin words on his blackboard. He copied out in blue chalk the parts of the words that changed according to declension or conjugation and in red chalk the part that never changed.

'I don't know if Cottard understood really, but he seemed interested and asked if he could have a red chalk. I was a little surprised, but then . . . Of course, I couldn't guess that he would use it in that way.'

Rieux asked what had been the subject of the second conversation. But the commissioner arrived, with his secretary, wanting to take Grand's statement. The doctor noticed that Grand, when speaking of Cottard, always referred to him as 'the desperate man'. At one point he even used the expression 'fatal resolve'. They discussed his motives for wanting to commit suicide and Grand was fussy about the form of words. They finally agreed on 'personal sorrows'. The commissioner asked if there had been anything in Cottard's attitude which could have indicated what he called 'his fixed intent'.

'He knocked on my door yesterday,' Grand said, 'to ask me for matches. I gave him my box. He apologized, saying that as we were neighbours . . . Then he promised to give the box back. I told him to keep it.'

The commissioner asked the civil servant if Cottard had not seemed odd.

'What seemed odd to me was that he appeared to want to start a conversation. But I was working.'

Grand turned towards Rieux and added self-consciously:

'Personal work.'

Meanwhile, the commissioner wanted to see the patient. But Rieux thought that it would be best to prepare Cottard for the visit. When he went into the room, the man was sitting up in bed, wearing only a greyish vest. He turned towards the door with an anxious look on his face.

'It's the police, isn't it?'

'Yes,' Rieux said. 'But don't get upset. Just two or three questions as a formality and they'll leave you in peace.'

But Cottard answered that there was no point to it and that he did not like the police. Rieux gave a sign of impatience.

'I'm not keen on them myself. All you have to do is to answer their questions briefly and politely, and get it over with.'

Cottard said nothing and the doctor turned back to the door. But the little man was already calling for him and took his hands as he approached the bed.

'They can't harm a sick man, a man who hanged himself, can they, doctor?'

Rieux looked at him for a moment and finally assured him that there had never been any question of anything like that – apart from which, he was there to look after his patient. The man seemed to relax and Rieux went to fetch the commissioner.

Grand's testimony was read to Cottard and they asked if he could tell them precisely why he had done what he did. He simply replied, without looking at the commissioner, that 'personal sorrows was quite right'. The commissioner urged him to say if he intended to try again. Cottard said, emphatically, that he did not and that all he wanted was to be left in peace.

'I must point out', the commissioner said, with irritation in his voice, 'that just now it is you who are disturbing the peace of others.'

He asked the doctor if the matter was serious and Rieux said that he had no idea.

'It's the weather, that's all,' the commissioner concluded.

And no doubt it was the weather. Everything stuck to one's hands as the day went on and Rieux felt a growing sense of foreboding with every visit he made. That same day, on the outskirts of the town, one of the old man's neighbours, delirious, pressed his groin and started to vomit. His lymph nodes were larger than the concierge's. One of them had already begun to suppurate and soon burst open like a rotten fruit. When he got home Rieux phoned the depot for pharmaceutical products for the *département*. His professional notes for the day in question merely state: 'Negative response.' And already he was being called out elsewhere to similar cases. Obviously, the abscesses had to be lanced. Two cuts with the scalpel in the form of a cross and the glands discharged a mixture of pus and blood. The patients bled, in agony. Dark patches appeared on the belly and the legs, a lymph node would cease to suppurate, then it swelled up again. More often than not, the patient died, with an appalling smell about him.

The press, which had had so much to say about the business of the rats, fell silent. This is because rats die in the street and people in their bedrooms; and newspapers are only concerned with the street. But the Prefecture and the Hôtel de Ville were starting to wonder. As long as each doctor was not aware of more than two or three cases, no one thought to do anything. But, after all, someone only had to decide to do an addition, and the tally was disturbing. In barely a few days the number of fatal cases multiplied, and it was clear to those who were concerned with this curious illness that they were dealing with a real epidemic. This was when Castel, one of Rieux's colleagues, though much older, came to see him.

'Of course,' he said, 'you know what it is, Rieux, don't you?'

'I'm waiting for the results of the tests.'

'Well, I know. And I don't need tests. I spent part of my life working in China, and I saw a few cases in Paris, twenty years ago – though no one dared put a name to it at that time. Public opinion is sacred: no panic, above all no panic. Then, as a colleague told me: "It's impossible, everyone knows it has vanished from the West." Yes, everyone knew that, except the dead. Come on, Rieux, you know as well as I do what it is.'

Rieux thought. Out of his study window he looked at the shoulder of the stony cliff that closed around the bay in the distance. Though the sky was blue it had a dull sheen that was softening as the afternoon went on.

'Yes, Castel,' he said. 'It's almost impossible to believe. But it appears that it must be the plague.'

Castel got up and went towards the door.

'You know what they'll tell us,' the old doctor said. ' "It disappeared from temperate lands years ago." '

'What does it mean, "disappeared"?' Rieux replied, shrugging his shoulders.

'Yes. And don't forget: in Paris, almost twenty years ago . . .'

'Fine. Let's hope that it won't be more serious now than it was then. But it's quite incredible.'

The word 'plague' had just been spoken for the first time. At this point in the story, leaving Bernard Rieux at his window, the narrator may be allowed to justify the doctor's uncertainty and surprise since, with a few slight differences, his reaction was the same as that of most of our townsfolk. Pestilence is in fact very common, but we find it hard to believe in a pestilence when it descends upon us. There have been as many plagues in the world as there have been wars, yet plagues and wars always find people equally unprepared. Dr Rieux was unprepared, as were the rest of the townspeople, and this is how one should understand his reluctance to believe. One should also understand that he was divided between anxiety and confidence. When war breaks out people say: 'It won't last, it's too stupid.' And war is certainly too stupid, but that doesn't prevent it from lasting. Stupidity always carries doggedly on, as people would notice if they were not always thinking about themselves. In this respect, the citizens of Oran were like the rest of the world, they thought about themselves; in other words, they were humanists: they did not believe in pestilence. A pestilence does not have human dimensions, so people tell themselves that it is unreal, that it is a bad dream which will end. But it does not always end and, from one bad dream to the next, it is people who end, humanists first of all because they have not prepared themselves. The people of our town were no more guilty than anyone else, they merely forgot to be modest and thought that everything was still possible for them, which implied that pestilence was impossible. They continued with business, with making arrangements for travel and holding opinions. Why should they have thought about the plague, which negates the future, negates journeys and debate? They considered themselves free and no one will ever be free as long as there is plague, pestilence and famine.

Even after Dr Rieux had acknowledged to his friend that a handful of sick people in different places had unexpectedly died of plague, the danger seemed unreal to him. It is just that when one is a doctor one has acquired some idea of pain and gained a little more imagination. As he looked through the window over his town, which was unchanged, the doctor could barely feel the first stirrings of that slight nausea with regard to the future that is known as anxiety. He tried to put together in his mind what he knew about the disease. Figures drifted through his head and he thought that the thirty or so great plagues recorded in history had caused nearly a hundred million deaths. But what are a hundred million deaths? When one has fought a war, one hardly knows any more what a dead person is. And if a dead man has no significance unless one has seen him dead, a hundred million bodies spread through history are just a mist drifting through the imagination. The doctor recalled the plague of Constantinople which, according to Procopius, claimed ten thousand victims in one day. Ten thousand dead equals five times the audience in a large cinema. That's what you should do. You should get all the people coming out of five cinemas, take them to a square in the town and make them die in a heap; then you would grasp it better. At least, one might put some known faces on this anonymous pile. But of course it would be impossible; apart from which, who knows ten thousand faces? In any event, people like Procopius were not able to count, as is well known. In Canton, seventy years ago, forty thousand rats died of plague before the pestilence affected the human inhabitants. But in 1871 they didn't have any means of counting rats. The calculation was a matter of approximation, of more or less, with an obvious margin for error. However, if one rat is thirty centimetres long, forty thousand rats, placed end-to-end, would make . . .

But the doctor was irritated with himself. He was letting himself go and he ought not to. A few cases are not an epidemic and it was a question of taking precautions. One had to stick with what one knew:

stupor and prostration, red eyes, furred mouth, headaches, the bubos, the dreadful thirst, delirium, patches on the body, the inner anguish and, at the end of it all . . . At the end of it all, some words came back to Dr Rieux, a sentence that happened to round off the list of symptoms in his medical textbook: 'The pulse becomes thready and death occurs as the result of some slight movement.' Yes, at the end of all that, one was hanging by a thread and three out of four people, that was the precise number, were so impatient that they made the slight movement that would carry them off.

The doctor was still looking out of the window. On one side of the glass was the cool, fresh sky of spring; on the other was the word that still resounded round the room: plague. The word contained not only what science had seen fit to put in it, but a long succession of extraordinary images that had nothing to do with this grey and yellow town, moderately busy at this time, humming rather than noisy, happy in short, if it is possible to be happy and drab at one and the same time. And such peaceful and unthinking tranquillity almost effortlessly contradicted the old images of pestilence: Athens stricken, abandoned by its birds; Chinese towns full of people dying in silence; the convicts of Marseille piling dripping corpses into holes; the building of the great wall in Provence in the hope of holding back the raging wind of plague; Jaffa and its ghastly beggars; beds, damp and rotten, sticking to the earth floor of the hospital in Constantinople; sick people dragged along by hooks; the carnival of masked doctors during the Black Death; the living copulating in the cemeteries of Milan; the carts of the dead in a London paralysed with terror; and days and nights filled, everywhere and always, with the endless cries of men. All this was not yet powerful enough to destroy the peace of the day. On the far side of the glass, the clank of an invisible tram resounded suddenly, in an instant contradicting cruelty and pain. Only the sea, beyond the dull chequerboard of houses, was evidence of all that is disturbing and forever restless in this world. And Dr Rieux, who was looking at the gulf, thought of the pyres that, Lucretius tells us, the Athenians built on the seashore when they were stricken with illness. The dead were brought there at night, but there was too little space and the living would fight each other with burning torches to put their loved ones on the pyres, engaging in bloody struggles rather than abandon their dead bodies on the beach. You could imagine the pyres glowing in front of the calm dark water, the torches struggling in a darkness crackling with sparks, and thick, poisonous fumes rising towards the waiting sky. And you could imagine it happening here . . .

But common sense dispelled this dizzying vision. It is true that the word 'plague' had been spoken, it is true that at that very moment the pestilence was tossing and beating down one or two victims. But that could end, couldn't it? What he must do was to acknowledge clearly what had to be acknowledged, drive away all needless shadows and take whatever measures were required. After that, the plague would cease because plague was inconceivable, or because it was wrongly conceived. If it did stop, as was most likely, then all would be well. Otherwise, they would understand what it was and know if there was some means by which they might come to terms with it, so as eventually to overcome it.

The doctor opened the window and the noise of the town swelled suddenly. From a nearby workshop came the brief, repeated sounds of a mechanical saw. Rieux shook himself. This was certainty: everyday work. The rest hang by threads and imperceptible movements; one could not dwell on it. The main thing was to do one's job well.

Dr Rieux had reached this point in his thoughts when Joseph Grand was announced. Although he was on the staff of the Hôtel de Ville and his duties there were very varied, he was occasionally used by the statistical service of the registry of births, marriages and deaths. Because of this he had been adding up the number of death certificates and, being naturally obliging, he had agreed to bring a copy of his results to Rieux in person.

The doctor saw Grand come in with his neighbour Cottard. The civil servant was waving a sheet of paper.

'The figures are rising, doctor,' he announced. 'Eleven deaths in forty-eight hours.'

Rieux greeted Cottard and asked him how he was. Grand explained that Cottard wanted to thank the doctor and to apologize for the trouble he had caused him. But Rieux was looking at the sheet of figures.

'Well, now,' he said. 'Perhaps we should make up our minds to call this disease by its proper name. So far, we have been kicking our heels. But come with me, I have to go to the laboratory.'

'Yes, yes,' Grand said, coming downstairs after the doctor. 'We must call things by their proper name. But what is the name?'

'I can't tell you. In any case, it would be no use to you.'

'You see,' the man said. 'It isn't that easy.'

They went in the direction of the parade-ground. Cottard was still not saying anything. The streets started to fill with people. The fleeting dusk that we have in our country was already giving way to night and the first stars had appeared on a still clear horizon. A few seconds later the lamps above the streets lit up and blocked out the sky. The sound of conversations seemed to rise a tone.

'Excuse me,' Grand said at the corner of the parade-ground. 'I have to catch my tram. My evenings are sacred. As they say where I come from: "One should never put off until tomorrow . . ."'

Rieux had already noted this habit that Grand had of quoting sayings from his part of the country – he was born in Montélimar – and then adding some cliché that came from nowhere in particular, like 'a peach of an evening' or 'fairytale lights'.

'Now there,' said Cottard, 'that's true. Nothing can drag him away from home after dinner.'

Rieux asked Grand if he was doing some work for the Hôtel de Ville; Grand answered no, he was working for himself.

'Ah,' said Rieux, for the sake of saying something. 'Is it progressing?'

'Inevitably, considering all the years I've been working on it. Although, in another sense, there isn't much progress.'

'But what exactly is it?' the doctor asked, stopping in his tracks.

Grand mumbled as he settled his round hat over his ears. Rieux got the vague idea that it was something about the development of a personality. But the civil servant was already leaving and walking briskly up the Boulevard de la Marne, between the fig trees. On the threshold of the lab Cottard told the doctor that he would like to see him to ask his advice. Rieux, who was fingering the page of statistics in his pocket, invited him to come to his consulting-room, then changed his mind and said that he would be in Cottard's neighbourhood the next day and would drop in to see him in the late afternoon.

After leaving Cottard the doctor noticed that he was thinking about Grand. He was imagining him in the midst of a plague, not this one which would doubtless not prove serious, but one of the great plagues of history. 'He's the kind of man who is spared in such cases.' He recalled having read that the plague spared those of weak constitution and mainly destroyed those of a robust nature. And the more he thought about him, the more the doctor considered that there was a little mystery surrounding the civil servant.

Indeed, at first sight Joseph Grand was nothing more than the minor clerk at the Hôtel de Ville that he appeared to be. Tall and thin, he was swamped by his clothes, always choosing them too large under the mistaken impression that this would give him more wear out of them. While he still had most of his teeth in the lower jaw, he had lost those in the upper one, so that his smile, which chiefly involved raising the upper lip, gave him a cavernous mouth. If you add to this portrait his manner of walking like a young priest, his ability to hug the walls and slide through doorways, his odour of smoke and cellars, and every appearance of insignificance, you will agree that he could not be imagined anywhere except behind a desk, earnestly revising the prices of public baths in the town or putting together the materials for a report, to be written by some young superior, about the new tax on the collection of household waste. Even for someone not in the know, he appeared to have been put in this world in order to carry out the unobtrusive but indispensable role of a temporary municipal clerk earning sixty-two francs thirty a day.

This was in fact the term that he said he put on employment forms after the words 'present post'. When, twenty-two years earlier, having completed a first degree but unable to study further because of lack of funds, he had accepted this job, he said that he had been led to hope that it would soon become a permanent appointment. It was just a matter of proving for a certain time that he was competent to deal with the delicate questions involved in administering our town. After that, he had been assured, he could not fail to be granted a post as report-writer which would give him a comfortable living. It was certainly not ambition that drove Joseph Grand, he vouched for that with a melancholy smile. But he was much gladdened by the prospect of a better life, supported by honest means, and as a consequence the possibility of indulging without compunction in his favourite pastimes. If he accepted the offer that was made to him, it was for honourable motives and one might even say out of fidelity to an ideal.

This provisional situation had lasted for many years, the cost of living had increased immeasurably and Grand's salary, despite some periodical increases, had remained derisory. He complained of this to Rieux, but no one else seemed to be aware of it. This is where Grand's eccentricity appears, or at least one indication of it; because he could at least have quoted the assurances he had been given, if not exactly his rights, about which he was unsure. But, to begin with, the chief who first employed him had died a long time ago and in any case the clerk did not remember the precise terms of the promise that he had been given. Finally, and most of all, words failed him.

As Rieux observed, this was the characteristic that best defined our fellow-citizen, Joseph Grand. This is what always prevented him from writing the letter of complaint that he had in mind or from taking whatever action the circumstances demanded. He claimed to feel especially inhibited in using the word 'right' when not sure of his rights, or 'promises' when this might imply that he was demanding something owed to him – which would, consequently, appear presumptuous and not appropriate from someone in the lowly post that he occupied. On the other hand, he refused to use the terms 'goodwill', 'request' and 'gratitude', which he considered incompatible with his personal dignity. This is why, unable to find the right words, he continued in his humble post until a fairly advanced age. Moreover, according to what he told Dr Rieux, he realized with time that his material existence was guaranteed, since all that was necessary in the end was for him to adapt his needs to his income. In this way he acknowledged the correctness of a favourite saying of the Mayor, a captain of industry in our town, who would insist that when it came down to it – and he emphasized the expression which bore the full weight of the argument – when it came down to it, then, no one had ever been known to starve to death. Anyway, the almost ascetic life led by Joseph Grand had at least, in reality, freed him from any such worry. He was still trying to find the right words.

In one sense, you could say that his life was exemplary. He was one of those men, as rare among us as anywhere else, who always have the courage of their better feelings. Indeed, the little that he revealed of himself testified to goodness and attachments that people nowadays are afraid to admit. He did not blush to acknowledge that he loved his nephews and his sister: she was the only relative that he still had left and he would go to visit her every two years in France. He confessed that he grieved over the memory of his parents, who had died when he was still young. He did not deny that most of all he liked a certain bell in his neighbourhood that rang softly around five in the evening. But even to find the words to express such simple emotions cost him an enormous effort. In the end this problem had become his main worry. 'Oh, doctor,' he would say. 'I wish I could learn to express myself.' He mentioned this to Rieux every time they met.

That evening, as he watched the civil servant leave, the doctor realized suddenly what Grand meant: he must surely be writing a book or something of that sort. This reassured Rieux all the way to the laboratory, where he did finally go. He knew that it was silly of him to feel like this, but he could not believe that the plague might really get a hold on a town where you could still find humble civil servants who devoted their free moments to honourable obsessions. More exactly, he could not imagine how such obsessions fitted into the context of the plague, and so concluded that, in practical terms, the plague had no future among the people of our town.

The following day, as a result of what was considered excessive insistence, Rieux persuaded the Prefect's office to appoint a health commission.

'It's true that people are starting to worry,' Richard agreed, 'and gossip exaggerates everything. The Prefect told me: "Let's act quickly if you like, but keep quiet about it." Anyway, he is sure that it's a false alarm.'

Bernard Rieux took Castel in his car when he went to the Prefecture.

'Do you know,' Castel said, 'that the *département* has no serum?'

'I know. I phoned the warehouse. The manager was flabbergasted. It has to be brought from Paris.'

'I hope it won't take long.'

'I've already sent a telegram,' Rieux replied.

The Prefect was pleasant, but nervous.

'Let's get started, gentlemen,' he said. 'Do I have to summarize the situation?'

Richard thought that there was no need. The doctors knew the situation already. The question was merely to decide on the proper course of action.

'The question,' old Castel said bluntly, 'is to decide whether we are dealing with the plague or not.'

Two or three doctors protested, while the others appeared hesitant. As for the Prefect, he leapt up in his seat and automatically turned towards the door, as though checking that it had really prevented this enormity from spreading down the corridor. Richard announced that in his opinion they should not give way to panic: all they could say for certain was that it was an infection with inguinal complications; and it was dangerous, in science as in life, to jump to conclusions. Old Castel, who was calmly chewing his yellow moustache, turned his clear eyes towards Rieux. Then he looked benevolently over the rest of the company and announced that he knew very well it was plague, but that, of course, if they were to acknowledge the fact officially, they would have to take stern measures. He knew that, underneath, this was what held his colleagues back and as a result, not to upset them, he was quite willing to state that it was not plague. The Prefect got annoyed and said that in any event that was not a sensible approach.

'The important thing,' Castel said, 'is not whether the approach is sensible, but whether it gets us thinking.'

As Rieux had said nothing, they asked his opinion.

'It's an infection, similar to typhoid, but with swelling of the lymph nodes and vomiting. I lanced some of the bubos. In that way I was able to have an analysis made in which the laboratory thinks it can detect the plague bacillus. However, to be precise, we must say that certain specific modifications of the microbe do not coincide with the classic description of plague.'

Richard emphasized that this meant they should not rush to judgement and that they would at least have to wait for the statistical result of the series of analyses, which had begun a few days earlier.

'When a microbe', Rieux said, after a brief silence, 'is capable of increasing the size of the spleen four times in three days, and of making the mesenteric ganglia the size of an orange and the consistency of porridge, that is precisely when we should rush to do something. The sources of infection are multiplying. At this rate, if the disease is not halted, it could kill half the town within the next two months. Therefore it doesn't matter whether you call it plague or growing pains. All that matters is that you stop it killing half the town.'

Richard felt that they should not paint too black a picture, and that in any case there was no proof of contagion since the relatives of his patients were still unaffected.

'But others have died,' Rieux pointed out. 'And, of course, contagion is never absolute, because if it were, we should have endless exponential growth and devastating loss of population. It's not a matter of painting a black picture; it's a matter of taking precautions.'

However, Richard thought he could sum the situation up by saying that if they were to halt the disease, assuming it did not stop of its own accord, they had to apply the serious preventive health measures provided for in law; that, to do so, they would have to acknowledge officially that there was an outbreak of plague; that there was no absolute certainty on that score; and consequently that they should consider the matter.

'The question', Rieux insisted, 'is not knowing whether the measures provided for under the law are serious but if they are *necessary* to prevent half the town being killed. The rest is a matter of administration and it is precisely in order to settle such questions that the State gives us a Prefect.'

'Naturally,' said the Prefect. 'But I need you to acknowledge officially that we do have an outbreak of plague.'

'If we don't acknowledge it,' said Rieux, 'it still threatens to kill half the population of the town.'

Richard interrupted nervously.

'The truth is that our colleague here believes in the plague. His description of the syndrome proves that.'

Rieux replied that he had not described a syndrome, he had described what he had seen. And what he had seen were ganglia, stains and delirious fevers, proving fatal in forty-eight hours. Was Dr Richard prepared to take responsibility for stating that the epidemic would stop without strict preventive health measures?

Richard hesitated and looked at Rieux.

'Sincerely, tell me what you think: are you certain that this is plague?'

'You're asking the wrong question. It is not a matter of vocabulary, but a matter of time.'

'Your opinion, then,' said the Prefect, 'is that even if this is not plague, then the preventive health measures that would be appropriate in the event of plague ought none the less to be applied?'

'If I really must have an opinion, then that is it.'

The doctors consulted one another and eventually Richard said:

'So we must take the responsibility of acting as though the disease were a plague.'

The form of words was warmly applauded.

'Is that also what you think, my dear colleague?' Richard asked.

'I don't mind the form of words,' Rieux said. 'Let's just say that we should not act as though half the town were not threatened with death, because then it would be.'

In the midst of general annoyance, Rieux left. A few moments later, in a suburb which smelled of frying oil and urine, a woman screaming to death, her groin covered in blood, was turning her face to him.

The day after the conference, the infection made another small advance. It even entered the newspapers, but under a harmless guise, since they merely made a few allusions to it. On the day after that Rieux could read some little white posters that the Prefecture had rapidly had stuck up in the least obtrusive corners of the town. From this poster it was hard to reach the conclusion that the authorities were confronting the situation. The measures were far from draconian and it appeared that a good deal had been done to avoid upsetting public opinion. The preamble to the decree announced that a few cases of a pernicious fever had been detected in the commune of Oran, though it was not yet possible to say whether or not it was contagious. These cases were not specific enough to be really disturbing and there was no doubt that the population would remain calm. None the less, for reasons of caution which everyone could understand, the Prefect was taking some preventive measures. If they were interpreted and applied in the proper way, these measures were such that they would put a definite stop to any threat of epidemic. As a result, the Prefect did not for a moment doubt that the citizens under his charge would co-operate in the most zealous manner with what he was doing.

After that, the poster announced some general measures, among them a scientific programme of rodent control by injecting toxic gas into the sewers, and strict supervision of the water supply. It advised the inhabitants to observe the most rigorous hygiene and finally invited anyone infested with fleas to attend a municipal dispensary. In addition, it was obligatory for families to declare any cases diagnosed by the doctor and agree to isolation of their patients in special wards in the hospital. These wards were suitably equipped to treat patients in the least amount of time and with the greatest possibility of a cure. A few additional provisions made it obligatory to disinfect the patient's room and the vehicle in which he or she was carried. And finally, relatives were simply advised to undergo a health test.

Dr Rieux turned sharply away from the notice and set off towards his surgery. Joseph Grand, who was waiting for him, once again raised his arms when he saw him.

'Yes,' said Rieux. 'I know. The figures are rising.'

The day before, around ten patients had died in the town. The doctor told Grand that he might see him that evening since he was going to visit Cottard.

'Good idea,' said Grand. 'You'll do him good: I think he has changed.'

'In what way?'

'He has become polite.'

'Wasn't he before?'

Grand hesitated. He couldn't say that Cottard was impolite, that wouldn't be correct. He was a reserved, silent man, a bit like a wild boar. His room, a plain restaurant, some rather mysterious outings . . . that was the whole of Cottard's life. Officially, he was a salesman, in wines and spirits. Occasionally, he would have a visit from two or three men, who must be his customers. Sometimes in the evening he would go to the cinema, which was opposite the house. The clerk had even noticed that Cottard seemed to prefer gangster films. In any event, the salesman was solitary and suspicious.

According to Grand, all this had changed:

'I don't know how to put it, but I have the impression, you see, that he is trying to get on the right side of people, that he wants to have everyone supporting him. He often talks to me, he invites me to go out with him and I'm not always able to refuse. In any case, he interests me and, after all, I did save his life.'

Since his suicide attempt Cottard had not had any more visits. In the streets, in shops, he appealed for sympathy. No one had ever spoken so kindly to grocers or shown such interest when listening to a tobacconist.

'That tobacconist,' Grand added. 'She's a real snake. I said as much to Cottard, but he told me that I was wrong and that she had good qualities if you knew where to look for them.'

Two or three times Cottard had also taken Grand into expensive restaurants or cafés in town. In fact, he had started to visit these places regularly.

'It's nice there,' he would say. 'And then, you're in good company.'

Grand had noticed that the staff were particularly attentive to the salesman and understood why when he saw the huge tips that Cottard left. He seemed particularly appreciative of the attention that he got in return. One day, when the maître d'hôtel had seen him to the door and helped him to put on his overcoat, Cottard said to Grand:

'He's a good lad, he would testify.'

'Testify to what?'

Cottard hesitated.

'Well, that I'm not a bad person.'

Apart from that, he had sudden moods. One day when the grocer had appeared less friendly, he returned home in a quite disproportionate fit of anger.

'He's going over to the others, that toad,' he said over and again.

'What others?'

'All of them.'

Grand had even witnessed a curious scene at the tobacconist's. In the middle of a heated conversation, she had spoken about a recent arrest that had caused a stir in Algiers. It involved a young company employee who had killed an Arab on a beach.

'If they put all that scum in prison,' the tobacconist said, 'respectable people could sleep easy.'

But she stopped when she saw Cottard suddenly become very agitated and rush out of her shop without a word of apology. Grand and the woman were left with their arms dangling, watching him vanish.

After that Grand would point out to Rieux other changes in Cottard's personality. Cottard had always held very liberal opinions; his favourite remark, 'big fish always eat little ones', proved that. But recently he had only been buying the most conservative paper in Oran and one could not help feeling that he quite deliberately read it in public places. Similarly, a few days after getting up, he asked Grand, who was going to the post office, to be kind enough to dispatch a postal order for the hundred francs that he sent every month to a sister, living somewhere far away. But just as Grand was leaving, Cottard said:

'Send her two hundred francs. It will be a nice surprise for her. She imagines that I never think about her, but the truth is that I'm very fond of her.'

Finally he had an odd conversation with Grand. Cottard was very intrigued by the work, whatever it was, that occupied Grand every evening, and had made Grand answer his questions about it.

'So,' Cottard said. 'You're writing a book.'

'If you like, but it's more complicated than that.'

'Oh!' Cottard exclaimed. 'I wish I could do what you're doing.'

Grand seemed surprised and Cottard stammered out that being an artist must make lots of things easier.

'Why?' Grand asked.

'Well, because an artist has more rights than other people, as everyone knows. He can get away with lots of things.'

'Come now,' Rieux told Grand on the day of the posters. 'This business of the rats has gone to his head, as it has with many other people, that's all. Or else he's afraid of infection.'

Grand replied:

'I don't think so, doctor, and if you want my opinion . . .'

The rodent-control lorry went past beneath the window with a loud noise from its exhaust. Rieux did not reply until he had some hope of being heard and casually asked the clerk for his opinion. Grand gave him a serious look.

'He's a man', he said, 'who has something on his conscience.'

The doctor shrugged his shoulders. As did the police commissioner, he had other fish to fry.

In the course of the afternoon Rieux had a meeting with Castel. The serum had not arrived.

'As for that,' Rieux said, 'would it be any use? This bacillus is very odd.'

'Oh, no,' said Castel. 'I don't agree. Those little brutes always look different from one another, but underneath they're the same.'

'So *you* think, anyway. In reality, we don't know a thing about it.'

'Of course not, I suppose we don't. But it's the same for everyone.'

Throughout the day, the doctor felt growing inside him the slight sense of dizziness that he got whenever he thought about the plague. Eventually he admitted that he was afraid. Twice he went into crowded cafés: like Cottard, he felt the need for human warmth. Rieux thought it was silly of him, but it did help remind him that he had promised to visit the salesman.

That evening the doctor found Cottard standing at his dining-room table. When Rieux came in there was an open detective novel in front of him, but it was already quite late in the afternoon and it would have been hard to read in the gathering darkness. Rather, a minute earlier, Cottard must have been meditating in the half-light. Rieux asked how he was. Cottard sat down and growled that he was well, but that he would be better still if he could be sure that no one was taking an interest in him. Rieux pointed out that one could not always be alone.

'Oh, it's not that. I'm talking about people who are interested in causing you trouble.'

Rieux said nothing.

'Mind you, this is not my situation, but I was reading this novel. Here is an unfortunate man who gets arrested suddenly one morning. People were taking an interest in him and he knew nothing about it. They were talking about him in offices, writing his name on index cards. Do you think that's fair? Do you think anyone has a right to do that to a man?'

'That depends,' Rieux said. 'Of course, in one sense, one never has that right. But all that is by the way. You shouldn't stay cooped up for too long. You ought to go out.'

Cottard seemed to get angry at this, saying that he was always going out and, if need be, he could get the whole neighbourhood to testify to it. Even outside the area, he had plenty of acquaintances.

'Do you know Monsieur Rigaud, the architect? He's a friend of mine.'

The room was getting darker. The suburban street was filling with people and a dull sigh of relief outside greeted the moment when the streetlamps came on. Rieux went out on the balcony and Cottard followed. From every nearby part of town, as every evening, a light breeze brought the hum of voices, the smell of grilled meat and the joyful, sweet-smelling buzz of freedom, little by little filling the street as noisy young people flowed into it. The great roars of invisible boats and the murmur that rose from the sea and from the swelling crowd by night, this moment that Rieux knew so well and once had loved, now seemed oppressive to him because of all that he knew.

'Can we put the light on?' he asked Cottard.

Once light had returned to the room the little man looked at him through blinking eyes.

'Tell me, doctor, if I were to fall ill would you take me in your hospital?'

'Why shouldn't I?'

At this Cottard asked if it had ever happened that a person was arrested when he was in a clinic or a hospital. Rieux said that it had occurred but that it depended on the state of the patient.

'I trust in you,' said Cottard.

Then he asked the doctor if he would kindly take him to town in his car.

In the centre of town the streets were already less crowded and the lights rarer. Children were still playing outside the doors. When Cottard asked him, the doctor stopped the car in front of a group of these children who were playing hopscotch and shouting. But one of them, with black hair stuck down, a perfect parting and a dirty face, stared at Rieux with his clear, intimidating eyes. The doctor looked away. Cottard, standing on the pavement, shook his hand; his voice was hoarse and he had difficulty forming the words. Two or three times he looked behind him.

'People are talking about an epidemic. Is it true, doctor?'

'People are always talking, that's normal,' Rieux said.

'You're right. And when a dozen people die, they'll say it's the end of the world. It's just what we don't need.'

The engine was already ticking over. Rieux's hand was on the gear-stick. But he looked once more at the child, who was still staring at him with a serious, unruffled air. Then suddenly, with no stopping halfway, the child gave him a beaming smile.

'So what do we need?' the doctor asked, smiling back at the child.

Cottard suddenly grasped the door and, before hurrying away, cried out in a voice full of tears and fury:

'An earthquake! A real one!'

There was no earthquake and, for Rieux, the following day passed merely in long trips to the four corners of town, discussions with his patients' families and talks with the patients themselves. Never had he found his job so hard to bear. Up to then, sick people had made it easy for him, they had come halfway to meet him. Now, for the first time, the doctor felt that they were reticent, retreating into the depths of their illness with a kind of suspicious astonishment. This was a struggle to which he had not yet become accustomed. Around ten o'clock, stopping his car in front of the house of the old asthma patient whom he always went to visit last, Rieux found it hard to rise out of his seat. He stayed there, looking at the dark street and the stars appearing and disappearing in the black sky.

The old asthmatic was sitting up in bed. He seemed to be breathing more easily and was counting chick-peas as he transferred them from one saucepan to another. He greeted the doctor cheerfully.

'So doctor, is it cholera?'

'Where did you get that idea?'

'In the paper. The radio says the same thing.'

'No, it's not cholera.'

'In any case,' the old man said, in a state of great excitement, 'they're exaggerating, aren't they, those bigwigs?'

'Don't believe any of it,' said the doctor.

He had examined the old man and was now sitting in the middle of the wretched dining-room. Yes, he was afraid. He knew that in this same part of town a dozen patients would be waiting for him the next day, bent double over their swollen glands. In only two or three cases had lancing the bubos brought about an improvement. But for most of them it would be hospital and he knew what hospital meant to the poor. 'I don't want him to be used for their experiments,' the wife of one sick man had told him. He would not be used for their experiments, he would die and that was all. The measures that had been taken were insufficient, that was quite clear. As for the 'specially equipped wards', he knew what they were: two outbuildings hastily cleared of other patients, their windows sealed up and the whole surrounded by a cordon sanitaire. If the epidemic did not stop of its own accord, it would not be defeated by the measures that the local administration had dreamed up.

However, that evening the official communiqués were still optimistic. The following day, the Infodoc agency announced that the steps taken by the Prefecture had been received calmly and that already some thirty patients had reported themselves. Castel phoned Rieux.

'How many beds are there in the outbuildings?'

'Eighty.'

'There must be more than thirty patients in the town?'

'There are the ones who are afraid and the others, the majority, who don't even have time to feel afraid.'

'Aren't burials being checked?'

'No. I phoned Richard to say we needed comprehensive measures, not fine words, and that either we must set up a real barrier to the epidemic, or nothing at all.'

'And?'

'He told me that he had no power. In my opinion, it will get worse.'

Sure enough, in three days the two buildings were full. Richard thought that they could requisition a school and provide an auxiliary hospital. Rieux waited for the vaccines to arrive and he lanced lymph nodes. Castel returned to his old books and spent a long time in the library.

'The rats died of the plague or of something very similar to it,' he concluded. 'They put tens of thousands of fleas in circulation and these will transmit the infection at an exponential rate if we do not stop it in time.'

Rieux stayed silent.

Around this time the weather seemed to settle. The sun drew up the puddles from the last showers. Fine, blue skies bursting with yellow light, the hum of aircraft in the gathering heat . . . it was a time when everything invited tranquillity. However, in four days the infection took four surprising leaps: sixteen dead, then twenty-four, twenty-eight and thirty-two. On the fourth day they announced the opening of the auxiliary hospital in an infants' school. The townspeople, who up to this point had continued to hide their anxiety behind jokes, seemed more depressed and less voluble in the streets.

Rieux decided to phone the Prefect.

'What we are doing is not enough.'

'I have the figures,' the Prefect said. 'They certainly are disturbing.'

'They are more than disturbing, they are quite unequivocal.'

'I'm going to ask for instructions from the State government.'

Rieux hung up in front of Castel.

'Instructions! What he needs is imagination.'

'And the serum?'

'It will arrive in less than a week.'

Through Richard, the Prefecture asked Rieux for a report which could be sent to the capital of the colony with a request for instructions. Rieux included a clinical description and figures. On that same day, they counted forty deaths. The Prefect took it upon himself, as he said, to step up the measures being taken, from the following day. It remained compulsory to declare the disease and isolate patients. Houses of sick people were to be closed and disinfected, their relatives put in preventive quarantine and burials organized by the authorities in conditions that will be described later. A day later the serum arrived by plane. There was enough for the cases currently being treated, but not if the epidemic were to spread. In reply to Rieux's telegram, he was told that the emergency supply was exhausted and that they had started to manufacture new stocks.

Meanwhile, from all the surrounding districts, spring was arriving in the market-place. Thousands of roses withered in the flower-sellers' baskets on the pavements, and their sugary scent wafted across the town. In appearance nothing had changed. The trams were always full in the rush hours, empty and dirty the rest of the day. Tarrou observed the little old man and the little old man spat on the cats. Grand returned home every evening to his mysterious work. Cottard went round in circles and M. Othon, the examining magistrate, was still showing off his menagerie. The old man with asthma moved his chick-peas from one saucepan to another and one might sometimes meet the journalist

Rambert looking calm and attentive. In the evenings the same crowd filled the streets and queues extended outside the cinemas. The epidemic seemed to be declining and for a few days they counted only ten or so deaths. Then, suddenly, it shot up. On the day when the death-toll once more reached thirty, Bernard Rieux looked at the official telegram which the Prefect had held out to him, saying: 'They're scared.' The telegram read:

'DECLARE A STATE OF PLAGUE STOP
CLOSE THE TOWN.'

Part II

From that point on, it could be said that the plague became the affair of us all. Up to then, despite the surprise and anxiety that these unusual events had brought us, everyone had gone on with his business, as well as he could, in the usual place. And that no doubt would continue. But, once the gates were closed, they all noticed that they were in the same boat, including the narrator himself, and that they had to adjust to the fact. This is how, for example, a quite individual feeling such as being separated from a loved one suddenly became, in the very first weeks, the feeling of a whole people and, together with fear, the greatest agony of that long period of exile.

One of the most remarkable consequences of the closing of the gates was, indeed, a sudden separation of people who were not prepared for it. Mothers and children, wives, husbands and lovers, who had imagined a few days earlier that they were embarking on a temporary separation, who had embraced on the platform of the station with some pieces of last-minute advice, sure that they would see one another a few days or a few weeks later, deeply entrenched in their idiotic human faith in the future, this parting causing barely a pause in the course of their everyday concerns, found themselves abruptly and irremediably divided, prevented from meeting or communicating with one another, because the gates were closed some hours before the prefectural decree was published and, of course, it was impossible to consider individual cases. One might say that the first effect of this sudden and brutal attack of the disease was to force the citizens of our town to act as though they had no individual feelings. In the first hours of the day when the decree took effect, the Prefecture was besieged by a crowd of applicants who, on the phone or face-to-face with the town officials, were explaining situations that were all equally interesting and at the same time equally impossible to consider. In truth, it was several days before we realized that we were in an extreme situation and that the words 'compromise', 'favour' and 'exception' no longer had any meaning.

Even the faint satisfaction of writing letters was denied us. On the one hand, the town was no longer linked to the rest of the country by the usual means of communication, and on the other, a new decree forbade the exchange of any correspondence, to prevent letters from transmitting the infection. At the beginning, a few privileged persons were able to get in contact with the sentries at the posts on the gates of the town and persuade them to take messages outside. This was in the early days of the epidemic, at a time when the guards found it normal to give in to compassionate impulses. But after a short while, when these same guards had become fully persuaded of the gravity of the situation, they refused to take responsibility for anything when they did not know where it might lead. Intercity telephone calls, permitted at first, caused such overcrowding in public phone booths and on the lines that they were entirely stopped for a few days, then strictly limited to what were described as urgent cases, such as deaths, births and marriages. So telegrams became our only recourse. Creatures bound together by mutual sympathy, by flesh and heart, were reduced to finding the signs of this ancient communion in a ten-word dispatch, all written in capitals. And since, as it happens, the forms of words that can be used in a telegram are quickly exhausted, before long whole lives together or painful passions were reduced to a periodic exchange of stock phrases such as 'Am well', 'Thinking of you', 'Affectionately yours'.

Some of us, meanwhile, insisted on writing, and endlessly dreamed up schemes for corresponding with the outside world, though they always proved illusory. Even if some of the methods that we thought of were successful, we knew nothing about it, for we never received any reply. Week after week we were reduced to starting the same letter over again and copying out the same appeals, so that after a certain time words which had at first been torn bleeding from our hearts became void of sense. We copied them down mechanically, trying by means of these dead words to give some idea of our ordeal. And in the end, the conventional call of a telegram seemed to us preferable to this sterile, obstinate monologue and this arid conversation with a blank wall.

Indeed, in a short while, when it became obvious that no one would manage to get out of the town, we thought to ask if those who had left before the start of the epidemic could be allowed to return. After a few days' consideration, the Prefecture replied in the affirmative. But it added that these returnees could not under any circumstances go back out of the town, and that while they were free to come in, they would not be free to leave again. Here again, a few families – though very few – took an optimistic view of the situation and invited their relatives to take advantage of this opportunity, sacrificing caution in their wish to be reunited with them. Very soon, however, those who were prisoners of the plague realized the danger to which they were exposing their loved ones and resigned themselves to enduring separation. At the worst point in the epidemic, we saw only one case where human feelings proved stronger than the fear of a horrible death. This was not, as you might imagine, a case of two young lovers induced to put love before suffering. It was old Dr Castel and his wife, who had been married for many years. A few days before the outbreak, Mme Castel had travelled to a nearby town. Theirs was not even one of those marriages which offer the world a picture of exemplary happiness and the narrator is in a position to say that in all probability the couple had not up to this point been sure that they were happy in their relationship. But a sudden and prolonged separation had convinced them that they could not live apart and, in the light of this startling revelation, the plague was a small thing.

Theirs was an exceptional case. In most cases it was clear that separation was to end only with the end of the epidemic. And for all of us, the feeling that governed our lives and which, none the less, we thought we knew well – as has already been said, the Oranais have simple passions – took on a fresh appearance. Husbands and lovers who had the greatest confidence in their partners found themselves becoming jealous. Men who thought they were frivolous in love found themselves loyal. Sons, who had lived close to their mothers and barely looked at them, instilled all their anxiety and longing into a line on her face that haunted their memories. This abrupt separation, without any halfway state and with no predictable future, left us disconcerted, unable to react against the memory of that presence, still so close, yet already so far away, that now filled our days. In reality, we suffered doubly: from our own suffering first and then from what we imagined to be that of the absent loved one, whether son, spouse or lover.

In other circumstances the people of the town would have found an outlet in a more external or more active life. But at the same time the plague left them idle, reduced to wandering round and round in their mournful town, day after day, engaged only in illusory games of memory; for in their aimless walks it was likely that they would always pass along the same paths, and, more often than not, in such a small town these paths were precisely the ones that in earlier times they had taken with their absent loved ones.

Thus, the first thing that the plague brought to our fellow-citizens was exile. The narrator is persuaded that he can set down here, in the name of everyone, what he then felt, since he experienced it at the same time as many of his fellows. Yes, that hollow that we carried constantly inside us, that precise emotion, that unreasonable desire to go backwards or, on the contrary, to speed up the march of time, those burning arrows of memory – all this really did amount to a feeling of exile. If sometimes we gave in to our imaginations and indulged in waiting for the ring of the homecoming bell or a familiar step on the stair, if at such moments we allowed ourselves to forget that the trains were at a standstill and if we then made sure to stay indoors at the time when, in normal circumstances, a traveller returning by the evening express might reach our neighbourhood, these games, of course, could not go on for long. Then we knew that our separation was going to last, and that we ought to try to come to terms with time. In short, from then on, we accepted our status as prisoners; we were reduced to our past alone and even if a few people were tempted to live in the future, they quickly gave it up, as far as possible, suffering the wounds that the imagination eventually inflicts on those who trust in it.

In particular, all of the people in our town very soon gave up, even in public, whatever habit they may have acquired of estimating the length of their separation. Why? It was when the most pessimistic had settled, say, on a figure of six months, when they had exhausted in advance all the bitterness of those months to come and raised their courage to the level of this trial, stretching themselves to the utmost to endure such suffering over such a long succession of days without weakening, and then, sometimes, a chance meeting with a friend, a view expressed in the newspaper, a fleeting suspicion or a sudden moment of foresight, gave them the idea that, after all, there was no reason why the disease should not last more than six months, perhaps a year, or even longer.

At that moment, the collapse of their morale, their will power and their patience was so abrupt that they felt they would never be able to climb back out of their hole. Consequently, they forced themselves never to think of the end of their suffering, never again to look towards the future and always, as it were, to keep their eyes lowered. But naturally this caution, this way of deceiving one's pain and dropping one's guard to refuse to fight, was ill-rewarded. At the same time as avoiding the collapse that they wished to avert at any price, they also deprived themselves of those moments, actually quite frequent, when they might have forgotten the plague by imagining their coming reunion with the ones they loved. Hence, foundering halfway between the abyss and the peak, they drifted rather than lived, given up to aimless days and sterile memories, wandering shadows who could only have found strength by resigning themselves to taking root in the soil of their distress.

Thus they endured that profound misery of all prisoners and all exiles, which is to live with a memory that is of no use to them. Even the past, which they thought of endlessly, had only the taste of remorse and longing. They would have liked to be able to add to it everything that they regretted not having done when they could do it, with the person for whom they were waiting – just as they brought the absent one into every situation of their life as prisoners, even the relatively happy ones, making them inevitably dissatisfied with what they now were. Impatient with the present, hostile to the past and deprived of a future, we really did then resemble those whom justice or human hatred has forced to live behind bars. In the last resort, the only way to escape this unbearable holiday was to make the trains run again in our imagination and to fill the hours with the repeated ringing of the doorbell, however silent it obstinately remained.

But, though this was exile, in most cases it was exile at home. And though the narrator only suffered an ordinary exile, he should not forget those, like the journalist Rambert and others, whose situation was different, and for whom the pain of separation was amplified by the fact that, being travellers surprised by the plague in the town, they were separated not only from the person to whom they could not return, but from their homes as well. In the midst of the general exile, they were the most exiled because while time aroused in them, as in all of us, that anguish peculiar to it, they were trapped in a particular space and were constantly running up against the barriers that separated this pestilential retreat from their lost homes. These no doubt were the people one saw wandering at any time of the day through the dusty town, silently invoking evenings that they alone could know and mornings in their own lands. They would nourish their pain with imponderable signs and disconcerting messages, like a flight of swallows, a rosy sunset or those peculiar rays that the sun sometimes casts on empty streets. They closed their eyes to the external world which can always offer an escape from anything, stubbornly nurturing their all-too-real fantasies and pursuing with all their strength the images of a land in which a certain light, two or three hills, a favourite tree and the faces of women composed a climate that nothing could replace.

To speak more particularly at last of lovers, who are the most interesting group and one about whom the narrator is perhaps better qualified to speak, they still found themselves tormented by other agonies, among which one should mention remorse. Their situation allowed them to consider their feelings with a sort of feverish objectivity, and it was rare, at such times, for them not to see their own shortcomings clearly. The first occasion of this was the difficulty they had in imagining precisely the absent person's actions and gestures. They deplored the fact that they knew nothing about how their loved ones spent their time;

they felt guilty about their past failure to find this out and about having pretended to believe that, for a person in love, the beloved's actions are not the source of every joy. From then on it was easy for them to go back through the story of their love and to examine its imperfections. In normal times we are all aware, consciously or not, that there is no love which cannot to be surpassed, yet we accept with a greater or lesser degree of equanimity that ours shall remain merely average. But memory is more demanding. And, in a highly significant way, the misfortune that attacked us from outside, and which affected a whole town, did not only bring us an unjust suffering, about which we might have complained, it also forced us to make ourselves suffer, and so made us consent to pain. This was one way that the disease had of distracting attention and confusing the issue.

Hence each one of us had to accept living from day to day, alone in the sight of heaven. This general abandonment, which might in the long run form character, began however by making life futile. For some of our fellow-citizens, for example, they were now subjected to another form of slavery that made them subservient to the sun and the rain. Seeing them, you would have thought that for the first time they were experiencing a direct impression of the weather. Their faces would light up at the simple appearance of golden light, while rainy days would cast a thick veil across their features and their thoughts. A few weeks earlier, they had been able to escape this weakness and this unreasonable subjection because they were not alone in the world, and to some extent the other person who lived with them stood at the front of their universe. From this moment, however, they seemed to have been handed over to the whims of the heavens, which is to say that they hoped and suffered without reason.

Finally, in these extremes of loneliness, no one could hope for help from his neighbour and everyone remained alone with his anxieties. If one of us, by chance, tried to confide in someone or describe something of his feelings, most of the time the reply that he received, whatever it was, would wound him. It was then that he realized that the other person and he were not talking about the same thing. He would be expressing himself from the depths of long days of meditation and suffering, the image that he wanted to communicate having been long tempered in the fire of waiting and passion. The other person, meanwhile, imagined a conventional emotion, the suffering that is hawked around the market-place, a mass-produced melancholy. Whether well-meant or not, the reply would always strike the wrong note and have to be abandoned. Or at least for those to whom silence was unbearable; since others could not find the true language of the heart, they resigned themselves to using the language of the market-place and themselves speaking in a conventional manner, that of the simple account or newspaper report, which is to some extent that of the daily chronicle of events. Here too the most authentic sufferings were habitually translated into the banal clichés of conversation. It was only at this price that the prisoners of the plague could obtain compassion from their concierges or gain the interest of their audience.

And yet the most important thing is that however painful these sufferings were, however heavy the heart was to bear (though empty), one can say that, in the first stage of the plague, these exiles were the privileged ones. At the very moment when the inhabitants of the town started to panic, their thoughts were entirely concerned with the person for whom they were waiting. The egotism of love protected them in the midst of the general distress and, if they did think about the plague, it was always and only to the extent that it risked making their separation eternal. Thus at the very heart of the epidemic they presented a salutary detachment that people were inclined to mistake for cool-headed com-posure. Their despair saved them from panic, so there was some good in their misfortune. For example, if it happened that one of them did succumb to the disease, it was almost always before he became aware of it. Dragged away from the long dialogue that he was holding inside himself with a shadow, he would then be cast forthwith into the still deeper silence of the earth. He had no time for anything.

While the townspeople were trying to come to terms with this sudden exile, the plague set guards at the gates and turned back ships that were making for the port of Oran. Since the town had been closed, not a vehicle had entered it. From that day onwards, you had the impression that cars had started to go round in circles. The port also took on an unusual appearance for those who looked at it from the height of the boulevards. The usual hustle and bustle which made this one of the leading ports on the coast had suddenly halted. One could still see a few ships which were held in quarantine, but on the quayside the huge idle cranes, the trucks turned on their sides and the solitary heaps of barrels or sacks showed that trade, too, had succumbed to the plague.

Despite these unusual scenes, the townspeople apparently found it hard to understand what was happening to them. There were those shared feelings, like separation or fear, but people also went on giving priority to their personal concerns. No one yet had really accepted the idea of the disease. Most were chiefly affected by whatever upset their habits or touched on their interests. They were annoyed or irritated by them, and these are not feelings with which to fight the plague. For example, their first reaction was to blame the authorities. The Prefect faced criticism that was echoed in the press ('Couldn't there be some relaxation in the measures proposed?'), and his reply was quite unexpected. Until then, neither the newspapers nor the Infodoc agency had had any official statistics for the disease. The Prefect passed them on to the agency, day by day, with the request that they should be published weekly.

Yet here too the public reaction was not immediate. The announcement that there had been 302 deaths in the third week of the plague did not stir the imagination. On the one hand, perhaps not all of them died of plague. And, on the other hand, no one in the town knew how many people died every week in ordinary times. The town had a population of two hundred thousand inhabitants. People had no idea if this proportion of deaths was normal. These are the sort of facts that no one ever bothers with, interesting though they clearly are. So in a sense the public had no point of comparison. It was only in the longer term, by noting the increase in the death rate, that people became aware of the truth. The fifth week produced 321 deaths and the sixth 345. These increases, at least, were convincing – but not enough for the townspeople, for all their anxiety, to abandon entirely the impression that it was merely an incident, annoying of course, but none the less temporary.

So they went on walking around the streets and sitting on the café terraces. On the whole, they were not cowardly, joking with each other more often than bewailing their fate, and pretending to accept with good humour discomforts that would clearly not last. Appearances were saved. Yet around the end of the month, more or less during the week of prayer that is mentioned below, more serious transformations altered the face of the town. First of all the Prefect took steps to deal with traffic and supplies. Supplies were limited and petrol rationed. Measures were even taken to save electricity. Only essential goods would be brought by road or air to Oran. As a result, traffic decreased progressively until it almost disappeared altogether, some shops selling luxury goods shut down overnight and others hung 'sold out' notices in their windows, while queues of customers formed in front of their doors.

So Oran took on an unusual appearance. The number of pedestrians rose and, at slack times, many people, who had been reduced to inactivity by the closing of shops and some offices, filled the streets and cafés. For the time being they were not yet unemployed, just on leave. This meant that, for example, at three in the afternoon on a sunny day Oran gave the deceptive impression of a town on holiday, in which the traffic had been halted and the shops closed to allow a public demonstration to march past, and the inhabitants had poured out into the streets to take part in the celebrations.

Of course the cinemas took advantage of this general holiday and did good business. But the circuits that the films followed in the *département* were interrupted. After two weeks, the theatres were forced to swap programmes, and, after a certain period of time, the cinemas ended up always showing the same film. However, their takings did not fall.

Finally, the cafés were able to carry on supplying their customers thanks to the considerable stocks they had put by in a town where wines and spirits are at the forefront of trade. It must be said that people drank a lot. After one café put up a notice saying that 'microbes hate the honest grape', the idea that alcohol protects you against infection – something that the public already found it natural to believe – became still more firmly anchored in their minds. Every night around two o'clock quite a large number of drunkards were thrown out of the cafés to fill the streets, where they delivered themselves of optimistic opinions.

But in one sense all these changes were so extraordinary and had happened so quickly that it was not easy to consider them as normal and lasting. The result was that we continued to give priority to our personal feelings.

Coming out of the hospital, two days after the closure of the gates, Dr Rieux met Cottard whose face expressed something close to satisfaction. Rieux congratulated him on how well he was looking.

'Yes, I'm fine,' said the little man. 'Tell me, doctor, this confounded plague, huh? It's starting to get serious.'

The doctor agreed, and the other man remarked with a sort of genial cheerfulness:

'There's no reason for it to stop now. Everything will be upside down.'

They walked along together for a moment. Cottard described how a big grocer in his district had stockpiled supplies so that he could sell them at a large profit, and they had found tins of food under his bed when they came to fetch him and take him to the hospital. 'He died there. You can't buy off the plague.' Cottard was full of stories like that, true or false, about the epidemic. For example, it was said that in the centre one morning a man with symptoms of the disease and at the delirious stage had rushed outside, thrown himself on the first woman he met and embraced her, shouting that he had the plague.

'Fine!' Cottard said, in a pleasant tone that was not at all in keeping with his words. 'We'll all go mad, that's for sure.'

Similarly, on the afternoon of the same day, Joseph Grand eventually confided a little in Dr Rieux. He had noticed Mme Rieux's photograph on the desk and looked at the doctor. Rieux replied that his wife was being treated elsewhere. 'In a sense', Grand said, 'it's a piece of luck.' The doctor replied that it certainly was and that they would just have to hope that his wife got better.

'Ah!' Grand said. 'I understand.'

Then, for the first time since Rieux had known him, he began to talk freely. Though he still had to hunt for his words, he almost always managed to find them, as though he had been thinking about what he was saying for a long time.

He had got married very young to a young girl of poor family from his neighbourhood. He had even interrupted his studies and taken a job so that he could get married. Neither Jeanne nor he ever went outside their part of town. He would go and see her at home, and Jeanne's parents would laugh a little at this silent, awkward suitor. Her father was a railway worker. When he was resting, you could always see him sitting in a corner by the window, thoughtful, watching the comings and goings in the street, his huge hands flat on his thighs. The mother was always busy around the house, where Jeanne would help her. She was so tiny that Grand could not see her cross a street without feeling afraid for her: at such times, the vehicles seemed disproportionately large. One day Jeanne was looking with wonderment at a shop window decorated for Christmas. She turned to him and said: 'Isn't it lovely!' He squeezed her hand. That's how they decided to marry.

The rest of the story, Grand said, was very simple. This is how it is for everyone: you get married, you stay in love for a little while and you work. You work so much that you forget to love. Jeanne worked too, because the head of his department's promises were not kept. Here it took some imagination to grasp what Grand meant. Partly because of tiredness, he had let himself go, he had become more and more silent and he had not convinced his young wife that she was loved. A working man, poverty, a narrowing of possibilities, the silent evenings around the table: there is no place for passion in such a universe. Jeanne must surely have suffered. Even so, she stayed: one can sometimes suffer for a long time without knowing it. The years went by. Later on, she left. Of course she did not leave by herself. 'I have been very fond of you, but now I am tired . . . I am not happy to go away, but one does not need to be happy to start again.' That, broadly speaking, is what she wrote to him.

Joseph Grand suffered in his turn. He could have started again, as Rieux pointed out to him. But, you see, he didn't believe in it.

Quite simply, he still thought about her. What he would have liked was to have written her a letter justifying himself. 'But it's hard,' he said. 'I've been thinking about it for a long time. As long as we were in love, we understood one another without words. But one is not always in love. At a certain moment I ought to have found the words that would have kept her, but I couldn't.' Grand blew his nose in a sort of chequered napkin; then he wiped his moustache. Rieux looked at him.

'Excuse me doctor,' the old man said. 'But – how can I put it? I trust you. With you, I can talk. And then I give way to my feelings.'

Grand, quite clearly, was a hundred miles from the plague.

That evening Rieux telegraphed his wife that the town was shut, that he was well, that she should go on looking after herself and that he was thinking about her.

Three weeks after the closing of the gates Rieux came out of the hospital to find a young man waiting for him.

'I expect you recognize me,' the man said.

Rieux thought he knew him, but was not sure.

'I came before all this happened,' the other said. 'I was asking you for information about the condition of the Arabs. My name is Raymond Rambert.'

'Oh, yes!' Rieux said. 'Well, now you have a good subject for a report.'

The young man seemed nervous. He said that it was nothing to do with that and he had come to ask for Dr Rieux's help.

'I'm sorry,' he added. 'But I don't know anybody in the town and unfortunately the correspondent of my paper is a half-wit.'

Rieux suggested that they should walk together to a dispensary in the centre of town because he had some orders to make. They went down through the narrow streets in the African quarter. Evening was coming, but the town, which had once been so busy at that time of day, seemed oddly deserted. Only a few bugle calls in the still golden sky showed that the army was pretending to do its job. Meanwhile, along the steeply descending streets, between the blue, ochre and violet walls of the Moorish houses, Rambert spoke in a state of great agitation. He had left his wife behind in Paris. Strictly speaking she was not his wife, but it was the same thing. He had sent her a telegram as soon as the town was closed. At first he thought it was just a temporary matter and he had simply tried to keep in touch with her. His colleagues in Oran had told him that there was nothing they could do, the police had sent him away and a secretary at the Prefecture had laughed in his face. Eventually, after waiting for two hours in a queue, he had managed to have a telegram accepted in which he said: 'ALL WELL STOP SEE YOU SOON.'

But the next day when he got up he suddenly thought that after all he had no idea how long it might last. So he decided to leave. Since he had influence (in his job, people can pull strings), he managed to reach the head of the Prefect's department and told him that he had nothing to do with Oran, that it was not his business to stay there, that he had found himself here by accident and that it was only right that he should be allowed to leave, even if, once he was outside, he had to be put in quarantine. The head of the department told him that he understood very well, but that there could be no exceptions; he would see, but the situation was serious and nothing could be decided.

'After all,' Rambert said to the doctor, 'I'm a stranger in this town.'

'Of course you are, but let's just hope that the epidemic will not last.'

In the end, he tried to console Rambert by pointing out that he could find the material for an interesting report in Oran and that, all things considered, there was no cloud without a silver lining. Rambert shrugged his shoulders. They were coming to the centre of the town.

'You see, doctor, it's ridiculous. I wasn't put on this earth to make reports; but perhaps I was put on earth to live with a woman. Doesn't that follow?'

Rieux said that to him it seemed reasonable.

On the boulevards in the centre there were none of the usual crowds. A few passers-by hurried towards their distant homes. None of them was smiling. Rieux thought it must be because this was the day for the Infodoc announcement. After another twenty-four hours the townspeople would start to hope again. But on the day itself, the figures were still too fresh in their memories.

'The thing is,' Rambert said, without warning, 'she and I met a short time ago and we get on well.'

Rieux said nothing.

'But I'm boring you,' Rambert went on. 'I just wanted to ask if you couldn't give me a certificate stating that I do not have this blasted disease. I think it could be useful to me.'

Rieux nodded, caught hold of a little boy who had collided with his legs and gently stood him back on his feet. They carried on as far as the parade-ground. The branches of fig trees and palms hung motionless, grey with dust, around a statue of the Republic, dirty and grimed. They stopped under this monument. Rieux stamped his shoes, which were covered with a whitish film, one after another on the ground. He looked at Rambert. With his felt hat pushed a little back on his head, his shirt collar unbuttoned under his tie, and badly shaved, the journalist looked morose and stubborn.

'Believe me, I understand you,' Rieux said at length. 'But you've got it wrong. I can't give you such a certificate because I do not in fact know if you have the disease and because, even if I did, I could not guarantee that between the moment when you left my surgery and the one when you entered the Prefecture, you would not be infected. And even if . . .'

'And even if?' asked Rambert.

'Even if I did give you this certificate, it would be of no use to you.'

'Why?'

'Because there are thousands of men in this town in your situation and they cannot be allowed to leave.'

'But what if they themselves don't have the plague?'

'That's not a good enough reason. I know very well that this whole business is stupid, but we are all involved. We must accept things as they are.'

'But I don't belong here!'

'I'm sorry to say that from now on you will belong here as everyone else does.'

The other man reacted excitedly:

'It's a question of humanity, I promise you. Perhaps you don't realize what a separation such as this means for two people who are fond of one another.'

Rieux did not answer at once. Then he said that he thought he did understand. He wanted with all his strength for Rambert to be back with his woman and for all those who loved one another to be reunited, but there were regulations and laws, and there was plague: his task was to do what had to be done.

'No,' Rambert said bitterly. 'You cannot understand. You are talking the language of reason, you are thinking in abstract terms.'

The doctor looked up at the Republic and said that he did not know whether he was speaking the language of reason, but he was speaking the language of the facts, which was not necessarily the same thing. The journalist adjusted his tie.

'So that means that I shall have to manage some other way, does it? In any case,' he said, with a sort of defiance, 'I shall leave this town.'

The doctor said that he understood that too, but it was none of his business.

'Yes, it is your business,' Rambert said, flaring up suddenly. 'I came to see you because I was told that you had a major role in the decisions that have been taken, so I thought that in one case at least you might undo what you had helped to do. But you don't care. You thought of no one. You didn't consider those who were kept apart.'

Rieux acknowledged that, in a sense, this was true: he did not want to consider such cases.

'Oh, I see!' said Rambert. 'You're going to tell me about public service. But the general good consists in the happiness of each.'

'Come, now,' said the doctor, who seemed to be emerging from a moment of absent-mindedness. 'It's that and it's other things. You should not judge. But you are wrong to feel angry. If you could get away from this business, I should be very happy indeed. It's just that there are certain things that my position forbids me to do.'

The other man shook his head impatiently.

'Yes, I was wrong to get annoyed. And I've taken up enough of your time already.'

Rieux asked him to let him know what he was up to and not to hold it against him. There was surely some common ground where they could meet. Suddenly, Rambert seemed bewildered:

'I think so,' he said after a pause. 'Yes, I think so, in spite of myself and in spite of everything you have told me.'

He paused again:

'But I cannot approve of your attitude.'

He pulled his hat down over his forehead and quickly walked away. Rieux saw him go into the hotel where Jean Tarrou was living.

After a moment the doctor shook his head. The journalist was right to be impatient for happiness. But was he right to accuse Rieux? 'You are thinking in abstract terms.' Was it truly an abstraction, spending his days in the hospital where the plague was working overtime, bringing the number of victims up to five hundred on average per week? Yes, there was an element of abstraction and unreality in misfortune. But when an abstraction starts to kill you, you have to get to work on it. And Rieux knew that this was not the easiest thing to do. It was not easy, for example, to manage this auxiliary hospital which was his responsibility – there were now three of them in all. He had had to convert one room, opening onto the consulting-room, into an admissions area. A pit dug into the floor formed a lake of disinfectant in the midst of which was a small island of brick. The patient was transported onto the island, quickly undressed and his clothes thrown into the water. Washed, dried and covered in the coarse hospital gown, he was passed on to Rieux, then taken to one of the wards. They had been forced to use the courtyard of a school which now contained five hundred beds in all, almost all of them occupied. After the morning admissions which he was in charge of himself, the patients were vaccinated and the swellings lanced. Then Rieux once again checked the figures before going back to his afternoon rounds. Finally, in the evening, he made his house visits and came home late at night. The previous night, when his mother handed him a telegram from the younger Mme Rieux, she had pointed out that the doctor's hands were shaking.

'Yes,' he said. 'But if I persevere, I shall be less nervous.'

He was healthy and tough. Really, he was not yet tired, but his house visits, for example, were becoming unbearable. Diagnosing the infection meant quickly removing the patient. And here the difficulty and the abstraction began because the family knew that they would not see the patient again until he or she was cured or dead. 'Have pity, doctor!' said Mme Loret, mother of the chambermaid who worked at Tarrou's hotel. What did that mean? Of course he had pity. But where did that get anyone? He had to telephone. Then the siren of the ambulance sounded. In the early days, the neighbours would open their windows and look out. Later, they hurriedly closed them. Then began struggles, tears, pleas, in short, abstraction. In these apartments, overheated by fever and anguish, scenes of madness were played out. But the sick person was taken away. Rieux could go.

On the first few occasions he had merely rung for the ambulance, then sped off towards other patients without waiting for it to arrive. But then the relatives locked their doors, preferring a tête-à-tête with the plague to a separation – knowing now what that meant. Shouts, orders, the arrival of the police, then, later, of the army, and the patient was seized by force. In the early weeks Rieux was obliged to wait until the ambulance came. After that, when every doctor was accompanied on his visits by a volunteer inspector, Rieux was again able to run from one patient to the next. But at the beginning, every evening was like the one when he had come into Mme Loret's, in a little apartment decorated with fans and artificial flowers, to be greeted by the mother who said with a forced smile:

'I do hope it's not that fever that everyone's talking about.'

And he, turning back the sheet and the nightdress, stared in silence at the red patches on the belly and the thighs, and the swollen lymph nodes. The mother looked between her daughter's legs and howled, unable to control herself. Every evening mothers would shout like that, in a distraught manner, at the sight of bellies displaying all their signs of death; every evening hands would grasp Rieux's arms, while useless words, promises and tears poured forth; and every evening the ambulance siren would set off scenes of distress as pointless as any kind of pain. At the end of a long succession of such evenings, each like the next, Rieux could no longer hope for anything except a continuing series of similar scenes, forever repeated. Yes, the plague, like abstraction, was monotonous. Only one thing may have changed, and that was Rieux himself. He felt it that evening, beneath the monument to the Republic, aware only of the hard indifference that was starting to fill him, still looking at the hotel door where Rambert had vanished.

At the end of these harrowing weeks, after all these evenings when the town poured into the streets to wander round them, Rieux realized that he no longer needed to protect himself against pity. When pity is useless one grows tired of it. And the doctor found his only consolation for these exhausting days in this feeling of a heart slowly closing around itself. He knew that it would make his task easier. That is why he welcomed it. When his mother, meeting him as he came in at two o'clock in the morning, was pained by the empty look he gave her, she was actually regretting the only comfort that Rieux by then could enjoy. To struggle against abstraction, one must come to resemble it a little. But how could Rambert be persuaded of that? Abstraction for Rambert was everything that stood in the way of his happiness. In truth, Rieux knew that in a certain sense the journalist was right. But he also knew that sometimes abstraction may become stronger than happiness, and that then, and only then, should one take it into account. This is what would happened to Rambert, and the doctor would learn of it in the details that Rambert would later confide in him. In this way, and at a different level, he would follow the sort of dreary struggle between the happiness of each individual and the abstractions of the plague, that was to make up the life of our town for this long period of time.

However, where some people saw abstraction, others saw truth. A cloud fell across the end of the first month of the disease because of a marked aggravation of the epidemic and an impassioned sermon by Father Paneloux, the Jesuit priest who had ministered to old Michel at the start of his illness. Father Paneloux had previously distinguished himself by his frequent contributions to the bulletin of the Geographical Society of Oran, with his authoritative reconstructions of epigraphs. But he had reached a wider audience than that of a mere specialist with a series of lectures that he gave on modern individualism. Here he had warmly defended a demanding form of Christianity which rejected both modern liberalism and the obscurantism of previous centuries. In these lectures he had not spared his listeners some hard truths. Hence his reputation.

Then, at the end of this same month, the ecclesiastical authorities of the town decided to wage war on the plague by their own means, by organizing a week of collective prayer. This demonstration of public piety was to end on the Sunday with a solemn mass under the auspices of Saint Roch, the saint who was a victim of plague. Father Paneloux was asked to preach on the occasion. For the preceding fortnight he had torn himself away from his work on Saint Augustine and the African Church which had won him a special place in his order. A man of fiery and passionate temperament, he had resolutely accepted the mission with which he was entrusted. A long time before the sermon, people in the town were talking about it and, in its way, it marked an important date in the history of that time.

The week of prayer was observed by many. It is not that ordinarily the people of Oran are especially pious. On Sunday mornings, for example, sea bathing offers serious competition to church-going. Nor was it the case that they had seen the light in a sudden conversion. But, on the one hand, with the town closed and the port barred, it was no longer possible to bathe; and, on the other, they were in a rather odd state of mind where, without having fully accepted in themselves the surprising events in which they were caught up, they did obviously believe that something had changed. However, many still hoped that the epidemic would end and that they and their families would be spared. As a result, they did not yet feel any sense of obligation. For them the plague was only an unpleasant visitor which would leave one day as it had entered. They were scared but not desperate and the time had yet to come when the plague would seem to them like the very shape of their lives and when they would forget the existence that they had led in the days before. In short, they were neither here nor there. As for religion, like several other problems, the plague had put them in a peculiar state of mind, as far removed from indifference as from passion, which might quite well have been defined by the word 'objectivity'. For example, most of those who followed the week of prayer could have subscribed to the observation that one of the faithful made to Dr Rieux: 'In any event, it can't do any harm.' Even Tarrou, having remarked in his notebook that the Chinese in such cases go and play the tambourine in front of the genie of the plague, noted that it was quite impossible in reality to know whether the tambourine was more effective than other preventive health measures. He added only that to decide the question one would need to be informed as to the existence of a genie of the plague and that our ignorance in the matter negated any opinion that one might have.

In any case, the cathedral of our town had a more or less full congregation throughout the week. On the first days many inhabitants still remained outside in the gardens of palm and pomegranate trees which extend in front of its porch, to listen to the wave of invocations and prayers that flowed out into the streets. Bit by bit, encouraged by example, the same listeners made up their minds to go in and timidly add their voices to the responses of the congregation. And on Sunday a considerable crowd poured into the nave, overflowing into the porch and the top steps. Since the evening before the sky had been overcast and rain was pouring down. Those who remained outside had opened umbrellas. As Father Paneloux climbed the steps into the pulpit, a scent of incense and damp clothing hovered in the air.

He was of medium height, but stocky. When he leant forward across the edge of the pulpit, his large hands clasping the wood, one could see nothing of him except a thick, black shape surmounted by the two patches of his cheeks, flushed red behind his steel-rimmed glasses. He had a strong, impassioned voice which carried a long way, so when he launched a single vehement and thundering attack on his listeners – 'My brethren, a calamity has befallen you; my brethren, you have deserved it' – a stir ran through the congregation as far as the west door.

Logically, what followed did not seem to tie in with this resounding first sentence. Only after the remainder of the oration did the people realize that, by a clever rhetorical device, like a boxer delivering a blow, the priest had imparted the theme of his entire sermon at a single stroke. Indeed, immediately after this sentence, Paneloux quoted the passage from Exodus concerning the plague in Egypt and said: 'The first time that this tribulation appeared in history, it was to strike down the enemies of God. Pharaoh opposed the designs of the Eternal and the plague brought him to his knees. Since the beginning of history, the scourge of God has brought down the proud and the blind beneath His feet. Think on this and fall to your knees.'

Outside the rain was coming down more heavily and this last sentence, delivered in the midst of total silence, made still deeper by the lashing of the rain on the cathedral windows, thundered forth with such power that after a moment's hesitation a few members of the congregation slipped from their chairs onto the prayer stools. Others felt that they should follow their example, with the result that, from one to another, with no noise except the creaking of some chairs, very soon the whole congregation was kneeling down. At this, Paneloux drew himself up, took a deep breath and continued in increasingly emphatic tones: 'If the plague affects you now, this means that the time has come to reflect. The just have no need to fear, but the unjust should tremble. In the vast granary of the universe, the implacable flail will thresh the human corn until the chaff is divided from the grain. There will be more chaff than grain, more called than chosen, and this misfortune was not willed by God. For too long this world has compromised with evil; for too long it has relied on divine mercy. Because one had only to repent, everything was permitted. And where repentance was concerned, each man felt he was strong. When the time came, one would surely repent. Until then, the easiest course was to let oneself go, and divine mercy would do the rest. Well, it could not last. God, who has so long bent the face of pity towards this town, is tired of waiting; disappointed in His eternal hope, He has turned away His face. And we, deprived of the light of God, will languish for a long time in the darkness of the plague!'

Someone in the hall snorted like an impatient horse. After a short pause, the priest carried on, lowering his voice: 'One may read in the *Golden Legend* that at the time of King Humbert, in Lombardy, Italy was ravaged by a plague so violent that there were hardly enough of the living to bury the dead, and that this plague raged above all in Rome and in Pavia. And a good angel appeared for all to see, giving orders to the bad angel who was carrying a hunting spear, and commanding him to strike the houses; and for as many blows as a house received, there were so many dead that came out of it.'

Here Paneloux extended his two short arms towards the west door as though pointing to something behind the moving curtain of rain. 'My brethren,' he said emphatically. 'The same mortal hunt is proceeding today through our streets. Can you see him, that angel of the plague, as fair as Lucifer and shining like evil itself, rising up above your rooftops, his right hand bearing the red spear level with his head and his left hand pointing to one of your houses. At this very moment, perhaps, his finger is stretching towards your door and the spear sounding on the wood. A moment later, and the plague is entering your home, sitting down in your room and awaiting your return. It is there, patient and watchful, as sure as the very order of the world. No earthly power − not even, note this well, vain human science − can shield you from this hand as it reaches out to you. Beaten on the bloody threshing floor of pain, you will be cast out with the chaff.'

Then the priest expanded even more on the poignant image of the flail. He suggested the image of the mighty piece of wood turning above the town, striking indiscriminately and returning covered in blood, only to scatter the blood and human misery 'in a sowing that would make way for a harvest of truth'.

At the end of this long development Father Paneloux stopped, his hair on his forehead and his body shaken by a tremor that his hands communicated to the pulpit; then he resumed in a duller but more accusing tone: 'Yes, the hour has come to reflect. You thought that it was enough for you to visit God on Sunday to be free to do as you wished for the rest of the week. You thought that a few genuflections would be sufficient compensation for your criminal lack of concern. But God is not lukewarm. Such a casual relationship is not sufficient for His all-devouring affection. He wanted to see you longer: this is His way of loving and, in truth, it is the only way. This is why, tired of waiting for you to come to Him, He has allowed the scourge to visit you as it has visit all the cities of sin since history began. You know now what sin is, as Cain and his sons knew, those before the Flood, those of Sodom and Gomorrah, Pharaoh and Job and all the accursed. And as they all did, now you have been looking with fresh eyes on people and on things, since the day when this town closed its walls around you and around the scourge. You know, at last, that you must arrive at the heart of the matter.'

A moist wind was now blowing along the nave and the candle flames guttered and bent. A thick smell of wax, coughs, a yawn rose up towards Father Paneloux who, resuming his analysis with much appreciated subtlety, went on calmly: 'Many of you, I know, are starting to wonder what I am leading to. I want to bring you to the truth and to teach you to rejoice, despite all that I have said. This is no longer the time for advice, it is not the time when a fraternal hand provided the means to steer you towards goodness. Today, truth is an order, and it is a red spear that points you down the way of salvation and drives you towards it. My brethren, this is where finally divine mercy is revealed, the mercy that has been put into everything good as well as evil, anger and pity, plague and salvation. This very scourge that assails you, raises you up and shows you the way.

'A long time ago, the Christians of Abyssinia saw in the plague an effective means to win eternity, a means sent by God. Those who were not infected would roll themselves in the bedclothes of the victims so as to ensure their own deaths. Of course, one would not recommend such zeal in search of salvation. It exhibits a regrettable haste, which is close to pride. One must not be in a greater hurry than God, and everything that aims to speed up the immutable order of things, which He has established once and for all, leads to heresy. But at least this example carries a lesson. To our more far-sighted minds it merely enhances the exquisite glimmer of eternity that shines in the depth of all suffering. This is the light that illumines the dim path which leads to deliverance. It manifests the divine will which unfailingly transforms evil into good. Today, through the paths of death, anguish and sighs, it still guides us towards the silence of God and the principle of all life. This, my brethren, is the immense consolation that I wished to bring you, so that what you take away from here should not only be the language of chastisement, but also the Word that brings peace.'

One could feel that Paneloux had finished. Outside the rain had ceased. A sky, in which water mingled with sunshine, was casting a fresher light across the square. Sounds of voices and the gliding of cars rose from the street – the language of a town as it wakes. The members of the congregation gathered their things in a muted jumble of sounds. Yet the priest was speaking again. He said that, after showing the divine origin of the plague and punitive nature of the scourge, he was finished with that and would not resort for his conclusion to an eloquence that would be misplaced, given the tragic character of the subject. He thought that everything must be clear to them all. He reminded them only that on the occasion of the great plague in Marseille, the historian Mathieu Marais had complained of being plunged into hell, of living without help and without hope. Well, Mathieu Marais was blind! Never before had Father Paneloux felt more intensely the aid of God and the Christian hope that was held out to them all. He hoped, against all hope, that despite the horror of these days and the cries of the dying, our fellow-citizens would offer heaven the only word that a Christian should, which was the word of love. God would do the rest.

Whether this sermon had any effect on our townspeople is hard to say. M. Othon, the examining magistrate, announced to Dr Rieux that he found Father Paneloux's analysis 'absolutely irrefutable'. But not everyone had such a categorical opinion. Quite simply, the sermon made some people more receptive to the notion – which had remained vague up to then – that they were condemned for some unknown crime to an unimaginable term of imprisonment. And while some carried on with their little lives and adapted to being shut in, for others on the contrary their sole idea from then on was to escape from this prison.

At first people had agreed to being cut off from the outside as they might have accepted any temporary irritation that would only interfere with a few of their habits. But, suddenly becoming conscious of a kind of incarceration beneath the lid of the sky in which summer was beginning to crackle, they felt in some vague way that this confinement threatened their whole lives, and, when evening came, the cool brought renewed energy and sometimes drove them to desperate actions.

First of all, whether or not by coincidence, it was from that Sunday onwards that a sort of fear arose that was general enough and deep enough for one to suspect that the people of the town were really starting to become aware of their situation. From that point of view, the climate in which we lived here was somewhat altered. But was the change really in the climate or in people's hearts and minds: that was the question.

A few days after the sermon Rieux, discussing the event with Grand as they walked towards the suburbs, ran into a man who was swaying around in front of them without making any effort to go forwards. At that very moment the street lamps, which were lighting up later and later in the town, suddenly came on. The high lamp right behind the two men suddenly lit up the stranger who was laughing noiselessly, with his eyes shut. Down his pale face, contorted by this silent mirth, sweat was pouring in large drops. They walked past him.

'A madman,' said Grand.

Rieux, who had just taken his arm to lead him forward, felt that the clerk was trembling with annoyance.

'Soon there will only be mad people in our town,' Rieux said.

Partly because he was tired, his throat felt dry.

'Let's have a drink.'

In the thick, reddish atmosphere of the little café that they entered, lit by a single lamp above the counter, people were talking in low voices, for no obvious reason. To Rieux's surprise, when they got to the counter Grand ordered a glass of brandy which he drank in a single gulp, saying that it was strong. Then he wanted to leave. Outside it seemed to Rieux that the night was full of sighing and moaning. Somewhere in the black sky above the street lights a dull whistle reminded him of the invisible scourge endlessly stirring in the warm air.

'Luckily, luckily . . . ,' Grand said.

Rieux wondered what he meant.

'Luckily,' the other man said, 'I have my work.'

'Yes,' said Rieux. 'It does help.'

And, deciding not to listen to the whistling sound, he asked Grand if he was satisfied with his work.

'Well, I think I'm on the right track.'

'Will it take you much longer?'

Grand seemed to become excited and the warmth of the alcohol passed into his voice.

'I don't know. But that's not the question, doctor, that's not the question. No.'

In the darkness, Rieux guessed that he was waving his arms. He seemed to be getting ready to say something that came abruptly and in a rush.

'You see, what I want, doctor, is that on the day when the manuscript reaches the publisher, he should stand up after reading it and say to his colleagues: "Hats off, gentlemen!"'

Rieux was surprised by this sudden declaration. He felt that his companion was making the gesture of taking off his hat, bringing his hand up to his head and raising his arm to a horizontal position. At this, the peculiar whistling sound seem to resume with even greater force.

'Yes,' Grand said. 'It must be perfect.'

Though he knew very little about customs and practice in the literary world, Rieux had the impression that things were not so simple, and, for example, that publishers would be bare-headed in their offices. But, in fact, one never knew and he preferred not to make any remark about it. Despite himself, he was listening to the mysterious noises of the plague. The two men were getting closer to Grand's neighbourhood and, since it was on a slight hill, they were cooled by a mild breeze which at the same time cleansed the town of all its noises. However, Grand went on talking and Rieux could not always follow what the good fellow was saying. He only understood that the work in question was already many pages long, but that the efforts the author was taking to bring it to perfection cost him dear. 'Whole evenings, whole weeks on one word . . . sometimes just a simple conjunction.' Here Grand stopped and took hold of the doctor by a button of his coat. The words stumbled out of his ill-adjusted mouth.

'You understand, doctor. At a pinch, it is easy enough to choose between *but* and *and*. It already becomes more difficult to opt for *and* or *then*. The difficulty grows with *then* and *afterwards*. But what is surely hardest of all is to decide whether one should put *and* or *not*.'

'Yes,' Rieux said. 'I understand.'

And he set off again. The other man seemed confused and once more caught up with him.

'Excuse me,' he stammered. 'I don't know what's wrong with me this evening!'

Rieux tapped him lightly on the shoulder and said that he wanted to help him, because his story interested him a good deal. Grand seemed a little calmer and when they arrived at his house hesitated for a moment, then invited the doctor to come up. Rieux accepted.

In the dining-room, Grand invited him to sit down at a table spread with papers, a manuscript in minute handwriting, which was covered with crossings-out.

'Yes, that's it,' Grand told the doctor, who was looking at him enquiringly. 'But would you like a drink? I have a little wine.'

Rieux refused, He was looking at the sheets of paper.

'Don't look,' said Grand. 'It's my first sentence. It's giving me trouble, a lot of trouble.'

He, too, was staring at all the sheets of paper and his hand seemed to be irresistibly drawn towards one of them, which he raised up until the light from the unshaded bulb was shining through it. The sheet trembled in his hand. Rieux noticed that the clerk's forehead was damp.

'Sit down', Rieux said, 'and read it to me.'

The other man looked at him with a kind of gratitude.

'Yes,' he said. 'I think I'd like to.'

He waited for a moment, still looking at the sheet of paper, then sat down. Rieux was listening at the same time to a sort of vague humming sound in the town, as if replying to the whistling flail of the plague. At this particular moment he had an extraordinarily acute perception of the town spread out at his feet, the enclosed world that it formed and the dreadful cries stifled in its night. He heard Grand's muffled voice: 'On a fine morning in the month of May, an elegant woman was riding a magnificent sorrel mare through the flowered avenues of the Bois de Boulogne.' Silence returned and with it the faint murmuring of the suffering town. Grand had put down the sheet of paper, but was still staring at it. After a pause, he looked up:

'What do you think of it?'

Rieux replied that this beginning made him curious to know what would follow. But the other man said with excitement that this was not the right way of looking at it. He slapped the flat of his hand down on the paper.

'That's only a rough idea. When I have managed to describe precisely the picture that I have in my imagination, when my sentence has the very same movement as that trotting horse, one-two-three, one-two-three, then the rest will be easy and above all the illusion will be such from the very start that it will be possible to say: "Hats off, gentlemen!"'

However, before he reached that point, there was still a lot of work to be done. He would never agree to hand over this sentence as it was to a printer because, though from time to time he did feel pleased with it, he realized that it still did not entirely accord with reality and that, to some extent, it had a certain facility of tone that made it sound distantly – but sound, for all that – like a cliché. At any rate, that was the sense of what he was saying when they heard some men running past below the window. Rieux got up.

'You see what I'll do with it,' Grand said. And, turning to the window, added: 'When all this is over.'

But the sounds of running feet returned. Rieux was already going downstairs and two men ran past him when he reached the street. They appeared to be going towards the town gates. In fact, some of our fellow-citizens, driven out of their minds by the heat and the idea of plague, had resorted to violence and tried to evade the guards on the barriers in order to flee the town.

Others, like Rambert, were also trying to escape from the atmosphere of increasing panic, though with more obstinacy and skill, if not more success. At first Rambert had continued to work through official channels. He had always said that he thought obstinacy would eventually triumph over anything and, in some ways, his job involved using his wits to get round problems. So he went to see a large number of civil servants and people whose competence one did not usually question. But, in the circumstances, this competence was useless to them. Most of the time they were men who had precise and fixed notions about everything to do with banking, or exports, or citrus fruits, or perhaps the wine trade. They had undeniable expertise in problems of litigation or insurance, not to mention excellent qualifications and evident good-will. You might even say that the most striking thing among all of them was their goodwill. But when it came to the plague, their knowledge was more or less nil.

However, Rambert had put his case to each of them, whenever it was possible. The basis of his argument remained the same: he said that he was a foreigner in our town and that, consequently, his case should be given special consideration. In general, those the journalist approached were willing to concede the point. But most of the time they argued that a number of other people were in this situation and so his case was not as exceptional as he imagined. To this Rambert might reply that it did not alter the substance of his argument at all, to which they answered that it did alter something in respect of administration, this being unfavourable to any measure of exemption that might tend to create what, with expressions of great repugnance, they called 'a precedent'. According to the classification which Rambert suggested to Dr Rieux, those who argued in this way belonged to the category of Formalists. In addition to these, there were also the Fine Words, who assured the client that none of this could last and who, full of good advice when what one wanted from them was a decision, consoled Rambert by telling him that all this was only a temporary inconvenience. There were also the High and Mighty, who requested the visitor to leave a note summarizing his case and told him that they would give a ruling on it; the Futile, who offered housing coupons or the addresses of cheap boarding houses; the Methodical, who got you to fill out a form, then filed it; the Overworked, who held their hands in the air; and the Interrupted, who looked in the other direction. And finally there were the Traditionalists, by far the greatest number, who directed Rambert to another office or suggested some alternative course of action.

So the journalist had exhausted himself with visits and gained a clear idea of how an hôtel de ville or a prefecture worked, after waiting on an imitation leather bench in front of large posters inviting him to subscribe to an issue of tax-free bonds or to join the colonial army, and going into one office after another where he could as easily foresee the faces that would greet him as the filing cabinets and the shelves of dossiers. The good thing about all this, as Rambert told Rieux, with a hint of bitterness, was that it hid the real situation from him. He was practically unaware of the spread of the plague. Not to mention that it made the days go by faster and, in the situation in which the whole town found itself, you might say that every day that went by brought each man, provided he did not die, closer to the end of his troubles. Rieux had to acknowledge that this was true, but that as truths go, it was rather a broad one.

At a particular moment, Rambert became hopeful. The Prefecture had sent him a blank form which they asked him to fill out precisely. The form enquired about his identity, his family situation, his former and present resources and that which they called his *curriculum vitae*. He got the impression that this was an enquiry designed to draw up a list of people who might be sent back to their usual place of residence. Some vague information, picked up in an office, confirmed this notion. But after a few precise questions he managed to find the office which had sent him the form and he was told that the information was being collected 'in the event . . .'.

'In the event of what?' Rambert asked.

They then told him that it was in the event of his falling ill with the plague and dying, in which case they could, on the one hand, inform his family, and on the other know whether the hospital fees should be charged to the budget of the town or whether they could request reimbursement from his relatives. Obviously, this proved that he was not altogether cut off from the woman who was waiting for him; society was taking an interest in them. But that was no consolation. What was more remarkable — and Rambert consequently remarked on it — was the way in which, in the very midst of a disaster, an office could carry on working and take initiatives appropriate to a quite different time, often unknown to the highest authorities, for the simple reason that it was designed to operate in this way.

For Rambert, the period that followed was both the easiest and the most difficult. It was a period of numbness. He had visited all the offices, made all the approaches, and for the time being the exits in that direction were blocked. He wandered from café to café. In the morning he would sit down on a terrace in front of a glass of warm beer, reading the newspaper and hoping to find in it some indication that the epidemic would soon be over, watching the faces of the passers-by in the street and turning away in disgust from their expressions of melancholy. Then after reading for the hundredth time the signs on the shops opposite and the advertisements for great aperitifs which were already no longer available, he would get up and walk aimlessly through the yellow streets of the town. In this way, with solitary walks to cafés and from cafés to restaurants, he would reach evening. Rieux noticed him, on one such evening, at the door of a café where the journalist seemed reluctant to enter. Then he appeared to make up his mind and went to sit at the back of the room. It was at the time when, in obedience to orders from above, they would delay as long as possible the moment of turning on the lights in public places. Dusk spread through the room like grey water, the pink of the evening sky was reflected against the windows and mirrors, and the marble tabletops shone faintly in the gathering darkness. In the middle of the empty room Rambert seemed like a lost shade and Rieux thought that it was his time for giving up. But it was also the moment when all the prisoners of the town felt their own sense of abandonment and something must be done to speed their delivery. Rieux turned away.

Rambert also spent long periods of time in the station. It was forbidden to go on to the platforms. But the waiting-rooms which could be reached from outside remained open; sometimes beggars would settle there when it was hot because the rooms were shady and cool. Rambert came to read old timetables, notices forbidding spitting and the railway by-laws. Then he would sit down in a corner. The room was dark. An old cast-iron stove had been cooling for months in the middle of figures-of-eight traced by old waterings. On the wall a few notices advertised a happy, free life in Bandol or Cannes. Here Rambert experienced the sort of fearful freedom that one finds in utter destitution. The pictures that were hardest for him to bear, at least according to what he told Rieux, were those of Paris. A landscape of old stone and water, the pigeons of the Palais-Royal, the Gare du Nord, the empty districts around the Panthéon and a few other places in a city that he had not been aware of loving so much, would pursue Rambert and prevent him from doing anything in particular. Rieux simply thought that he identified these images with those of his beloved. And, on the day when Rambert told him that he liked to wake up at four in the morning and to contemplate his city, the doctor had no difficulty in deciding, on the basis of his own experience, that this was when Rambert liked to think about the woman he had left behind. This was, actually, the time when he could grasp hold of her. In general, at four in the morning, one does nothing but sleep, even if the night has been one of betrayal. Yes, this is the time when one sleeps and that is reassuring because the great wish of the uneasy heart is endlessly to possess the being that it loves and, when the time of absence arrives, to be able to plunge that being into a dreamless sleep which can only come to an end on that day when the two are reunited.

Shortly after the sermon the warm weather began. It was approaching the end of June. The day after the late rainstorms that marked the Sunday of the sermon, summer all at once burst across the sky and above the houses. First of all a great burning wind arose and blew for a day, drying off the walls. The sun settled in the sky. All day long, uninterrupted waves of heat and light flooded the town. With the exception of streets with arcades and people's flats, it seemed that there was no point in the town that was not subject to the most blinding glare. The sun pursued our fellow-citizens into every corner of the street and, if they stopped, then it struck them. Since this first heatwave coincided with a sharp increase in the number of victims, which rose to nearly seven hundred a week, the town was seized with a kind of despairing exhaustion. In the working-class districts, between the flat streets and the terraced houses, in neighbourhoods where people always used to live on their front doorsteps, this bustle of life began to die down: the doors were all shut and the blinds drawn, though no one could tell whether the idea was to protect oneself from the plague or the sun. However, groans and cries could be heard from a few of the houses. Before, when this happened, you could often see curious bystanders in the street, listening. But after this long period of anxiety it seemed that their hearts had hardened, and everyone walked by or lived alongside these moans as though they were the natural language of mankind.

Skirmishes at the gates, in the course of which the gendarmes had to use their weapons, created a vague atmosphere of unrest. People had certainly been wounded, but in town there was talk of deaths, everything there being exaggerated by the effects of heat and fear. In any case, it is true to say that discontent continued to grow and that the authorities feared the worst, seriously considering what measures were to be taken in the event of the inhabitants of our town turning to revolt if the pestilence continued to hang over them. The newspapers published decrees repeating the prohibition against going out and threatening the disobedient with prison. Patrols scoured the town. Often, in empty, over-heated streets, one would see mounted police, after first hearing the sound of their horses' hoofs on the paved roadway, passing between rows of closed windows. Once the patrol had vanished, a heavy, suspicious silence fell over the threatened town. Every now and then there was the sound of gunfire from the special teams whose job it was, under a recent regulation, to kill cats and dogs which might pass on fleas. These sharp discharges helped to create an atmosphere of alarm in the town.

In the terrified minds of our fellow-citizens, and in the heat and silence, everything became more important. For the first time, all of us became aware of the colours of the sky and the smells of the earth which mark the passage of the seasons. Each person realized with anxiety that warmth would favour the epidemic and, at the same time, each one saw that summer was settling in. The call of the swifts in the evening sky became sharper above the town, and the sky itself had grown too small for those dusks of June that push back the horizon in our country. In the markets the flowers no longer arrived as buds but were already blooming, and, after the morning sale, their petals littered the dusty pavements. It was clear to see that spring had exhausted itself, giving of its bounty in the thousands of flowers to be seen everywhere around, and that now it was going to fade away, slowly crushed beneath the double weight of the plague and the heat. This summer sky and these streets paling beneath the colours of dust and boredom had the same sinister meaning for everyone as the hundred additional deaths that weighed daily upon the town. This incessant sunshine, this season with its flavour of sleep and holidays, no longer invited one to the pleasures of water and the body, as they once had. On the contrary, in the silent, enclosed town, they gave a hollow sound. They had lost the resonant shine of happier times. The plague sun extinguished all colours and drove away all joy.

This was one of the profound changes brought about by the epidemic. Normally, all our fellow-citizens rejoiced at the coming of summer. The town used to open itself towards the sea and spill its young people out on to the beaches. This summer, however, the nearby sea was out of bounds and the body no longer had the right to enjoy it. In these circumstances, what could one do? Once more, Tarrou was the person who gave the most accurate picture of our life as it was then. Naturally he was following the course of the plague in general, accurately observing that a turning point in the epidemic was marked by the radio no longer announcing some hundreds of deaths per week, but 92, 107 and 120 deaths a day. 'The newspapers and the authorities are engaged in a battle of wits with the plague. They think that they are scoring points against it, because 130 is a lower figure than 910.' He would also note the touching or impressive aspects of the epidemic, like the woman who, in an empty district, with closed shutters, had suddenly thrown open a window above her and let out two great cries before pulling the shutters closed again on the deep shadows of her room. In addition, he pointed out that peppermints had vanished from chemists' shops because a lot of people sucked them as a defence against infection.

And he continued to observe his favourite characters. He learned that the little old man with the cats was experiencing a tragedy of his own. What had happened was that one morning some shots had rung out and, as Tarrou described it, splinters of lead had killed most of the cats and terrorized the rest, who left the street. That same evening, the little old man had gone out onto his balcony at the usual time, shown some indication of surprise, leant over to look up and down the street and then settled down to wait. His hand tapped lightly against the railing of the balcony. He waited a bit longer, tore up a piece of paper, went back inside, came out again, then, after a while, suddenly vanished, slamming his french windows angrily behind him. In the days that followed, the same scene was repeated, but you could read clearer and clearer signs of sadness and dismay on the face of the old man. When a week had gone by, Tarrou waited in vain for his daily appearance, but the windows remained obstinately closed against a very understandable feeling of grief. 'In times of plague, it is forbidden to spit at cats,' was what Tarrou's notebooks concluded.

On the other hand, when Tarrou came back in the evening he was always sure to meet the sombre figure of the night-watchman walking up and down in the hall. The man never ceased to remind everyone that he had foreseen what was happening. Tarrou would acknowledge that he had heard him predict a misfortune, but would remind him of his idea that it would be an earthquake, to which the old watchman would reply: 'Ah! If only it had been an earthquake! A good shake and that's it . . . One counts the dead, one counts the living and the whole thing's over and done with. But this rotten bastard of a disease! Even those who don't have it, carry it in their hearts.'

The hotel manager was no less overcome by it all. At the beginning, travellers who were unable to leave the town were kept in the hotel by the closing of the gates. But little by little, as the epidemic continued, many of them chose to stay with friends. So now the same reasons that had filled all the rooms in the hotel kept them empty, since no new travellers were arriving in town. Tarrou remained one of the few tenants and the manager never let slip an opportunity to remind him that, were it not for his eagerness to please his last customers, he would have closed the place long ago. He often asked Tarrou to estimate the probable length of the epidemic: 'They say', Tarrou noted, 'that cold is unfavourable to this sort of illness.' The manager was appalled: 'But it's never really cold here, Monsieur. In any case, it would mean waiting for several months more.' Quite apart from that, he was sure that travellers would take a long time to come back to the town. This plague was the ruination of tourism.

In the restaurant, M. Othon, the owl man, reappeared, but only followed by his two performing dogs. After enquiry it was learned that the wife had cared for and buried her own mother, and was now in quarantine.

'I don't like it,' the manager said to Tarrou. 'Quarantine or not, she is suspect, and in that case so are they.'

Tarrou pointed out that, if you considered it in that way, everyone was suspect. But the other man was insistent and saw the whole question in black and white.

'No, Monsieur. Neither of us is suspect, while *they* are.'

But a trifle such as this would not change M. Othon: here, the plague was wasting its time. He came into the restaurant in the same manner, sat down before his children and proceeded to deliver well-turned, hostile remarks to them. Only the little boy had altered in appearance. Dressed in black like his sister and a little more shrunk into himself, he looked like the smaller shadow of his father. The night-watchman, who did not like M. Othon, told Tarrou:

'No, that one, he'll die fully dressed. Like that, no need to lay him out; he'll go as he is.'

Paneloux's sermon was also noted down by Tarrou, but with the following commentary: 'I understand the appeal of such ardour. At the start of a pestilence, and when one is over, people always indulge in a little rhetoric. In the first case, the habit is not yet lost and, in the second, it has already returned. It is at the moment of misfortune that one becomes accustomed to truth, that is to say to silence. Let us wait.'

Finally, Tarrou observed that he had had a long conversation with Dr Rieux of which all he could remember was that it had a good outcome, he noted in this context the light brown colour of Mme Rieux senior's eyes, rather oddly stated on that subject that a face in which one could read so much goodness would always be stronger than the plague and, finally, he devoted quite a lot of space to the old asthmatic who was being treated by Rieux.

He had been to see him with the doctor after their talk. The old man had greeted Tarrou by giggling and rubbing his hands. He was in bed, propped up against his pillow, above his two saucepans of chick-peas. 'Ah, another one,' he said, when he saw Tarrou. 'It's the world turned upside down, more doctors than patients. That means it's going fast, huh? The priest is right, it's well deserved.' The next day, without warning, Tarrou came back.

If one is to believe the notebooks, the old asthmatic, a draper by trade, had decided at the age of fifty that he had done enough. He had gone to bed and not got up since. His asthma, however, was better suited to a standing position. A small private income had carried him on to the seventy-five years which now sat lightly on him. He could not stand the sight of a watch and, indeed, had not a single one in his house. 'A watch', he would say, 'is expensive and stupid.' He judged time, especially mealtimes – the only ones that really mattered to him – by his two saucepans, one of which was full of peas when he woke up. He filled the other, pea by pea, with a single, regular and assiduous movement. In this way he found his bearings through a day measured saucepan by saucepan. 'Every fifteen pans,' he said, 'I need a snack. It's quite simple.'

In fact, if one was to believe his wife, he had given signs of his vocation quite early in life. Nothing had really interested him – work, friends, cafés, music, women or walks. He had never left his home town, except one day when he was obliged to go to Algiers on some family business and had stopped at the closest station to Oran, unable to carry on with the adventure. He returned home by the first train.

When Tarrou expressed astonishment at the cloistered existence he led, he explained, more or less, that the first half of a man's life was an ascent and the other half a descent, and that in the descent a man's days no longer belonged to him, that they could be taken away from him at any moment, that consequently there was nothing he could do and that the best thing was in fact to do nothing. Beside that, he was not afraid of contradiction, because he told Tarrou shortly after this that God certainly did not exist since, if he did, there would be no need for priests. But, from a few remarks that followed, Tarrou realized that this philosophy was closely connected with his irritation at the frequent collections of money in his parish. And the thing that completed the old man's portrait was a desire, apparently profound and several times repeated in front of Tarrou: he hoped to live to a great age.

'Is he a saint?' Tarrou asked himself; and he answered: 'Yes, if sanctity is a set of habits.'

At the same time, Tarrou began quite a minute description of one day in the plague-ridden town, so giving an accurate idea of how our fellow-citizens lived and spent their time during that summer: 'No one laughs except drunks,' Tarrou wrote, 'and they laugh too much.' Then he started his description:

'In the early hours, light breezes blow through the town, which is still empty. At this time, between the last to die at night and the first dead of the day, it seems as though the plague relaxes its efforts for a moment and pauses for breath. All the shops are shut, but on some of them the sign "Closed because of plague", shows that they will not be opening with the rest, at the usual time. Newspaper sellers, still asleep, are not shouting the news, but sit with their backs to the wall on street corners and offer their wares to the street lamps with the gestures of sleepwalkers. Soon, woken by the first trams, they will spread across the whole town, holding out at arm's length sheets from which the word "plague" leaps out. "Will there be an autumn of plague? Professor B answers: 'No'", "One hundred and twenty-four dead: the total for the ninety-fourth day of the plague."

'Despite the paper shortage which is becoming more and more severe, forcing certain periodicals to cut down on the number of pages, a new paper has been launched, *The Courrier of the Epidemic*, with the aim of "informing our fellow-citizens, in a spirit of total objectivity, about the advances or decline in the illness; to provide them with the most authoritative accounts of the future of the epidemic; to lend the support of its columns to all those, well-known or otherwise, who may be able to fight this pestilence; to sustain the morale of the inhabitants, to pass on directives from the authorities and, in short, to bring together all well-intentioned persons to undertake an effective struggle against the scourge which has fallen upon us." In reality, the paper very soon confined itself to publishing advertisements for new products which were infallible in protecting against plague.

'Around six in the morning, all these newspapers started to be sold in the queues forming at the doors of shops more than an hour before opening, then in the packed trams that arrived from the outlying districts. Trams have become the only means of transport and they can hardly move, their footboards and rails loaded to breaking point. An odd thing, however: all the passengers, as far as possible, turn their backs on one another, to avoid infection. At stops, the tram unloads its cargo of men and women, all in a hurry to get away and be on their own. Rows often break out due purely to bad temper, which is becoming chronic.

'After the first trams have gone by, the town wakes up bit by bit and the first taverns open their doors with counters laden with notices: "No more coffee", "Bring your own sugar", etc. Then the shops open and the streets fill. At the same time the light increases and the heat gradually builds up its leaden weight in the July sky. This is the time when those who have nothing to do venture out onto the boulevards. Most of them seem to have resolved to ward off the plague by an ostentatious display of wealth. Every day, at around eleven o'clock in the major thorough-fares, there is a parade of young men and women among whom one can sense that passion for life which flourishes in the midst of great disasters. If the epidemic extends, so will the bounds of morality. We shall see the Milanese saturnalia beside the tombs.

'At noon the restaurants fill in the twinkling of an eye. Small groups of people who have not managed to find a seat rapidly form at the door. The sky starts to lose its luminescence because of the excessive heat. Candidates for food wait their turn in the shade of the great awnings, on the edge of streets bursting with sunshine. The reason why the restaurants are packed out is that, for many people, they simplify the problem of getting food. But they leave unaltered their anxieties about infection. Diners spend several minutes patiently wiping their knives and forks. Not long ago some restaurants would announce: "Here, the cutlery has been boiled." But, bit by bit, they gave up advertising of any sort, because the customers were obliged to come. Moreover, the customers are happy to spend. Fine wines – or allegedly fine ones – and the most expensive supplements to the menu are snapped up in a frantic rush. It also seems that scenes of panic broke out in one restaurant because a customer felt unwell, went pale, staggered to his feet and rushed out of the door.

'Around two o'clock the town gradually empties and this is the moment when silence, dust, sun and plague meet in the street. The heat pours relentlessly all over the great grey houses. These are long hours of imprisonment which end in blazing evenings breaking over the populous, chattering city. During the first days of hot weather, occasionally, no one knows why, the evenings were deserted. But now the first cool air brings with it a sense of relaxation, even of hope. So everyone comes down into the streets, they deafen each other with talk, argue or lust after one another – and the town, under the red July sky, filled with couples and noise, drifts towards breathless night. In vain, every evening on the boulevards, a cranky old man, wearing a felt hat and a large tie, walks through the crowd repeating endlessly: "God is great, come to Him" – while everyone is rushing, on the contrary, towards something that they are unaware of, but which seems to them more urgent than God. At the beginning, when they thought that it was a sickness like any other, religion had its place. But when they saw that it was serious, they remembered pleasure. So in the dusty, blazing dusk all the anguish imprinted on their faces during the day resolves itself into a sort of crazed excitement, an uneasy freedom that enflames a whole population.

'I, too, am like them. And yet! Death is nothing for men like myself. It's an event that proves us right.'

It was Tarrou who had asked Rieux for the talk that he mentions in his notebooks. On the evening when Rieux was expecting him, the doctor happened to be looking at his mother, who was quietly sitting in a corner of the dining-room on a chair. This is where she spent her days when she had finished the household chores. With her hands crossed on her knees, she waited. Rieux was not even sure that he was what she was waiting for. However, something changed in his mother's face when he appeared. At that moment, all the taciturnity that a hard-working life had imposed on it seemed to lift. Then she would relapse into silence. That evening, she was looking out of the window into the now deserted street. The street lighting had been reduced by two-thirds; and here and there a very weak light cast its glow into the shades of the town.

'Are they going to keep the lighting low until the plague's over?' Mme Rieux asked.

'Probably.'

'As long as it doesn't go on until winter. That would be dreary.'

'Yes,' said Rieux.

He saw that his mother was looking at his forehead. He knew that the anxiety and overwork of the past few days had lined his face.

'You haven't had a good day, then?' said Mme Rieux.

'Oh, much as usual.'

As usual! That meant that the new serum they had sent from Paris seemed to be less effective than the previous one and that the death-toll was rising. There was still no possibility of vaccinating with preventive serum except in families already affected by the disease: a general inoculation would have required industrial quantities. Most of the swellings refused to let themselves be lanced, as though the season had come for them to harden, and they tormented their victims. The previous day, two new forms of the epidemic had appeared in the town. Here the plague was starting to affect the lungs. The same day, in a meeting between the harassed doctors and a confused Prefect, the doctors had asked for and got his agreement to new measures to prevent mouth-to-mouth infection from this pulmonary plague. As usual, no one knew anything.

He looked at his mother. Her fine chestnut eyes brought back years of tenderness in him.

'Are you afraid, mother?'

'At my age, one no longer fears anything much.'

'The days are very long and I'm never here now.'

'I don't mind waiting for you if I know that you will be coming. And when you aren't here, I think about what you are doing. Do you have any news?'

'Yes, everything's all right, according to her latest telegram. But I know that she says that to stop me worrying.'

The doorbell rang. The doctor smiled at his mother and went to open it. In the half-light on the landing, Tarrou looked like a great bear dressed in grey. Rieux told the visitor to sit down in front of his desk while he remained standing behind his chair. They were separated by the only lamp that was lit in the room, the one on the desk.

'I know that I can talk quite openly with you,' Tarrou said without any preamble.

Rieux nodded.

'In a fortnight or a month you will not be of any use here, you will be unable to cope.'

'That's true,' said Rieux.

'The health service is badly organized. You don't have enough staff or time.'

Once again, Rieux agreed that it was true.

'I am told that the Prefecture is thinking about a sort of community service under which fit men will be obliged to take part in general rescue work.'

'You're very well informed; but there is already a lot of public dissatisfaction and the Prefect is not sure whether to go ahead.'

'Why not ask for volunteers?'

'We did, but not many came forward.'

'It was done through official channels, rather half-heartedly. What they need is imagination. They never rise to the challenge of a disaster. And the cures that they dream up would hardly cope with a head cold. If we leave them to their own devices, they'll perish and so will the rest of us.'

'Quite likely,' said Rieux. 'I must say though that they also thought about using prisoners for what I would call the heavy work.'

'I'd rather it was done by free men.'

'So would I; but why, after all?'

'I hate the death penalty.'

Rieux looked at Tarrou:

'So?' he said.

'So I have a plan for organizing voluntary health teams. Appoint me to take charge and we can leave the authorities out of it. In any case, they are too busy to cope. I have friends all over the place, and they will form the core. And, naturally, I shall take part myself.'

'Of course,' Rieux said, 'as you can imagine, I am only too happy to accept. One needs help, especially in this job. I will be responsible for getting the Prefecture to accept the idea. In any case, they have no choice. But . . .' Rieux thought. 'But the work might be fatal, you know that. I still have to warn you. Have you really thought about it?'

Tarrou looked at him with his grey eyes.

'What did you think of Paneloux's sermon, doctor?'

The question was naturally put and Rieux replied to it naturally.

'I've spent too much of my life in hospitals to like the idea of collective punishment. But, you know, Christians sometimes talk in that way, without really believing it. They are better than they appear to be.'

'And yet you think, as Paneloux does, that the plague has its benefits because it opens people's eyes and forces them to think.'

The doctor shook his head impatiently.

'Like every sickness in this world. But what is true of the ills of this world is also true of the plague. It may serve to make some people great. However, when you see the suffering and pain that it brings, you have to be mad, blind or a coward to resign yourself to the plague.'

Rieux had barely raised his voice, but Tarrou waved his hand as though to calm him. He smiled.

'Yes,' Rieux said, shrugging his shoulders. 'But you still haven't answered me. Have you thought about it?'

Tarrou sat back a little further in his chair and leant forward so that his head was in the light.

'Do you believe in God, doctor?'

Once again, the question was asked quite naturally, but this time Rieux hesitated.

'No, but what does that mean? I am in darkness, trying to see the light. I stopped a long time ago thinking there was anything unusual in that.'

'Isn't that the thing that makes you different from Paneloux?'

'I don't think so. Paneloux is a scholar. He has not seen enough people die and that is why he speaks in the name of eternal truths. But the least little country priest who administers to his parishioners and who has heard the breath of a dying man thinks as I do. He would treat suffering, not try to demonstrate what a fine thing it is.'

Rieux got up; his face was now in shadow.

'Let's leave the matter,' he said, 'since you don't wish to reply.'

Tarrou smiled, not moving from his chair.

'Can I answer you with a question?'

The doctor smiled in his turn.

'You like mystery,' he said. 'Carry on.'

'Well then,' said Tarrou. 'Why are you yourself so dedicated when you don't believe in God? Perhaps your answer will help me in my own.'

Without emerging from the shadows, the doctor said that he had already answered that: if he believed in an all-powerful God, then he would stop healing people and leave it up to Him. But since no one in the world believed in a God of that kind – not even Paneloux who *thought* that was what he believed – because no one abandoned himself entirely to Him, in this at least Rieux felt he was on the right path, in struggling against the world as it was.

'Ah!' said Tarrou. 'So that's your idea of your job?'

'More or less,' the doctor said coming back into the light.

Tarrou whistled softly and the doctor looked at him.

'Oh, yes,' he said. 'You're telling yourself that it takes some pride. But, believe me, I have only the pride that it takes. I don't know what awaits me or what will come after all this. For the time being, there are patients who have to be cured. Afterwards, they can reflect on it all and so can I. But the immediate task is to cure them. I am defending them as best I can, that's all.'

'Against whom?'

Rieux turned towards the window. In the distance, where the horizon condensed into a darker mass, he sensed the presence of the sea. All he could feel was his exhaustion and at the same time he was struggling against a sudden, unreasonable desire to confide a little more in this man, this unusual man, but one whom he felt to be a friend and a brother.

'I don't know at all, Tarrou, I promise you, I don't know. When I first took up this profession, I did so in a sense abstractly, because I needed to, because it was a career like any other, one of those that young people consider for themselves. And, perhaps, also because it was especially hard for someone like myself, a working-man's son. And then I had to see people die. Do you know that there are people who refuse to die? Have you ever heard a woman cry out "Never!" at the moment of death? I have. And I realized then that I could not get used to it. I was young and my disgust thought that it was directed against the very order of the world. Since then I have become more modest. Quite simply I am still not used to seeing people die. I don't know anything more than that. But, after all . . .'

Rieux paused and sat down again. His mouth felt dry.

'After all?' Tarrou said softly.

'After all . . . ,' the doctor continued, hesitating again and looking closely at Tarrou. 'And this is something that a man like yourself might understand; since the order of the world is governed by death, perhaps it is better for God that we should not believe in Him and struggle with all our strength against death, without raising our eyes to heaven and to His silence.'

'Yes,' Tarrou agreed, 'I can understand. But your victories will always be temporary, that's all.'

A cloud seemed to pass over Rieux's face.

'Always, I know that. But that is not a reason to give up the struggle.'

'No, it's not a reason. But in that case I can imagine what this plague must mean to you.'

'Yes,' said Rieux. 'An endless defeat.'

Tarrou stared at the doctor for a moment, then got up and walked stiffly towards the door. Rieux followed. He was about to catch him up when Tarrou, who seemed to be staring at his feet, said:

'Who taught you all that, doctor?'

The reply was instantaneous.

'Suffering.'

Rieux opened the door of his office and, in the corridor, told Tarrou that he would come down as well, since he had to see one of his patients on the outskirts of town. Tarrou offered to accompany him and the doctor accepted. At the end of the corridor they met Mme Rieux, and the doctor introduced Tarrou to her.

'A friend,' he said.

'Oh!' Mme Rieux exclaimed. 'I am very pleased to meet you.'

When she left, Tarrou turned his back on her again. The doctor tried in vain to put the landing lights on, but the stairway remained plunged in darkness. He wondered if this was as the result of some new economy measure. It was impossible to tell. For some time now everything in homes and in the town had been breaking down. Perhaps this was simply because the concierges and people in general no longer took care of things. But the doctor did not have time to wonder about it because Tarrou's voice was echoing behind him:

'One more thing, doctor, even if it seems ridiculous to you: you are quite right.'

In the darkness, Rieux shrugged his shoulders – for his own benefit.

'I really don't know about that. Do you?'

'Ah,' the other man said, calmly. 'I know most things.'

The doctor stopped and behind him Tarrou's foot slipped on a stair. He recovered his balance by putting a hand on Rieux's shoulder.

'Do you think you know everything about life?' the doctor asked.

The reply came though the darkness, in the same tranquil tones:

'Yes.'

When they came out into the street they realized that it was quite late, perhaps eleven o'clock. The town was silent, inhabited only by rustling noises. Far, far away, the siren of an ambulance sounded. They got into the car and Rieux turned on the engine.

'You must come to the hospital tomorrow,' he said. 'To get your preventative vaccine. But, once and for all, before you become involved, tell yourself that you have a one-in-three chance of surviving.'

'Calculations like that are meaningless, doctor, and you know it as well as I do. A hundred years ago, an outbreak of plague killed all the inhabitants of a town in Persia, except the man who washed bodies, who had carried on with his job throughout.'

'He got his one chance in three, that's all,' Rieux said; and suddenly the sound of his voice was duller. 'But it's true: we still know nothing about this matter.'

They were reaching the outskirts of town. The headlights shone on empty streets. The car stopped. When he was standing next to it, Rieux asked Tarrou whether he wanted to come in. The other man said he did. A brief light in the sky lit up their faces and suddenly Rieux gave a friendly laugh.

'Come now, Tarrou,' he said. 'What makes you want to get involved in all this?'

'I don't know. My sense of morality, perhaps?'

'What morality?'

'Understanding.'

Tarrou turned towards the house and Rieux did not see his face again until they were in the old asthmatic's flat.

Tarrou started work the very next day and mustered a first team that was to be followed by many others.

However, it is not the narrator's intention to attribute more significance to these health groups than they actually had. It is true that nowadays many of our fellow-citizens would, in his place, succumb to the temptation to exaggerate their role. But the narrator is rather inclined to believe that by giving too much importance to fine actions one may end by paying an indirect but powerful tribute to evil, because in so doing one implies that such fine actions are only valuable because they are rare, and that malice or indifference are far more common motives in the actions of men. The narrator does not share this view. The evil in the world comes almost always from ignorance, and goodwill can cause as much damage as ill-will if it is not enlightened. People are more often good than bad, though in fact that is not the question. But they are more or less ignorant and this is what one calls vice or virtue, the most appalling vice being the ignorance that thinks it knows everything and which consequently authorizes itself to kill. The murderer's soul is blind, and there is no true goodness or fine love without the greatest possible degree of clear-sightedness.

This is why the health teams that were organized thanks to Tarrou should be viewed with satisfaction, but also objectivity; so the narrator will not become an over-eloquent eulogist of a determination and heroism to which he attaches only a moderate degree of importance. But he will continue to be the historian of the heartaches and soul-searching that the plague imposed on all our fellow-citizens at this time.

In reality, it was no great merit on the part of those who dedicated themselves to the health teams, because they knew that it was the only thing to be done and not doing it would have been incredible at the time. The teams helped the townspeople to get further into the plague and to some extent convinced them that, since the disease was here, they had to do whatever needed to be done to overcome it. So, because the plague became the responsibility of some of us, it appeared to be what it really was – a matter that concerned everybody.

This is all very well; but no one congratulates a schoolmaster for teaching that two and two make four. One might perhaps congratulate him on choosing a fine profession; so let us say that it was laudable of Tarrou and others to have chosen to show that two and two make four rather than otherwise, but let us also say that they shared this good impulse with the schoolmaster and with all those who think as he does – who are more numerous than people think, to the credit of humanity; at least, that is the narrator's view. Moreover, he is well aware of the objection that you might make to him, namely that those men were risking their lives. But there always comes a time in history when the person who dares to say that two and two make four is punished by death. The schoolmaster knows this quite well. And the question is not what reward or punishment awaits the demonstration; it is knowing whether or not two and two do make four. For those of the townspeople who risked their lives, they had to decide whether or not they were in a state of plague and whether or not they should try to overcome it.

A lot of new moralists appeared in the town at this moment, saying that nothing was any use and that we should go down on our knees. Tarrou, Rieux and their friends could answer this or that, but the conclusion was always what they knew it would be: one must fight, in one way or another, and not go down on one's knees. The whole question was to prevent the largest possible number of people from dying and suffering a definitive separation. There was only one way to do this, which was to fight the plague. There was nothing admirable about this truth, it simply followed as a logical consequence.

This is why it was natural for old Castel to put all his trust and energy into making serums on the spot, with whatever was to hand. Rieux and he hoped that a serum made with cultures from the very microbe that was infecting the town would be more directly effective than any serum brought in from outside, since the microbe differed very slightly from the bacillus of plague as traditionally defined. Castel hoped to have his first serum quite soon.

This is also why it was natural for Grand, who had nothing heroic about him, to be in charge of a sort of secretariat of health organizations. One section of the teams set up by Tarrou was engaged in the task of preventive assistance in over-populated districts. They were trying to encourage essential hygiene, and were checking out lofts and cellars that had not been visited by the disinfection squads. Another section of the health teams helped doctors during home visits, transported plague victims and even, later, when there were no longer any trained staff, drove ambulances and hearses. All this required registration and statistical tasks which Grand had agreed to do.

From this point of view the narrator thinks, even more than Rieux and Tarrou, that Grand was the real representative of the quiet virtue that inspired the health teams. He said yes without hesitating, with his habitual goodwill. He asked only to be useful in small ways. He was too old for anything more than that. He could give his time from six in the evening until eight. And when Rieux thanked him warmly, he was surprised: 'There's nothing hard about that. We have the plague and we must get rid of it. Ah, if only everything were so simple!' And he went back to his sentence. Sometimes, in the evening, when work on the card index was finished, Rieux spoke to Grand. Eventually, they brought Tarrou into their conversation and Grand confided in his two comrades with more and more evident pleasure. They were interested to follow the patient work that Grand continued in the midst of the plague. Eventually, they too found a sort of outlet in it.

'How is the horsewoman?' Tarrou often asked; and Grand would invariably reply with a pained smile: 'Trotting along, trotting along.' One evening Grand said that he had finally abandoned the adjective 'elegant' for his rider; from now on, he would describe her as 'slender', adding: 'It's more concrete.' Another time, he read his two listeners the first sentence, with this alteration: 'On a fine May morning, a slender woman was riding a magnificent sorrel mare through the flowered avenues of the Bois de Boulogne.'

'You can see her better, don't you think?' Grand said. 'And I preferred "on a May morning" because "in the month of May" draws it out too much.'

After that, he became very concerned about the adjective 'magnificent'. It was not evocative enough, he said, so he was hunting for the word that would capture in a single snapshot the splendid animal that he had in mind. 'Plump' was not right: it was concrete, but somewhat pejorative. 'Lustrous' had tempted him for a while, but the sound was not right. One evening, he announced triumphantly that he had found it: 'a black sorrel mare'. Blackness, he felt, discreetly suggested elegance.

'It's not possible,' Rieux said.

'Why not?'

'Because sorrel is not a breed, it describes a colour.'

'What colour?'

'Well, a colour that is not black in any case!'

Grand seemed very touched.

'Thank you,' he said. 'I'm so glad you were there. But you see how hard it is.'

'What do you think about "resplendent"?' Tarrou asked.

Grand looked at him thoughtfully.

'Yes,' he said. 'Yes!'

And a smile slowly crossed his face.

Shortly after this, he confessed that the word 'flowered' was bothering him. Since he had only ever been to Oran and Montélimar, he would sometimes ask his friends for details about how flowery were the avenues of the Bois de Boulogne. Quite honestly, neither Rieux nor Tarrou had ever had the impression that there were flowers there, but the civil servant's conviction made them doubt. He was astonished by their uncertainty: 'Only artists know how to use their eyes.' Then one day the doctor found him in a state of great excitement. He had replaced 'flowered' by 'full of flowers'. He rubbed his hands: 'At last, we can see them, we can smell them. Hats off, gentlemen!' Triumphantly, he read out the sentence: 'On a fine May morning, a slender woman was riding a resplendent sorrel mare through the avenues full of flowers of the Bois de Boulogne.' But when it was read aloud, the repetition of 'of' at the end of the sentence sounded ugly and Grand stumbled a little over it. He sat down, seeming crushed. Then he asked the doctor's permission to leave. He needed to think for a while.

It was around this time, as they learned later, that he started to show signs of absent-mindedness at the office, which was considered unfortunate at a moment when the demands on the Hôtel de Ville were overwhelming and they had to manage with a reduced staff. His work was suffering and his head of department seriously criticized him, with a reminder that he was paid to carry out duties that he was not in fact carrying out. 'It appears', the head of department had said, 'that you are doing voluntary service in the health teams, in addition to your work. This does not concern me. What does concern me is your work; and the first way to make yourself useful in these dreadful circumstances is for you to do your work for us well. Otherwise, all the rest is pointless.'

'He's right,' Grand told Rieux.

'Yes, he is right,' the doctor agreed.

'But I can't concentrate; I don't know how to resolve the end of my sentence.'

He had thought of lightening it by dropping 'de Boulogne', assuming that everyone would understand 'the Bois'. But then the sentence appeared to attach the flowers to the Bois instead of to the avenues:

'flowers of the Bois'. He also considered writing: 'the avenues of the Bois full of flowers'; but this left one uncertain whether the flowers belonged with the Bois or with the avenues, and this tormented him. It is true that some evenings he seemed even more tired than Rieux.

Yes, he was exhausted by this study that entirely absorbed him, but he continued none the less to do the calculations and statistics that the health teams needed. Patiently, every evening, he sorted out the card index, translated it into diagrams and slowly endeavoured to present the situation in as precise a way as possible. He would often go to join Rieux in one of the hospitals, where he would ask for a table in some office or ward. He settled down there with his papers, exactly as though he was sitting at his table in the Hôtel de Ville and, in air thick with the smell of disinfectant and of the disease itself, would shake his papers to dry the ink on them. At such times he tried honestly not to think of his slender horsewoman and to do only what had to be done.

Yes, if men really do have to offer themselves models and examples whom they call heroes, and if there really has to be one in this story, the narrator would like to offer this insignificant and self-effacing hero who had nothing to recommend him but a little goodness in his heart and an apparently ridiculous ideal. This would be to give truth its due, to give the sum of two and two its total of four, and to give heroism the secondary place that it deserves, just after – but never before – the generous demand of happiness. It would also define the nature of this chronicle, which is to be that of an account made up of good feelings, which is to say feelings that are neither visibly bad nor designed to arouse emotion in the unpleasant manner of a stage play.

This at least was the opinion of Dr Rieux when he read in the newspapers or heard on the radio the appeals and encouragement that the outside world got through to the stricken town. At the same time as aid by air or by road, every evening on the airwaves or in the press, pitying or admiring comments rained down on this now solitary town; and, every time, the doctor was irritated by the epic note or the tone of a prize-giving address. Of course he knew that the concern was genuine, but it could only express itself in the conventional language in which men try to explain what unites them with the rest of humanity. Such language could not be applied to the little, daily efforts of Grand, for example, and could not describe Grand's significance in the midst of the plague.

Sometimes at midnight, in the great silence of the deserted town, just as he got into bed to catch an all-too-short moment of sleep, the doctor switched on his radio. And from distant parts of the world, across thousands of miles, unknown but fraternal voices tried awkwardly to express their solidarity – and did, indeed, express it, while at the same time exhibiting the dreadful powerlessness of all men who truly endeavour to share a pain that they cannot see. 'Oran, Oran!' In vain the appeal crossed the seas and in vain Rieux stood by, waiting; then, soon, eloquence would well up and make still plainer the fundamental division that made Grand and the speaker strangers to one another. 'Oran, yes, Oran! But no,' thought the doctor. 'To love or to die together, there is nothing else to be done. They are too far away.'

And what precisely remains to be told before we come to the height of the plague, while the pestilence was gathering all its strength for an assault on the town, so that it could take hold of it for good, are the long, desperate, monotonous efforts that a few individuals like Rambert made to rediscover happiness and to preserve from the plague that part of themselves that they defended against all assault. This was their way of resisting the threat of slavery, and even though this resistance was evidently not as effective as the other, the narrator's opinion is that it had its own logic and, in its very futility and contradictions, also bore witness to the element of pride in each of us at the time.

Rambert struggled to prevent the plague from taking him. When it had been proved to him that he could not leave the town by legal means, he decided, as he told Rieux, to try the other sort. The journalist started with waiters: a waiter in a café always knows everything that is going on. But the first ones he questioned were especially well informed about the very serious penalties imposed for this kind of venture. In one case, he was even mistaken for an *agent provocateur*. It was not until he met

Cottard at Rieux's that he made some headway. That day Rieux and he had been talking once again about the journalist's fruitless efforts with the authorities. A few days later Cottard met Rambert in the street and greeted him with the directness that nowadays characterized all his behaviour with others:

'Still nothing?' he asked.

'No, nothing.'

'You can't count on officials; they're not trained to understand.'

'That's true. But I'm looking for another way. It's hard.'

'Ah!' said Cottard. 'I see.'

He did know certain channels and explained to Rambert, who expressed astonishment at this, that he had for a long time been frequenting all the cafés in Oran, that he had friends and that he knew about the existence of an organization which took care of this kind of operation. The truth was that Cottard, whose expenditure nowadays exceeded his income, had been involved in smuggling rationed goods: he traded in cigarettes and cheap spirits, the prices of which were constantly going up. The business brought in a small fortune.

'Are you sure?' Rambert asked.

'Yes, since the proposition was made to me.'

'Why didn't you take advantage of it?'

'Don't be so suspicious,' Cottard said, good-naturedly. 'I didn't take advantage of it because I don't myself want to leave. I have my reasons.'

And after a pause he added:

'Why don't you ask what those reasons are?'

'I assume,' said Rambert, 'that it's none of my business.'

'In a sense, no, it isn't. But in another . . . Well, in any case, the one thing that's clear is that I feel much better here since we've had the plague.'

The other man listened to him speaking.

'How does one join this organization?'

'Oh, it's not easy,' Cottard said. 'Come with me.'

It was four o'clock in the afternoon. The town was slowly cooking beneath a leaden sky. All the shops had their blinds down. The roads were empty. Cottard and Rambert took streets with arcades and walked along for some time without saying anything. It was one of those times when the plague became invisible. This silence, this death of colours and movement, could belong to summer as much as to the pestilence. One could not tell if the air was heavy with menace, or with dust and scorching heat. You had to look and think yourself back to the plague, which only betrayed its presence by negative signs. Cottard, who had some affinity with it, pointed out to Rambert, for example, that there were no dogs around, though normally they would have been lying on their sides, panting, just inside doorways, in search of some unattainable coolness.

They took the Boulevard des Palmiers, crossed the parade-ground and went down towards the area of the port. On the left there was a green-painted café shaded by a slanting awning made of coarse yellow cloth. As they went in Cottard and Rambert wiped their foreheads. They sat down on folding garden chairs in front of green, cast-iron tables. The room was entirely empty. Flies buzzed in the air and in a yellow cage standing on the rickety counter a parrot was slumped on its perch with all its feathers drooping. Old pictures showing battle scenes hung on the walls, covered with dirt and the thick filaments of cobwebs. Bird droppings were drying on all the metal tables, including the one in front of Rambert; he was unable to explain quite where they came from until, after a little commotion in a dark corner, a splendid cockerel hopped out.

Just then the heat seemed to increase even further. Cottard took off his jacket and banged on the table. A small man, swamped in a long blue apron, came out from the back-room, greeted Cottard as soon as he saw him, walked over kicking the cockerel aside sharply and asked, amid the clucking of the fowl, what he could get these gentlemen. Cottard wanted white wine, and he asked after a certain Garcia. The midget said that he had not seen him in the café for a few days.

'Do you think he'll come this evening?'

'Puh!' the man said. 'I'm not his minder. Do you know his usual time?'

'Yes, but it's not very important. It's just that I have a friend to introduce to him.'

The waiter wiped his damp palms on the front of his apron.

'Ah! Is Monsieur in business, too?'

'Yes,' said Cottard.

The little man sniffed:

'Well then, come back this evening. I'll send the kid for him.'

As they went out Rambert asked what the business was.

'Contraband, of course. They get merchandise through the town gates, then sell at high prices.'

'Fine,' said Rambert. 'Are they in collusion with the police?'

'You bet.'

That evening, the awning was raised, the parrot was squawking in its cage and the metal tables were surrounded by men in shirt-sleeves. One of them, with a straw hat pushed back on his head and a white shirt open on a chest the colour of burnt earth, got up when Cottard came in. He had regular, tanned features, small black eyes, white teeth and two or three rings on his fingers. He appeared to be aged around thirty.

'Hi,' he said. 'We're drinking at the bar.'

They drank three rounds in silence, then Garcia said:

'Why don't we go outside?'

They walked down towards the port and Garcia asked what they wanted of him. Cottard said that he didn't precisely want to introduce him to Rambert for business, but just for what he called 'an exit'. Garcia walked straight ahead, smoking. He asked a question, using 'he' to refer to Rambert, as though unaware of his presence.

'What does he want to do?'

'He has a wife in France.'

'Ah!'

Then, after a pause:

'What job does he do?'

'Journalist.'

'That's a profession where they talk a lot.'

Rambert said nothing.

'He's a friend,' said Cottard.

They went on in silence. They had reached the docks, access to which was barred by large iron fences. But they walked over to a little canteen where fresh sardines were sold, the smell of which was wafting towards them.

'In any case,' Garcia said in conclusion, 'I'm not the one who deals with that, it's Raoul. I'll have to find him. It won't be easy.'

'Ah!' said Cottard. 'Is he in hiding?'

Garcia did not answer. Near the canteen he stopped and turned to Rambert for the first time.

'The day after tomorrow, at eleven, on the corner of the customs officials' barracks, at the top of town.'

He made as though to leave, then turned towards the two men.

'There'll be expenses,' he said.

It was a simple statement of fact.

'Of course,' Rambert agreed.

Shortly afterwards the journalist thanked Cottard.

'Oh, no,' the other man said cheerfully. 'It's a pleasure to be of service. And, of course, you're a journalist, so you'll pay it back to me some day or another.'

The day after next Rambert and Cottard were climbing up the wide, unshaded streets that led to the upper part of town. Part of the customs officers' barracks had been transformed into an infirmary and, in front of the large door, people were stationed, having come in the hope of making a visit which could not be permitted, or seeking news that from one hour to the next would be overtaken by events. In any case, this gathering gave the opportunity for many comings and goings, and one might assume that this consideration was not unconnected with the manner in which Garcia and Rambert's meeting had been arranged.

'It's odd,' Cottard said, 'this determination to leave. When it comes down to it, what's happening is very interesting.'

'Not for me,' said Rambert.

'Oh, of course there's a risk. But after all before the plague there was just as much risk in crossing a busy road junction.'

At that moment Rieux's car stopped beside them. Tarrou was driving and Rieux seemed to be half asleep. He woke himself up to do the introductions.

'We know one another,' said Tarrou. 'We live in the same hotel.'

He offered to drive Rambert into town.

'No, we've got a rendezvous here.'

Rieux looked at Rambert.

'Yes,' Rambert said.

'Oh!' said Cottard in astonishment. 'Does the doctor know?'

'Here comes the examining magistrate,' Tarrou warned, looking at Cottard.

The latter's face fell. M. Othon was indeed coming down the street towards them with a brisk but even step. He raised his hat as he passed the little group.

'Good day, Monsieur le Juge,' said Tarrou.

The magistrate returned the greeting from the occupants of the car and, looking at Cottard and Rambert, who had stayed in the background, nodded gravely at them. Tarrou introduced Cottard and Rambert. The magistrate looked at the sky for a second and sighed, remarking that these were indeed sad times.

'They tell me, Monsieur Tarrou, that you are engaged in applying preventive measures. I cannot applaud this enough. Doctor, do you think that the disease will spread?'

Rieux said that they could only hope that it would not and the magistrate replied that one must always hope, but the designs of Providence are unknowable. Tarrou asked him if the events had brought him an excess workload.

'On the contrary, what we call common-law cases are in decline. Nowadays, all I have to examine are serious breaches of the new regulations. Never have people shown such respect for the old laws.'

'This is because, by comparison, they seem good, inevitably,' Tarrou said.

The magistrate abandoned the reflective air that he had assumed, with his gaze apparently suspended in mid-air. Now he examined Tarrou coldly.

'What does that matter?' he said. 'What counts is not the law, but the sentence imposed. We can do nothing about it.'

'That man', Cottard said, when the magistrate had left, 'is Enemy Number One.'

The car started.

Shortly afterwards Rambert and Cottard saw Garcia coming. He walked towards them without any sign of recognition and said, instead of a greeting: 'We must wait.'

Around them the crowd, the majority of whom were women, were standing in complete silence. Almost all of them were carrying baskets in the vain hope that they could get them across to their sick relatives and with the still more foolish notion that these relatives could make use of the provisions. The door was guarded by armed sentries and from time to time an odd cry could be heard from across the yard which separated the barracks from the door. At such moments worried faces among those waiting would turn towards the infirmary.

The three men were watching this scene when a 'hello', curt and deep, behind them made them turn round. Despite the heat, Raoul was smartly dressed. Tall and strong, he was wearing a dark check suit and a felt hat with a turned-up brim. His face was rather pale. Tight-lipped, with brown eyes, Raoul spoke rapidly and precisely:

'We'll go down into town,' he said. 'Garcia, you can leave us.'

Garcia lit a cigarette and let them walk away. They did so quickly, adjusting their steps to keep up with Raoul who had placed himself between them.

'Garcia explained to me,' he said. 'It can be done. In any case, it will cost you ten thousand francs.'

Rambert replied that he accepted.

'Have lunch with me tomorrow at the Spanish restaurant in the harbour.'

Rambert said that was understood and Raoul shook his hand, smiling for the first time. After he had gone, Cottard made his apologies. He was not free the following day and in any case Rambert no longer needed him.

When the following day the journalist entered the Spanish restaurant, all heads turned as he went past. This shady cellar, situated below the level of a little sun-dried, yellow street, was only frequented by men, mostly of Spanish appearance. But as soon as Raoul, who was at a table at the back of the room, had made a sign to Rambert and the journalist had started to walk over to him, all curiosity vanished from the faces, which turned back to their plates. At the table with him Raoul had a tall fellow, thin and badly shaved, with excessively broad shoulders, a horsy face and thinning hair. Long slender arms covered in black hair emerged from rolled-up shirt-sleeves. He nodded three times when Rambert was introduced to him. His name had not been spoken and Raoul only referred to him as 'our friend'.

'Our friend thinks he may be able to help you. He's going to . . .'

Raoul stopped because the waitress had come over to take Rambert's order.

'He's going to put you in touch with two of our friends who will introduce you to some sentries who are in our pay. That won't be the end of it. The sentries have to decide themselves on the right moment. The easiest thing would be for you to stay for a few nights with one of them who lives near the gates. But before that our friend must give you the necessary contacts. When everything is arranged, you will settle up the fee with him.'

Once again, the friend nodded his horse's head, while continuing to munch away at the salad of tomatoes and peppers that he was stuffing into himself. Then he started speaking, with a slight Spanish accent. He suggested that he and Rambert should meet the day after next, at eight in the morning, under the porch of the cathedral.

'Two more days,' Rambert observed.

'It's not so easy,' said Raoul. 'People have to be found.'

The horse nodded again and Rambert accepted without any show of feeling. The rest of lunch was spent looking for a subject of conversation. It all became very easy when Rambert discovered that the horse was a footballer. He himself had played the game a lot. So they spoke about the French championship, the standard of English professional teams and the 'W' tactic in passing the ball. At the end of the meal, the horse had become quite excited and started to call Rambert *tu* while trying to persuade him that there was no finer place in a team than centre-half. 'You see,' he said, 'the centre-half is the one who positions the game and that's what football is about.' Rambert agreed, though he had always played centre-forward. This discussion was interrupted only by a radio set which had been softly droning out sentimental songs, then announced that on the previous day the plague had claimed 137 victims. No one among the listeners reacted to this. The man with the horse's head shrugged his shoulders and got up. Raoul and Rambert followed suit.

As he was leaving, the centre-half shook Rambert's hand vigorously: 'My name's Gonzales,' he said.

The two days seemed endless to Rambert. He went to see Rieux and gave him a detailed account of what had gone on. Then he accompanied the doctor on one of his house calls. He said goodbye at the front door beyond which a suspected victim was waiting. In the corridor there was a sound of voices and hurrying steps: the family was being told that the doctor had arrived.

'I hope Tarrou won't be long,' Rieux muttered. He seemed tired.

'Is the epidemic progressing too quickly?' Rambert asked.

Rieux replied that that was not the problem; even the graph was levelling out. It was just that they did not have enough weapons with which to fight the plague.

'We don't have the equipment,' he said. 'Generally, in every army in the world, when *matériel* runs short, it is replaced by men. But we don't have enough men either.'

'Doctors and health workers have been brought in from outside.'

'Yes,' Rieux said. 'Ten doctors and around a hundred men. This is a lot, apparently. But it's barely enough in the present state of the disease. If the epidemic spreads, it will be too few.'

Rieux listened to the noises from inside, then smiled at Rambert.

'Yes,' he said. 'You ought to hurry up and get out.'

A cloud passed over Rambert's face.

'You know,' he said in a dull voice. 'That's not the reason I'm going.'

Rieux answered that he knew that, but Rambert went on:

'I don't think I'm a coward, most of the time at least. I have had the opportunity to test it. Only, there are some ideas that I cannot bear.'

The doctor looked directly at him.

'You'll see her again,' he said.

'Perhaps, but I cannot bear the idea of this going on and of her getting older all that time. At thirty, you are starting to get old and you have to take advantage of everything. I don't know if you can understand that.'

Rieux was saying quietly that he thought he understood when Tarrou came up, very excited.

'I've just asked Paneloux to join us.'

'Well?' said the doctor.

'He thought it over and said yes.'

'I'm glad,' said the doctor. 'I'm glad to find out that he is better than his sermon.'

'Everyone is like that,' said Tarrou. 'You just need to give them the opportunity.'

He smiled and winked at Rieux.

'It's my task in life, that: to give opportunities.'

'Excuse me,' said Rambert. 'I must be leaving.'

The Thursday when he was due to meet Gonzales, Rambert went to the porch of the cathedral, five minutes before eight o'clock. The air was still quite cool. Little round white clouds were travelling across the sky which would shortly be swallowed up by the heat. A vague scent of humidity was still rising from the lawns, dry as they were. The sun, rising behind the houses in the East, only warmed Joan of Arc's fully gilded helmet which decorated the square. A clock struck eight. Rambert walked back and forth a little under the empty porch. Faint sounds of chanting were emerging from within, mixed with old perfumes of cellars and incense. Suddenly, the singing stopped. A dozen small black shapes came out of the church and began to trot along in the direction of the town. Rambert was starting to get impatient. Other black forms were walking up the broad stairways towards the porch. He lit a cigarette, then thought that perhaps this was not the proper place for it.

At quarter past eight the cathedral organ started to play softly. Rambert went into the dark vault. After a moment, he could make out in the nave the black shapes that had gone in ahead of him. They were all gathered in one corner around a sort of improvised altar on which someone had set up a statue of Saint Roch, hastily carved in one of the town workshops. Kneeling down, they seemed still more hunched and shrivelled up, lost in the semi-darkness like pieces of coagulated shadow, scarcely more substantial here and there than the mist in which they hovered. Above them the organ played endless variations.

As Rambert came out Gonzales was already going back down the stairway towards the town.

'I thought you'd gone,' he told the journalist. 'It's normal.'

He explained that he had been expecting his friends at another meeting-place, not far away, where he had arranged to meet them at ten to eight. He had waited for twenty minutes, in vain.

'There's some problem, that's for sure. Things don't always go smoothly in our line of work.'

He suggested another rendezvous, the next day at the same time in front of the war memorial. Rambert sighed and pushed back his hat.

'It's nothing,' Gonzales assured him. 'Think of all the moves, crosses and passes that have to be made before you score a goal.'

'Of course,' Rambert agreed. 'But a match only lasts an hour and a half.'

The war memorial in Oran is situated at the only place from which one can see the sea, a sort of promenade which for quite a short distance runs along the cliffs overlooking the port. The following day Rambert, first to arrive at the meeting-place, was attentively reading the list of those who had died on the field of honour. A few minutes later, two men came over, looked at him without any particular interest, then went over to lean on the parapet of the promenade, seeming altogether absorbed in contemplating the bare, deserted quays. Both men were the same height, each wearing blue trousers and a dark blue, short-sleeved pullover. The journalist moved a short distance away and sat down on a bench where he could keep them in view. This was when he noticed that they could surely not be more than twenty years old. Just then, he saw Gonzales walking towards him, apologizing.

'Here are our friends,' he said, leading him towards the young men whom he introduced as Marcel and Louis. From the front they looked very alike and Rambert guessed that they must be brothers.

'Here we are,' said Gonzales. 'Now you know each other. We have to make the actual arrangements.'

Marcel and Louis said that their turn at sentry duty began in two days and lasted a week. They would have to look out for the most convenient day. Four of them guarded the West Gate and the other two men were professional soldiers; there was no question of involving them in the business: they could not be trusted and, in any case, it would put up the cost. But occasionally these two colleagues would go and spend part of the night in the back-room of a bar that they knew. So Marcel and Louis suggested to Rambert that he should come and stay with them, near the gates, and wait for someone to come and fetch him. In these circumstances the crossing would be quite easy. But they would have to hurry because there was talk recently of setting up double sentry posts outside the town.

Rambert agreed and handed round some of his last cigarettes. The one of the pair who had not yet spoken asked Gonzales if the matter of expenses had been settled and if they could have an advance.

'No,' said Gonzales. 'There's no need. He's a friend. The account will be settled on departure.'

They fixed a new meeting. Gonzales suggested dining in the Spanish restaurant the day after next. From there they could go to the sentries' house.

'For the first night,' he told Rambert, 'I'll keep you company.'

The next day Rambert was going up to his room in the hotel when he met Tarrou on the staircase.

'I'm going to see Rieux,' Tarrou said. 'Would you like to come?'

Rambert hesitated and said: 'I never know if I'm getting in his way.'

'I don't think so. He often talks to me about you.'

The journalist thought, then said: 'Listen, if you have a moment after dinner, however late it is, both of you come to the hotel bar.'

'It depends on him and on the plague,' said Tarrou.

Even so, at eleven o'clock that evening, Rieux and Tarrou came into the narrow little bar. About thirty people were there, pressed together, talking in very loud voices. Coming from the silence of the stricken town, the new arrivals halted, slightly stunned. They understood the agitation when they saw that spirits were still being served. Rambert was at one end of the counter, waving to them from a bar stool. They gathered round, Tarrou calmly pushing aside a noisy neighbour.

'You're not worried about drinking alcohol?'

'No,' Tarrou said. 'Far from it.'

Rieux sniffed the smell of bitter herbs in his glass. It was hard to speak in this tumult, but what Rambert seemed to care most about was drinking. The doctor could not say if he was drunk. At one of the two tables which occupied the rest of the narrow room, a naval officer with a woman on each arm was telling a fat man with a florid complexion about an outbreak of typhus in Cairo: 'Camps,' he said. 'They set up camps for the natives, with tents for the victims and a line of sentries all round who would open fire on the families when they tried to sneak in their old wives' remedies. It was hard, but fair.' The conversation at the other table, occupied by elegant young people, was incomprehensible and swallowed up by the sound of 'Saint James's Infirmary Blues', pouring out from a gramophone perched up near the ceiling.

'Are you pleased?' Rieux asked, raising his voice.

'It's getting close,' said Rambert. 'Within a week, perhaps.'

'Pity,' Tarrou shouted.

'Why?'

Tarrou looked at Rieux.

'Ah!' the doctor said. 'Tarrou says that because he thinks you could have been useful to us here. But I understand only too well how much you want to leave.'

Tarrou paid for another round. Rambert got off his stool and looked him directly in the face for the first time:

'How would I have been useful to you?'

'Well,' Tarrou answered, unhurriedly reaching out for his glass. 'In our health teams.'

Rambert resumed his usual air of stubborn reflection and got back up on his stool.

'Don't you think that the teams are of any use?' Tarrou said. He had just taken a drink and was now looking closely at Rambert.

'Very useful,' said the journalist, drinking in his turn.

Rieux noticed that his hand was trembling and decided that, undoubtedly, he was altogether drunk.

The next day, when Rambert came into the Spanish restaurant for the second time, he passed through a small group of men who had taken chairs outside in front of the door and were enjoying a green and gold evening, where the heat was only just starting to subside. They were smoking bitter-smelling tobacco. Inside, the restaurant was almost empty. Rambert went and sat down at the table at the back where he had met Gonzales the first time. He told the waitress that he would wait. It was seven thirty. Bit by bit, the men came back into the dining-room and settled down at the tables, while their orders started to be brought in and the low vaulted ceiling filled with the noise of cutlery and muffled conversations. At eight, Rambert was still waiting. They put on the lights. New customers sat down at his table. He ordered his dinner. By eight thirty he had finished, without any sign of Gonzales or the two young men. Outside, night was falling rapidly. A warm breeze from the sea gently lifted the curtains over the french windows. By nine o'clock Rambert noticed that the room was empty and that the waitress was looking at him in astonishment. He paid and went out. There was a café open across from the restaurant. At half past nine, he walked back to his hotel, wondering how on earth he could contact Gonzales when he did not have the man's address, and his heart failing at the idea of having to start the whole business over again.

It was at this moment, in the night full of fleeting ambulances, that, as he would later tell Dr Rieux, he noticed that in all this time he had to some extent forgotten his wife, applying his mind entirely to the search for a breach in the walls that separated them. But it was also at this moment, when all roads were once more blocked, that he found her once again at the centre of his desires, with such a sudden outbreak of pain that he started to run towards his hotel in an attempt to flee this dreadful burning which, none the less, he carried with him and which was eating away at his temples.

However, very early the next day, he went to see Rieux, to ask him how he could find Cottard.

'The only thing left for me,' he said, 'is to follow the same leads.'

'Come tomorrow evening,' said Rieux. 'Tarrou asked me to invite Cottard, I don't know why. He should be here at ten. You come at half past.'

When Cottard arrived at the doctor's the next day, Tarrou and Rieux were talking about an unexpected cure involving one of the doctor's patients.

'One out of ten. He was lucky,' Tarrou was saying.

'Oh, well,' said Cottard. 'Then it wasn't plague.'

They assured him that it really had been the disease.

'It can't be so, if he recovered. You know as well as I do, the plague is merciless.'

'On the whole, it is,' said Rieux. 'But if you persevere, you can have some pleasant surprises.'

Cottard laughed.

'It doesn't seem like it. Have you seen this evening's figures?'

Tarrou, who was giving the man of means a kindly look, said that he knew the figures and the situation was serious, but what did that prove? It proved that they needed still more emergency measures.

'You've taken them already.'

'Yes, but everyone has to take them on his own account.'

Cottard looked at Tarrou without understanding. The other man explained that too many people were not doing anything, that the epidemic was everybody's business and that they all had to do their duty. The voluntary health teams were open to all.

'It's an idea,' said Cottard. 'But it won't do any good. The plague is too strong.'

'We'll find out,' said Tarrou, patiently. 'When we've tried everything.'

Meanwhile Rieux was at his desk copying some figures. Tarrou was still looking at the man of means, who was shifting about on his chair.

'Why don't you join us, Monsieur Cottard?'

Cottard got up looking offended and picked up his round hat.

'It's not my job.'

Then, with a tone of bravado:

'In any case, this plague is doing me a favour, so I don't see why I should be involved in getting rid of it.'

Tarrou struck his forehead, as though suddenly realizing something:

'Of course, I'm forgetting; you would be arrested otherwise.'

Cottard started and grabbed the chair as if about to fall over. Rieux had stopped writing and was looking at him in a solemn, interested way.

'Who told you that?' said the man of means.

Tarrou seemed surprised and said:

'You did. Or, at least, that's what the doctor and I thought you meant.'

And, while Cottard stammered out an incomprehensible stream of words, suddenly overcome by an uncontrollable fit of rage, Tarrou added:

'Don't get excited. Neither the doctor nor I will denounce you. Your background doesn't concern us. And then, we've never much liked the police. Come now, sit down.'

The man of means looked at his chair, hesitated and sat down. After a moment, he sighed.

'It's an old story', he agreed, 'which they dredged up. I thought it was all forgotten, but someone talked. They called me in and told me to remain available until the inquiry was over. I realized that, in the end, they would arrest me.'

'Is it serious?' Tarrou asked.

'Depends what you mean. It's not a murder, anyway.'

'Prison or forced labour?'

Cottard seemed very downcast.

'Prison, if I'm lucky.'

Then, after a short pause, he went on emphatically:

'It's a mistake. Everyone makes mistakes. But I can't stand the idea of being taken in for that, separated from my home, my way of life, all the people I know . . .'

'I see,' said Tarrou. 'Is that why you had the idea of hanging yourself?'

'Yes, a silly idea, of course.'

Rieux spoke for the first time and told Cottard that he could understand his anxiety, but that perhaps everything would work out.

'Oh, for the time being, I know I have nothing to fear.'

'I see that you are not going to join our teams,' said Tarrou.

The other man, twisting his hat between his hands, gave him a hesitant look.

'Don't hold it against me.'

'Certainly not. But at least,' Tarrou added with a smile, 'try not to spread the microbe knowingly.'

Cottard protested that he didn't want the plague, it had come of its own accord and it was not his fault if it temporarily got him out of a mess. And when Rambert arrived at the door, he added, with a lot of emphasis:

'In any case, what I think is that you won't achieve anything.'

Rambert learned that Cottard did not know Gonzales's address, but that they could always go back to the little café. They arranged a meeting for the next day. And when Rieux indicated that he would like to know what was going on, Rambert invited him, with Tarrou, to come to his room that weekend at any time of the day.

In the morning Cottard and Rambert went to the little café and left a message for Garcia to meet them that evening or, if that was impossible, the next day. In the evening they waited in vain, but the following day Garcia was there. He listened to Rambert's story in silence. He had not been informed, but he did know that whole districts had been put out of bounds for twenty-four hours while the police made house-to-house searches. It was possible that Gonzales and the two young men had been unable to get past the roadblocks. The only thing that could be done was to put them in touch with Raoul. Of course, it could not be done overnight.

'I see,' said Rambert. 'We have to go back to square one.'

The day after next, at the corner of a street, Raoul confirmed Garcia's supposition: the lower districts had been sealed off. It would be necessary to establish contact with Gonzales again. Two days later Rambert was having lunch with the footballer.

'It's ridiculous,' he said. 'We should have settled on some way of contacting one another.'

Rambert could only agree.

'Tomorrow morning we'll go and see the kids and try to arrange it all.'

The next day the kids were not at home. A meeting was arranged for the following day at noon on the Place du Lycée and Rambert went home with a look on his face that struck Tarrou when he met him that afternoon.

'Something wrong?' Tarrou asked.

'It's having to start over again,' Rambert said.

And he repeated his invitation: 'Come over this evening.'

That evening when the two men came into Rambert's room he was stretched out on the bed. He got up and filled some glasses that he had ready. Rieux, taking his drink, asked if things were going well. The journalist said that he had once more completed a full round, got back to the same point and would soon have his final meeting. He drank, and added:

'Of course, they won't come.'

'You mustn't make a regular thing out of it,' said Tarrou.

'You still haven't understood,' Rambert replied, shrugging his shoulders.

'What haven't we understood?'

'The plague.'

'Ah!' said Rieux.

'You haven't understood that it's all about starting again.'

Rambert went into a corner of the room and put on a little record player.

'What is that record?' asked Tarrou. 'I know it.'

Rambert replied that it was 'Saint James's Infirmary Blues'.

In the middle of the record they heard two shots ring out in the distance.

'A dog, or an escape,' said Tarrou.

A moment later the record ended and the sound of an ambulance became clearer, got louder, passed under the windows of the hotel room, decreased, then finally died away.

'That record is not funny,' said Rambert. 'And I've heard it at least ten times today.'

'Do you like it that much?'

'No, it's the only one I have.'

And, a moment later:

'I tell you – it's about starting again.'

He asked Rieux how the health teams were working. There were five of them in operation, but they hoped to form others. The journalist was sitting on his bed and appeared to be concentrating on his nails. Rieux looked at his stocky, powerful shape on the corner of the bed. He suddenly became aware that Rambert was looking at him.

'You know, doctor,' he said, 'I've thought a lot about your organization. If I haven't joined you, there's a reason for it. Anyway I think I could still put my life on the line, I fought in Spain.'

'On which side?' Tarrou asked.

'On the losing one. But since then I've reflected a bit.'

'On what?'

'On courage. I know now that man is capable of great actions. But if he is not capable of great feeling, then he doesn't interest me.'

'One has the impression he is capable of anything,' said Tarrou.

'Not at all; he's not capable of suffering or of being happy for long. So he's not capable of anything worthwhile.'

He looked at them, then asked:

'Come Tarrou, are you capable of dying for love?'

'I don't know, but I doubt it, now.'

'There. Yet you are capable of dying for an idea, that's patently obvious. Well, I've had enough of people who die for ideas. I don't believe in heroism, I know that it's easy and I've found out that it's deadly. What interests me, is living or dying for what one loves.'

Rieux had been listening closely to the journalist. Still looking at him, he said gently:

'Man is not an idea, Rambert.'

The other man jumped up from the bed, his face contorted with emotion.

'He is an idea and a very brief one, just as soon as he turns away from love. And that's the trouble: we are no longer capable of love. Let's resign ourselves, doctor, let's wait until we are capable of it and if it's really not possible, wait for the general deliverance, without playing at heroes. As for me, I'm not going any further.'

Rieux stood up with a look of sudden tiredness.

'You're right, Rambert, quite right and I wouldn't want to divert you from what you intend to do for anything in the world, because it seems to me good and proper. But I have to tell you this: this whole thing is not about heroism. It's about decency. It may seem a ridiculous idea, but the only way to fight the plague is with decency.'

'What is decency?' Rambert asked, suddenly serious.

'In general, I can't say, but in my case I know that it consists in doing my job.'

'Ah!' said Rambert, furiously. 'I don't know what my job is. Perhaps I really am wrong to choose love.'

Rieux stood in front of him.

'No!' he said emphatically. 'You are not wrong.'

Rambert looked thoughtfully at them.

'I suppose the two of you have nothing to lose in all this. It's easier to be on the right side.'

Rieux emptied his glass.

'Come on,' he said. 'We've work to do.'

And he went out.

Tarrou followed, but seemed to have second thoughts just as he was leaving. He turned to the journalist and said:

'Do you know that Rieux's wife is in a sanatorium a few hundred miles from here?'

Rambert gave a gesture of surprise, but Tarrou had already left.

Very early the next morning, Rambert telephoned the doctor:

'Would you agree to let me work with you until I find the means to get out of town?'

There was a silence on the end of the line, then:

'Yes, Rambert. Thank you.'

Part III

So, week in, week out, the prisoners of the plague struggled along as best they could. As we have seen, a few, like Rambert, even managed to imagine that they were acting as free men and that they could still choose. But in reality one could say, at that moment, in the middle of August, that the plague had covered everything. There were no longer any individual destinies, but a collective history that was the plague, and feelings shared by all. The greatest of these were feelings of separation and exile, with all that that involved of fear and rebellion. This is why the narrator feels it appropriate, at this high point of heat and sickness, to describe the general situation and, for the sake of examples, the violence of our living fellow-citizens, the burials of the dead and the suffering of parted lovers.

It was in the middle of that year that the wind rose and blew for several days on the plague-ridden town. The inhabitants of Oran have a particular dread of the wind because it encounters no natural obstacle on the plateau where the town lies and consequently sweeps along the streets with full force. After those long months in which not a drop of water had refreshed the town, it was covered by a grey coating which peeled off when the wind blew on it. In this way, it raised clouds of dust and papers, which wrapped around the legs of what had become rare passers-by. One saw them hasten down the street, bent forward, with a handkerchief or a hand across their mouths. In the evening, instead of the gatherings in which people tried to prolong contact as far as possible these days, each of which could be the last, one met small groups of people hurrying to return home or get into cafés, so much so that for some days, at dusk which fell much faster at that time of the year, the streets were deserted and only the wind moaned continually down them. A smell of seaweed and salt rose from the wind-tossed, always invisible sea. This empty town, white with dust, saturated with sea smells, loud with the howl of the wind, would groan at such times like an island of the damned.

Up to now the plague had claimed many more victims in the outlying districts, which were more crowded and less affluent than the centre of town. But suddenly it seemed to get closer and to take up residence in the business quarters as well. The inhabitants accused the wind of carrying the seeds of infection. 'It is shuffling the cards,' said the manager of the hotel. Whatever the cause, the town centre learned that its turn had come when its people heard with increased frequency at night the throbbing of ambulances sounding the dreary, passionless call of the plague beneath their windows.

Inside the town someone had the idea of quarantining certain districts which had been especially hard hit and only allowing people whose services were indispensable to leave them. Those who had lived there until that time were bound to consider this measure as a form of victimization particularly directed against them; in any case, they considered the inhabitants of other areas to be free men. Meanwhile, people from these other areas found some consolation in hard times in the idea that there were those still less free than themselves. 'There's always someone more captive than I am,' was the statement that summed up the only possible hope at that time.

In roughly this same period, there was an increased number of fires, especially in the leisure districts around the west gates of the town. Investigation showed that these were due to people who had come back from quarantine and, driven mad by grief and misfortune, set light to their houses under the illusion that this would kill the plague. It was very hard to fight these endeavours, which were frequent enough to put whole districts in permanent danger because of the violence of the wind. After it had been demonstrated, to no avail, that disinfection of houses by the authorities was enough to protect against any risk of contamination, it became necessary to impose very harsh penalties on these innocent pyromaniacs. It was apparently not the idea of prison itself that discouraged these unfortunates, but the idea that they shared with everyone else, namely that a prison term was equivalent to a death sentence, because of the very high mortality rate found in the municipal jail. Of course, this belief was not without foundation. For obvious reasons, the plague seemed to fasten particularly on all those who had become accustomed to living in groups: soldiers, members of religious orders or prisoners. Despite the isolation of some inmates, a prison is a community, and what proves this is the fact that in our municipal prison the warders were as likely as the prisoners to succumb to the disease. From the higher point of view adopted by the plague, everyone, from the prison governor to the least of the inmates, was condemned, and perhaps for the first time absolute justice reigned inside the jail.

The authorities tried in vain to introduce a hierarchy into this levelling and had the idea of decorating prison warders who had died carrying out their duties. As a state of siege had been declared and, from some points of view, it might be said that prison warders were on active service, they were awarded a military medal, posthumously. Yet, while the prisoners raised no objection, the military reacted badly and correctly pointed out that an unfortunate confusion might arise in the public mind. Their objection was accepted and it was decided that the simplest thing was to give warders who died the Medal of the Epidemic. But, in the case of the first among them, the harm had been done and there could be no question of taking away their decoration, though the military authorities continued to press their point of view. In any case, as far as the epidemic medal was concerned, it had the disadvantage of not producing the effect on morale which resulted from the award of a military decoration, since it was quite routine to get such a decoration in the event of an epidemic. So no one was happy.

Moreover, the prison authorities could not act in the same way as the religious and, to a lesser extent, military authorities. The monks from the only two convents in the town had been dispersed and housed provisionally in pious families. In the same way, wherever possible, small groups of men had been taken out of barracks and billeted on schools or public buildings. In this way, the disease which had apparently brought the inhabitants of Oran together in the solidarity of people under siege, at the same time broke up traditional associations and drove individuals back into solitude. There was dismay.

As you might imagine, all these circumstances, together with the wind, inflamed some people's minds. Again, the gates of the town were repeatedly attacked at night, but this time by small armed groups. There were exchanges of fire, a few wounded and some escapes. The sentry posts were reinforced and such attacks quite quickly ceased. They were enough, however, to raise a breath of revolt in the town, which led to some scenes of violence. Houses that had been set on fire or shut up for health reasons were pillaged. In fact, it was hard to believe that such actions were premeditated. Most often, a sudden opportunity would lead hitherto honest citizens to reprehensible actions, which were promptly imitated. So it might happen that some maniacs would dash into a still burning house, right in front of the owner, who was dazed and distressed. Seeing that he did nothing, several onlookers would follow the example of the first vandals and by the light of the fire, in this dark side-street, silhouettes could be seen fleeing in all directions, deformed by the dying flames and by the objects or the furniture which they carried on their shoulders. It was these incidents that forced the authorities to compare the plague to a state of siege and to apply the appropriate laws. Two thieves were shot, but it is doubtful whether this made much impression on the rest, since, in the midst of so much death, these two executions passed unnoticed – they were a drop in the ocean. And the truth was that similar events occurred quite frequently without the authorities giving any sign of intervention. The only measure that seemed to impress all the inhabitants was the imposition of a curfew. After eleven o'clock, plunged into darkness, the town was like a monument.

Under a moonlit sky, its whitish walls and regular streets extended in straight lines, never broken by the black shape of a tree, never disturbed by the steps of a passer-by or the howl of a dog. The silent town was henceforth a heap of massive, motionless cubes between which the mute statues of forgotten benefactors or former great men, stifled for ever in bronze, were left alone trying with their imitation faces in stone or iron to suggest a degraded image of what the man used to be. These mediocre idols reigned beneath a heavy sky on lifeless crossroads, unfeeling brutes who evoked rather well the state of immobility into which we had drifted – or at least its final state, that of a necropolis in which plague, stone and night would finally have silenced every voice.

But night was also in every heart, and the facts, as well as the myths, that were passed around about burials were not likely to reassure our fellow-citizens. It really is necessary to speak about burials, and the narrator apologizes for the fact. He is well aware of the criticism that might be levelled against him in this respect, and his only justification is that there were burials throughout this time and that, in a sense, he was forced, like all the other people of the town, to concern himself with them. It is not that he has a taste for this kind of ceremony – on the contrary, he prefers the company of the living and, if you want an example, likes sea bathing. But the fact is that sea bathing had been forbidden and the company of the living was in constant fear of being obliged to give way to that of the dead. This is obvious. Of course one could always try not to see, cover one's eyes and reject the obvious, but it has a terrible force that eventually carries all before it. For example, how can you avoid burials when the day comes when someone you love has need of one?

Well, the main feature of our ceremonies at the start was speed! All the formalities were simplified and in general funerary pomp and circumstance were discarded. Victims died far from their families and the ritual watch over the dead was banned, so the person who died in the evening passed the night alone and the one who died in the day was buried as quickly as possible. Of course, the family was informed, but in most cases its members could not attend, since they were in quarantine if they had been living with the sick person. In cases where the family had not lived with the deceased, they would arrive at the appointed time for departure towards the cemetery, the corpse having already been laid out and put in the coffin.

Suppose this formality had taken place in the auxiliary hospital where Dr Rieux was in charge. The school had an exit sited behind the main building and there were coffins in a large box-room off the corridor. In the corridor itself, the family discovered a single coffin, already closed.

Immediately, they got on with the most important task, which was to have some documents signed by the head of the family. After that the coffin was loaded into a motor vehicle, which was either a proper hearse or a large ambulance appropriately modified. The relatives got into one of the taxis still allowed to operate and the cars headed for the cemetery at full speed, taking a route that avoided the town centre. At the gate the convoy was halted by gendarmes who stamped an official pass, without which it was impossible to have what our townsfolk called a 'last home', then the gendarmes stepped back and the cars pulled up beside a square where a number of graves were waiting to be filled. A priest met the party because funeral services in church had been banned. The coffin was brought out to the accompaniment of prayers, ropes were placed around it, it was dragged along, slipped, hit the bottom of the grave. The priest shook the holy water over it and already the first clods of earth were crashing against the lid. The ambulance had left a short time before to be washed down with disinfectant and, while the shovelfuls of clay gave off an increasingly dull sound, the family piled back into the taxi. A quarter of an hour later they were back home.

In this way everything really happened with the greatest speed and the minimum of risk. And needless to say, at least at the start, it is clear that the natural feelings of the relatives were offended. But in time of plague, these are considerations which cannot concern us: everything was sacrificed to efficiency. Moreover, while at the start the morale of the people was affected by such practices – because the desire to be decently buried is more widespread than you might think – luckily, after a short while, there was an urgent problem of food supplies and the attention of the inhabitants turned towards more immediate concerns. Taken up with queuing, pulling strings and filling forms if they wanted to eat, people did not have time to worry about how others were dying around them and how they themselves would one day die. So these material difficulties which seemed like an affliction would eventually be seen to have been a boon. All would have been for the best if the epidemic had not spread, as we have seen.

For coffins were starting to be in short supply, and there was not enough cloth for shrouds or space in the cemetery. Something had to be done. The simplest thing, still for reasons of efficiency, seemed to be to group funerals together and when necessary to increase the number of journeys between the hospital and the cemetery. So, as far as Rieux's hospital was concerned, they had five coffins for the time being. Once these were full, the ambulance loaded them. At the cemetery the coffins were emptied, the corpses, grey as iron, were loaded on stretchers and waited in a specially prepared hanger, the coffins were sprayed with an antiseptic solution and taken back to the hospital, then the process began again, as often as necessary. The whole thing was well organized and the Prefect expressed his satisfaction. He even told Rieux that, when all was said and done, this was preferable to hearses driven by black slaves which one read about in the chronicles of earlier plagues.

'Yes,' Rieux said. 'The burial is the same, but we keep a card index. No one can deny that we have made progress.'

Despite these successes for the authorities, the unpleasant character that the formalities had now taken on forced the Prefecture to keep relatives away from the ceremony. They were allowed to come to the gate of the cemetery – though even that was not official, because where funerary rites were concerned, things had changed a bit. At the far end of the cemetery, in a featureless area covered in mastic trees, two huge pits had been dug. There was a men's grave and a women's grave. From this point of view, the authorities respected convention and it was only later when force of circumstances caused even this vestige of modesty to disappear and men and women were buried haphazardly, one on top of the other, with no thought of decency. Luckily, this extreme confusion affected only the final moments of the pestilence. At the time which concerns us now, there was a separation of pits and the authorities were very keen on it. At the bottom of each, a thick layer of quicklime smoked and boiled, while around the edges of the hole a small mound of the same chemical bubbled in the open air. When the ambulances had completed their journey, the stretchers were brought in procession and the naked, slightly twisted corpses were allowed to slip to the bottom, more or less side-by-side. After that, they were covered with quicklime, then earth, but only up to a certain height, in order to leave room for more occupants to come. The following day, the relatives were invited to sign a register – which just showed the difference that there may be between men and, for example, dogs: you can keep check of human beings.

These operations needed staff and manpower was always on the verge of running out. Many of the male nurses and the gravediggers, who were at first official, then casual, died of the plague. Whatever precautions were taken, one day infection occurred. Though, when you think about it, the most surprising thing was that there was never a shortage of men to do the job, for as long as the epidemic lasted. The critical period occurred shortly before the plague reached its peak and then Dr Rieux's fears were well founded. There were not enough people either for supervision or for what he called 'heavy work'. But from the time when the plague really took hold of the town, its very immoderation had one quite convenient outcome, because it disrupted the whole of economic life and so created quite a large number of unemployed. In most cases, they did not supply supervisors, but when it came to the dirty work, recruitment became much easier as a result. Indeed, from this time onwards, poverty always triumphed over fear, to the extent that work was always paid according to the risk involved. The health services were able to draw up a list of those seeking work and as soon as a vacancy occurred, the first on the list were informed and – assuming that they had not gone vacant themselves in the meantime – did not fail to turn up. In this way, the Prefect, who had long refused to make up his mind about employing the condemned (to death, or life) for this kind of work, was able to avoid having recourse to them. As long as there were men unemployed, he considered that such a decision could wait.

So, for better or worse, up to the end of August, the townspeople could be taken to their last resting-place, if not decently, at least in good enough order for the authorities to feel that they were carrying out their duties with a clear conscience. We must jump a little ahead of events to note the steps that had finally to be taken. When the epidemic levelled out after August, the accumulated number of victims was far greater than the capacity of our little cemetery. It was all very well knocking down walls and giving the dead an outlet into the surrounding land, but something else had to be done, and soon. First of all, they decided to bury the dead at night, which simply allowed them to do without certain forms and ceremonies. More and more bodies could be piled up in the ambulances. The few late strollers who, against all the rules, were still wandering around in the outlying districts after the curfew (or those who had to go there for work), sometimes came across long white ambulances which drove past at full speed, making the hollow night-time streets echo with their dull sirens. The bodies were hastily thrown into pits. They had barely come to rest before spadefuls of quicklime were landing on their faces and the anonymous earth covered them in holes that were being dug ever more deep.

However, after a short time, they were obliged to go and look elsewhere and gain some more space. A decree from the Prefect expropriated the occupants from graves leased in perpetuity and all the remains dug up were sent off to the crematorium. Soon it was also necessary to take those who had died from the plague off for cremation. But for this they had to use the old incinerating ovens to the east of the town, outside the gates. The guard post was moved further out and a town hall employee made the task of the authorities much easier by advising them to use the tramline which had formerly served the seaside promenade but was now lying idle. To this end, they made some alterations to the interior of the trucks and engines by taking out the seats, and redirected the track to the oven which now became the end of the line.

In the middle of the night, through the whole of the rest of the summer and beneath the autumn rains, one could see strange convoys of trams without passengers proceeding down the front, rattling along above the sea. Eventually, the people discovered what was going on; and despite patrols preventing anyone from reaching the promenade, some groups did quite often manage to get among the rocks right above the sea and throw flowers into the carriages as the trams went past. One could hear the vehicles still bumping along on a summer's night, laden with flowers and corpses.

By morning, at least in the early days, a thick, foul-smelling vapour would be drifting over the eastern quarter of the town. All doctors were of the opinion that these emissions, though unpleasant, could not harm anyone. But the inhabitants of those districts immediately threatened to evacuate them, convinced that the plague would rain down on their heads from the sky, so much so that the authorities were forced to redirect the fumes by means of a complicated system of piping; then the inhabitants were pacified. Only on very windy days would a vague smell from the east remind them that they were living under a new order and that the flames of the plague devoured their sacrifice every evening.

These were the extreme consequences of the epidemic. Fortunately, it did not increase any further, because one may imagine that the ingenuity of our administration, the talents of the Prefecture and even the capacity of the oven might have been overwhelmed. Rieux knew that in this case desperate measures had been envisaged, for example throwing bodies into the sea, and he could easily picture this monstrous foam on the blue waves. He also knew that if the figures went on rising, no organization, however excellent, could withstand it and that men would come and die in heaps and rot away in the streets, despite the Prefecture, and that the town would see the dead on the public squares clinging to the living with a mixture of justified hatred and ridiculous hope.

It was this kind of evidence or fear which meant that our fellow-citizens had a continuing feeling of exile and separation. At this juncture the narrator is perfectly well aware how unfortunate it is that he cannot here describe something truly spectacular, for example some reassuring hero or an impressive action, similar to those that one finds in old stories. The trouble is, there is nothing less spectacular than a pestilence and, if only because they last so long, great misfortunes are monotonous. In the memory of those who have lived through them, the dreadful days of the plague do not seem like vast flames, cruel and magnificent, but rather like an endless trampling that flattened everything in its path.

No, the plague had nothing in common with the great elevating images that obsessed Dr Rieux at the start of the epidemic. First of all, it was a shrewdly designed and flawless system, which operated with great efficiency. Incidentally – not to give anything away and especially not to give himself away – this is why the narrator has tended towards objectivity. He has tried to change almost nothing for artistic ends, except when it came to the basic requirement of giving a more or less coherent account. And it is objectivity itself that requires him to say here that while the greatest suffering of the time, the most widespread and the deepest, was separation, and while it is necessary in all conscience to give a new description of it at this point in the plague, it is also quite true that even this suffering lost all its pathos.

Did our fellow-citizens, at least those who suffered the most from this separation, ever get used to the situation? It would not be quite correct to say that they did. Rather, they suffered a kind of spiritual and physical emaciation. At the start of the plague they remembered the person whom they had lost very well and they were sorry to be without them. But though they could clearly recall the face and the laugh of the loved one, and this or that day when, after the event, they realized they had been happy, they found it very hard to imagine what the other person might be doing at the moment when they recalled her or him, in places which were now so far away. In short, at that time they had memory but not enough imagination. At the second stage of the plague the memory also went. Not that they had forgotten the face, but (which comes to the same thing) it had lost its flesh and they could only see it inside themselves. And while in the early weeks they tended to complain at only having shadows to deal with where their loves were concerned, they realized later that these shadows could become still more fleshless, losing even the details of colour that memory kept of them. After this long period of separation, they could no longer imagine the intimacy that they had shared nor how a being had lived beside them, on whom at any moment they could place their hands.

From this point of view, they had entered into the very system of the plague which was all the more efficient for being mediocre. No one among us experienced any great feelings any more, but everyone had banal feelings. 'It's time it ended,' they said, because, in a period of pestilence, it is normal to wish for the end of collective suffering and because they really did want it to end. But the words were spoken without the anger or bitterness of the early days, and only with the few arguments that still remained clear to us, which were feeble ones. The great, fierce surge of feeling of the first weeks had given way to a dejection that it would be wrong to confuse with resignation, but which was despite that a kind of provisional assent.

The townspeople had adapted, they had come to heel, as people say, because that was all they could do. Naturally, they still had an attitude of misfortune and suffering, but they did not feel its sting. Dr Rieux, for one, considered that the misfortune lay precisely in this, and that the habit of despair was worse than despair itself. Previously, those separated had not really been unhappy, their suffering had a brightness that had just gone out. Now one could see them on the corner of the street, in cafés or with their friends, placid, their minds wandering and their eyes so bored that, thanks to them, the whole town seemed like a waiting-room. Those who had jobs did them at the pace of the plague, meticulously and prosaically. Everyone was simple and unpretentious. For the first time, those separated did not mind speaking about their absent ones, adopting the language of all and studying their separation just as they would study the statistics of the epidemic. While up to this point they had fiercely subtracted their suffering from the sum of collective misfortune, now they accepted it as part of the whole. Without memory and without hope, they settled into the present. In truth, everything became present for them. The truth must be told: the plague had taken away from all of them the power of love or even of friendship, for love demands some future, and for us there was only the here and now.

Of course, none of this was absolute. Though it was true that all the separated reached this point, one should also add that they did not all reach it at the same time and that, once they had settled into this new attitude, flashes of memory and sudden relapses of lucidity brought the sufferers back to a younger and more painful sensibility. They needed these momentary losses of concentration in which they made plans for something that implied that the plague might have ceased. They needed the unexpected boon of feeling the pangs of undirected jealousy. Others also experienced sudden revivals and would emerge from their torpor on certain days of the week – on Sunday, of course, and Saturday afternoon – because those days had been devoted to certain rituals when they were still with the absent one. Or otherwise a certain melancholy that took hold of them at the end of the day would give warning (not always correctly, as it happened) that memory was about to return. That time in the evening, which for believers is the occasion for an examination of conscience, is hard for the prisoner or the exile who has only the void to examine. It held them for a moment in suspense; then they returned to insensibility and locked themselves up in the plague.

It is already understood that this consisted of giving up what was most personal to them. While in the early days of the plague they were struck by the number of small things that meant a great deal to them, though they had no significance to others, and they thus had a limited outlook on life, now, on the contrary, they had only the most general ideas and their love itself had taken on the most abstract appearance for them. They were so far abandoned to the plague that they might sometimes even hope for nothing more than the sleep of plague and catch themselves thinking: 'Let's have the bubos and be done with it!' But in truth they were already sleeping and this whole time was nothing more than a long sleep. The town was inhabited by people asleep on their feet, who did not really escape from their fate except on rare occasions when, in the night, their apparently healed wound would suddenly open. Then, waking with a start, they would feel around in a kind of stupor, their lips smarting, at one stroke rediscovering their pain which was suddenly revived, and with it the devastated features of their love. In the morning, they would return to the pestilence, that is to say, to routine.

But what did they look like, these separated people, you ask. Well, the answer is simple: like nothing. Or, if you prefer, they looked like everyone, part of the general scene. They shared the placidity and puerile agitation of the town. They lost any appearance of critical sense, while retaining an appearance of sang-froid. For example, you could see the most intelligent among them pretending to search the newspapers, or radio broadcasts, for reasons to believe that the plague would shortly end; and apparently they built imaginary hopes or felt unfounded terrors on reading the views that some journalist had set down more or less by chance, while yawning with boredom. Otherwise, they drank their beer or looked after the sick, lazed or exhausted themselves, filed cards or played gramophone records without otherwise distinguishing themselves from each other. In other words, they no longer made choices. The plague had suppressed value judgements. This could be seen in the way that no one cared any longer about the quality of the clothes or the food that they bought. Everything was accepted as it came.

Finally, one might say that the separated no longer had this peculiar privilege that had protected them at the start. They had lost the egoism of love and the advantages that they gained by it. At least, now, the situation was clear, the pestilence affected everybody. All of us, in the midst of the shots that could be heard at the gates of the town, the thump of rubber stamps that beat the rhythm of our lives, or our deaths, in the midst of fires and filing cards, terror and formalities, destined for an ignominious – but registered – death, amid horrifying smoke and the tranquil notes of ambulances, we ate the same bread of exile, waiting (though we did not know it) for the same devastating reunion and the same devastating peace. No doubt our love was still there, but quite simply it was unusable, heavy to carry, inert inside us, sterile as crime or condemnation. It was no longer anything except a patience with no future and a stubborn wait. From this point of view, the attitude of some of our fellow-citizens reminded one of those long queues in all parts of the town, in front of food shops. There was the same resignation and the same forbearance, at once limitless and without illusions. It was merely that where separation was concerned the feeling had to be measured on a scale a thousand times greater, because another kind of hunger was involved, one that might devour everything.

In any case, should anyone wish to have an accurate notion of the state of mind of the separated in our town, one must once more describe those eternal, golden, dusty evenings which descended on the treeless town while men and women poured out into every street. Because, oddly, what rose at such times towards the still sunlit terraces, in the absence of the sounds of vehicles and machinery that usually make up the language of towns, was only the vast noise of footsteps and muffled voices, the painful groan of thousands of shoes marching to the rhythm of the pestilence in the heavy sky, an endless and eventually stifling trample which gradually filled the whole town and which, evening after evening, was the most faithful and most melancholy expression of the blind obstinacy which at that time replaced love in our hearts.

Part IV

During the months of September and October the plague kept the town bent beneath it. As it was a case of marking time, many hundreds of thousands of people were still kicking their heels for endless weeks. Mist, heat and rain followed one another in the sky. Silent flocks of starlings and thrushes, coming from the south, flew overhead, but skirted around the town as though kept at a distance by Paneloux's flail, that strange piece of wood which whistled as it swung above the houses. At the beginning of October great storms of rain swept through the streets. And all the while, nothing more important happened than this great marking of time.

Rieux and his friends now discovered how tired they were. Indeed, the members of the health teams could no longer overcome their tiredness. Dr Rieux noticed it when he observed the steady growth of a strange indifference in himself and in his friends. For example, men who up to now had shown such a lively interest in any news about the plague, no longer bothered with it. Rambert, who had been provisionally put in charge of running one of the quarantine houses, which had been set up in his hotel, knew exactly the number of people whom he had under observation. He was informed of the minutest details of the plan for immediate evacuation that Rieux had drawn up for anyone who suddenly showed signs of the disease. The statistics of the effects of the serum on those in quarantine were engraved on his memory. But he was unable to tell you the weekly total of plague victims and genuinely had no idea if it was rising or falling. Yet he, despite everything, clung to the hope that he would shortly escape.

As for the others, they were absorbed day and night in their work, not reading the newspapers or listening to the radio. If someone told them a figure, they would pretend to be interested, but in fact greet it with that absent-minded indifference that one imagines to be the attitude of soldiers in great wars, exhausted by toil and simply determined not to fail in their daily duties, while looking forward to the final push or the day of the armistice.

Grand, who went on making the necessary calculations on the plague, would surely have been unable to give you any general trends or outcomes. His health had never been good, unlike that of Tarrou, Rambert and Rieux, who were evidently tough and fit; yet he carried out his duties as assistant at the Hôtel de Ville, his secretarial work for Rieux, and his own work at night. As a result, he could be seen in a continual state of exhaustion, sustained by two or three fixed ideas, for example that he would give himself a complete holiday after the plague, for at least one week, so that he could work in a positive way, 'hats off', on his project. He was also liable to sudden moments of emotion; and, on such occasions, he readily spoke to Rieux about Jeanne, wondering where she might be at that moment and if, when she read the newspapers, she thought of him. Rieux was surprised one day to find himself speaking to Grand about his own wife in the most casual way, something that he had never previously done. As he was not sure how much faith he should put in the always reassuring telegrams that his wife sent, he had decided to cable the head doctor at the sanatorium where she was being treated. In the reply he was informed that the patient's condition had worsened and that everything would be done to halt the advance of the disease. He kept the news to himself and could not understand what, unless it was tiredness, had induced him to confide in Grand. The civil servant, after talking about Jeanne, had questioned him about his wife and Rieux answered him. 'You know,' Grand had said, 'it can be cured very well nowadays.' Rieux had agreed, saying simply that the separation was getting long and that he might have been able to help his wife to overcome her illness, but that now she must feel all alone. After that, he fell silent and would only give evasive answers to Grand's questions.

The others were in the same state. Tarrou was holding up best, but his notebooks show that, while his curiosity had not lessened in depth, it had lost some of its diversity. Indeed, throughout that period he appeared only to be interested in Cottard. In the evening, at Rieux's house, where he had eventually moved in after the hotel was transformed into a place of quarantine, he would barely listen to Grand or the doctor as they delivered the results. He would immediately bring the conversation back to the small details of Oran life that usually occupied his attention.

As for Castel, on the day when he came to tell the doctor that the serum was ready, and after they had decided to make the first trials on M. Othon's little boy who had just been brought to the hospital and whose case seemed to Rieux hopeless, the doctor was just telling his old friend the latest statistics when he noticed that the other man had fallen fast asleep sunk in the bottom of his chair. Seeing this face to which usually an air of gentleness and irony gave a look of perpetual youth, now suddenly abandoned, a thread of saliva running between the half-open lips, revealing the effects of age and wear, Rieux felt a lump in his throat.

By such weaknesses Rieux could assess his own fatigue. His sensibility was getting out of hand. Held back most of the time, hardened and dried out, it would occasionally collapse and abandon him to feelings that he could no longer control. His only defence was to resort to hardening himself and tightening the knot which had formed in him. He knew full well that this was the correct way to proceed. For the rest, he had few illusions and tiredness took away even those that he still had. He knew that for a period of time, the end of which he could not see, his role was no longer that of a healer; it was that of a diagnostician. Discovering, seeing, describing, noting and then condemning – that was his task. Wives would seize him by the wrist and scream: 'Doctor, give him life!' But he was not there to give life, he was there to order isolation. What use then was the hatred that he could read on people's faces? 'You have no heart,' someone once told him. But he did have one. He used it to bear the twenty hours a day in which he saw men dying who were made for life. He used it to start again day after day. For the time being, he had just enough heart for that. How could his heart have been big enough to give life?

No, it was not help that he handed out through the day, but information. Of course, you couldn't call that a man's job. But when all's said and done, who in this terrorized, decimated mass was free to exercise a man's job? Thank goodness, at least, that he was tired. If Rieux had been more alert, this smell of death everywhere might have made him sentimental. But there is no room for sentimentality when you have only slept for four hours. You see things as they are, that is to say in the light of justice – ghastly and ridiculous justice. And those others, the condemned, also feel it. Before the plague, he was greeted like a saviour. He would fix everything with three pills and a hypodermic, so they squeezed his arm and led him along corridors. This was flattering, but dangerous. Now, on the contrary, he would appear with soldiers and it would take some blows with the butt of a rifle before the family would agree to let them in. They would like to have dragged him and to have dragged all humankind with them into death. Oh, it was quite true that men could not do without other men, that he was as helpless as these unfortunates and that he deserved that same shudder of pity that he allowed to rise in him when he had left them.

Such at least were the thoughts that Dr Rieux pursued over these interminable weeks, along with others concerning his status as a separated person. They were the same thoughts that he could see reflected in the faces of his friends. But the most dangerous effect of the exhaustion that gradually overtook all those who carried on this struggle against the affliction was not this indifference to outside events and the feelings of others, but the neglect to which they gave way. They tended at this time to avoid any gesture that was not absolutely necessary or which seemed to them to tax their strength too much. As a result, these men came increasingly to neglect the very rules of hygiene that they had drawn up, to overlook some of the various disinfecting procedures that they ought to apply to themselves; they would sometimes hurry to see patients suffering from pulmonary plague without taking the necessary precautions, because they had been informed at the last moment that they would have to visit an infected house and had considered it too exhausting to go back to the proper place in order to take the necessary drops or injections. This is where the real danger lay, because it was the very struggle against the plague that made them more vulnerable to the plague; in short, they were gambling on chance and chance is on nobody's side.

There was, however, one man in the town who never appeared exhausted or discouraged and remained a living image of satisfaction. This was Cottard. He continued to keep himself to himself, while maintaining his relations with others. But he chose to see Tarrou as often as Tarrou's work permitted, on the one hand because Tarrou was well informed about his case and on the other, because he would welcome the little man of means with consistent cordiality. It was a never-ending miracle, but Tarrou, despite the amount of work that he did, always remained friendly and considerate. Even after those evenings when he was dropping with tiredness, by the next day he had recovered new energy. 'You can talk with that one,' Cottard told Rambert. 'Because he's a man. He always understands you.'

This is why Tarrou's notes at this period more or less centre on the figure of Cottard. Tarrou tried to give a picture of Cottard's reactions and reflections, either as they were confided to him by the man himself or as he interpreted them. Under the heading 'Cottard's Relationship with the Plague', this portrait occupies a few pages in the notebook and the narrator thinks it would be useful to give an idea of it here. Tarrou's general opinion about the little man of means can be summed up in this opinion: 'He is a man who is growing in stature.' Moreover, it appears that he also grew in good humour. He was not unhappy with the turn of events. He would sometimes summarize how he felt in remarks of the following sort: 'Of course, it's not getting any better, but at least everyone is in the same boat.'

'Naturally,' Tarrou added, 'he is threatened just as everyone else is, but what matters is that he is with everybody else. And then I am sure that he does not seriously think that he might be infected. He appears to survive with the idea – which is not such a foolish one – that a man who is suffering from a great illness or a great fear is automatically relieved of all other illnesses or anxieties. "Have you noticed," he asked me, "that you cannot accumulate illnesses? Suppose you have a serious or incurable disease, a serious cancer or a good bout of TB, you will never catch plague or typhus; it's impossible. Moreover, it goes further than that, because you never see a cancer victim die in a car accident." Whether this notion is true or false, it puts Cottard in a good mood. The one thing that he does not want is to be separated from other people. He would rather be under siege with everybody than a prisoner all alone. With the plague going on, there are no more secret invest- igations, files, index cards, mysterious instructions and imminent arrest. Properly speaking, there is no longer any police, no more old or new crimes, no more guilty people; there are only the condemned awaiting the most arbitrary reprieve – and that includes the police themselves.' So Cottard (still as interpreted by Tarrou) was right to consider the symptoms of anxiety and confusion manifested by our fellow-citizens with the complete and indulgent satisfaction that might be expressed in the phrase: 'Carry on talking, I've already had it before you.'

'It was all very well for me to tell him that the only way not to be separated from others was, in the end, to have a clear conscience; but he gave me a wicked look and said: "Well, on that score, no one is ever with anybody." And then: "Think what you like, I'm telling you, the only way to bring people together is to send them the plague. Just look around." I have to admit that I can very well understand what he means and how pleasant life must appear to him today. How could he fail to recognize the reactions in others that had also been his: the attempt that each person makes to have everyone on his or her side; the consideration that one sometimes displays when showing a lost passer-by the way and the irritation that one shows on other occasions; the way that people hasten to expensive restaurants, their satisfaction in being there and staying there; the chaotic crowds who queue every day at the cinema, fill all the theatres and dance halls and spread like an uncontrolled tide through all public places; the shrinking from any contact and yet the hunger for human warmth that draws people towards one another, elbow to elbows and sexual organs to sexual organs? Cottard had clearly experienced all this before them. Except for women, because with looks like that . . . I expect that when he felt inclined to go with a prostitute, he denied himself, so as not to acquire a vulgar reputation that might harm him later.

'In short, the plague suits him. It has made an accomplice out of a solitary man who did not want to be solitary. Because he is clearly an accomplice and an accomplice who delights in it. He has a complicity in everything he sees: the superstitions, the unjustified terrors and the susceptibilities of these vigilant souls. He is a party to their manner of trying to talk about the plague as little as possible, while never ceasing to speak of it; to their panic and terror at the least headache once they know that the illness begins with cephalgia; to their overexcited, touchy and unstable sensibilities, which can transform an oversight into an offence and grieve at the loss of a trouser button.'

It often happened that Tarrou would go out in the evening with Cottard. He later described in his notebooks how they would plunge into the dark crowds of dusk or night-time, shoulder to shoulder, immersing themselves in a black and white crowd, lit here and there by the occasional lamp; and they would accompany the human herd towards the warm pleasures that protected it against the cold of the plague. A whole people was now indulging in what a few months earlier Cottard had been looking for in public places, in luxury and an abundant life, which he dreamed of without being able to satisfy his need, that is to say unbridled pleasure. Even though the price of goods was rising inexorably, people had never wasted so much money and while most of them lacked the essentials, they had never more effectively dissipated the superfluous. You could see them indulging in all the games of an idleness that was in reality nothing but unemployment. Sometimes Cottard and Tarrou would follow for minutes at a time behind one of those couples who had previously taken trouble to hide what united them and who now, pressed one against the other, would march stubbornly through the town without noticing the crowd that surrounded them, with the slightly obsessive absorption of great passion. Cottard would gush over them: 'Oh, what lusty young things!' he would say. And he said it aloud, becoming expansive in the midst of the collective fever, the huge tips clanging on the tables around them and intrigues concocted before their eyes.

However, Tarrou felt that there was little malice in Cottard's attitude. His 'I experienced that before them' was said more in misfortune than in triumph. 'I think', Tarrou said, 'that he is starting to love these people imprisoned between the sky and the walls of their town. For example, if he could, he would happily explain to them that it is not as bad as all that: "Can't you hear them?"' he asked. '"After the plague, I'll do this, after the plague I'll do that . . ." They're ruining their lives, instead of staying calm. And they don't even realize what they have going for them. Could I say: "After my arrest, I'll do this or that? An arrest is a beginning, not an end. While, the plague . . . Do you want to know what I think? I think they're miserable because they don't let themselves go. And I know what I'm talking about."

'He does know what he's talking about,' Tarrou added. 'He has a clear assessment of the contradictions in the inhabitants of Oran, who, while they feel a deep need for warmth, which brings them together, at the same time cannot surrender to it entirely because of the suspicion that keeps them apart. You know very well that you cannot trust your neighbour, that he is quite capable of giving you the plague without knowing it and taking advantage of your lowered guard to infect you. When, like Cottard, you have spent your days looking for possible police spies in everyone, even people you liked being with, you can understand the feeling. One can very well sympathize with those people who live with the idea that from one day to the next the plague might touch them on the shoulder and that it is perhaps getting ready to do so just as one is congratulating oneself on still being safe and sound. As far as one can be, Cottard is at ease in terror. But because he has felt all this before them, I think that he cannot really feel how cruel this uncertainty is. In short, with us, who have not yet died of the plague, he is aware that his freedom and his life are on the brink of destruction at any moment. But since he has himself lived in terror, he considers it normal that others should experience it in their turn. Or, more precisely, terror seems to him a less heavy burden than if he were all alone. This is where he is wrong and he is harder to understand than some others. But after all that is why he deserves, more than others, that we should try to understand him.'

Finally, Tarrou's account ends with a story which illustrates the peculiar awareness that came at the same time to Cottard and to victims of the plague. This story captures the difficult atmosphere of the time, which is why the narrator attaches some importance to it.

They had gone to the Municipal Opera House where they were playing *Orpheus and Eurydice*. Cottard had invited Tarrou. The company was one that had arrived in the spring of the plague year to give some performances in our town. Trapped by the disease, they found themselves obliged – with the agreement of the Opera House – to keep on giving the same performance, once a week. Thus, for some months now, every Friday, the municipal theatre rang to the melodious sighs of Orpheus and the powerless pleas of Eurydice. However, the opera was still a success with the public and continued to take a lot of money at the box-office. Sitting in the most expensive seats, Cottard and Tarrou looked out over an audience packed with the most elegant of their fellow-citizens. Those who came into the auditorium obviously made an effort not to spoil their entrance. The silhouettes stood out clearly beneath the dazzling lights on the apron stage as they moved from one row to another, bowing gracefully, while the musicians tuned their instruments. In the slight hum of polite conversation, the men recovered the self-confidence they had lost a few hours earlier in the black streets of the town. Evening dress drove away the plague.

Throughout the first act, Orpheus sighed and moaned without difficulty, a few women in Grecian tunics commented elegantly on his plight, love was sung about in little arias. The audience responded with moderately warm applause. Hardly anyone noticed that, in his aria in the second act, Orpheus introduced some unscheduled tremolos and put rather too much pathos into his voice when singing to the master of the Underworld as he begged him to be moved by his tears. When he let slip a few jerky movements, the more sophisticated considered this to be a touch of stylization and an improvement to the singer's interpretation of the role.

It was not until the great duo of Orpheus and Eurydice in the third act – this is the moment where he loses Eurydice – that the audience showed some surprise. And, as though the singer had been expecting this stir among the spectators, or, more probably, as though the murmur rising from the stalls confirmed what he was feeling, he chose that moment to walk towards the footlights in a grotesque manner, arms wide and bow-legged in his classical costume, and collapse in the midst of an eighteenth-century pastoral décor that had always been inappropriate, but which, in the eyes of the audience, now became so for the first time and in the most dreadful way. At the same moment, the orchestra stopped playing, the people in the stalls got up and slowly started to leave the theatre, firstly in silence, as one does on leaving a church when the service is over or a funerary chamber after a visit, the women gathering up their skirts and leaving with lowered heads, the men guiding their female companions by the elbow and steering them past the folding seats. But little by little, the movement speeded up, the whisperings turned into exclamations and the crowd poured out in the direction of the exits, hurrying through them and eventually pushing and shouting. Cottard and Tarrou, who had merely risen to their feet, remained alone before an image of what their life was at that time: the plague on the stage in the person of a performer like a limp puppet; and, in the auditorium, luxury that had become useless in the form of fans and lace stoles left behind on the red plush of the seats.

In the early days of September Rambert worked conscientiously beside Rieux. He merely asked for a day's leave when he was to meet Gonzales and the two young men in front of the boys' school.

That day, at noon, Gonzales and the journalist saw the two lads laughing as they approached. They said that they'd been unlucky last time, but it was only to be expected. In any case, it wasn't their week on guard duty. They'd have to wait until the next week; then they could start all over again. Rambert said that was certainly how he would put it. So Gonzales suggested meeting the following Monday, but this time they would lodge Rambert in Marcel and Louis's house. 'We'll arrange a meeting, you and I. Then if I'm not there, you can go directly to their place. We'll tell you where they live.' But Marcel (or Louis) said at that point that the simplest thing was to take the comrade there at once. If he wasn't fussy, there was enough to eat for all four of them. In this way, he'd know how things stood. Gonzales said that was a very good idea and they set off towards the port.

Marcel and Louis lived on the outskirts of the Maritime district, near houses which looked out over the front. Theirs was a little Spanish house, with thick walls, painted wooden shutters and bare, shady rooms. The young men's mother, an old Spanish woman, with a smile and lots of wrinkles, served them rice. Gonzales was amazed, because there was already a shortage of rice in town. 'We have ways, at the gates,' said Marcel. Rambert ate and drank, and Gonzales said he was a real friend, while the journalist could only think of the week he had ahead of him.

In fact, he had two weeks, because the shifts of guard duty were extended to a fortnight, to reduce the number of teams. And, during that fortnight, Rambert worked unstintingly and continuously, from dawn to night, as it were with his eyes shut. He would go to bed late at night and sleep a heavy sleep. The sudden transition from idleness to this exhausting labour left him more or less without dreams and without strength. He spoke little about his forthcoming escape. One notable fact: after a week, he confided in the doctor that for the first time, the previous night, he had got drunk. On coming out of the bar, he suddenly had the impression that his groin was swelling and that his arms were stiff around the armpits. He thought it was the plague. And the only thing he could think of doing at that point – something which he agreed with Rieux was not reasonable – was to run up to the highest part of the town and there, from a little square from which you could still not see the sea, but could at least see a bit more sky, he called to his wife with a great cry across the town walls. When he got home, he found no sign of infection on himself and was not particularly proud of succumbing to this sudden panic. Rieux said that he understood his acting like that very well: 'In any case,' he said, 'it's the sort of thing you might want to do.'

'Monsieur Othon talked to me about you this morning,' Rieux added suddenly just as Rambert was leaving. 'He asked me if I knew you. "Then advise him," he said, "not to frequent smugglers. People are starting to notice him."'

'What does that mean?'

'It means that you'd better hurry.'

'Thank you,' said Rambert, shaking the doctor's hand.

At the door, he suddenly turned round. Rieux saw that for the first time since the outbreak of the plague he was smiling.

'So why don't you stop me leaving? You could if you wanted to.'

Rieux shook his head in his usual way and said that this was a matter for Rambert: he had chosen happiness and Rieux could not argue against that. He felt unable to judge what was right or wrong in the matter.

'So in that case why are you telling me to hurry?'

It was Rieux's turn to smile.

'Perhaps it's because I, too, would like to do something for happiness.'

The next day they did not discuss anything, but worked together. The following week Rambert was finally settled in the little Spanish house. They made up a bed for him in the living-room. Since the young men did not come home for meals, and since he had been told to go out as little as possible, he lived alone, most of the time, or made conversation with the old mother. She was dry, energetic, dressed in black, with a wrinkled brown face under very clean grey hair. She kept quiet, but would smile with her eyes sparkling when she looked at Rambert.

At other times she would ask if he wasn't afraid of taking the plague to his wife. He thought this was a risk they had to take, but a minute one, while if he stayed in the town there was a chance of them being separated for ever.

'She's nice?' the old woman asked with a smile.

'Very nice.'

'Pretty?'

'I think so.'

'Ah! That's why,' she said.

Rambert thought about it. Of course, that was why, but it couldn't only be for that reason.

'Don't you believe in God?' said the old woman. She attended mass every morning.

Rambert admitted that he didn't and she said again that this was why.

'You have to get back to her, you're right. Otherwise, what's left for you?'

The rest of the time, Rambert walked round and round within the naked, roughcast walls, stroking the fans nailed to them or else counting the woollen balls in the fringe around the tablecloth. In the evening the two boys came home. They said very little except to tell him that it was not yet time. After dinner Marcel played the guitar and drank an aniseed liqueur. Rambert seemed to be thinking.

On Wednesday Marcel came back saying: 'It's tomorrow evening, at midnight. Be ready.' One of the two men who kept guard with them had caught the plague, and the other who usually shared a bedroom with him was under observation. So for two or three days Marcel and Louis would be alone. During the night they would make the final arrangements. The next day it would be possible. 'Are you pleased?' the old woman asked. Rambert said that he was, but he was thinking of other things.

The following day, the sky was heavy, the air humid and stifling. There was bad news of the plague. However, the old Spanish woman remained calm: 'There is sin in the world,' she said. 'So naturally . . .' Like Marcel and Louis, Rambert was stripped to the waist. But whenever he moved, the sweat ran between his shoulder blades and across his chest. In the half-light of the house with its closed shutters, their torsos looked brown and shiny. Rambert walked about the house without speaking. Suddenly, at four o'clock in the afternoon, he got dressed and said he was going out.

'Watch out,' said Marcel. 'It's for midnight. Everything's set up.'

Rambert went to see Dr Rieux. The doctor's mother told him that he could be found in the hospital in the upper town. Around the guard post, the same crowd was constantly going round and round. 'Move on!' said a gendarme with protruding eyes. The crowd did move on, but in circles. 'There's nothing to see,' said the gendarme, the sweat soaking through his jacket. Everyone agreed, but they stayed even so, despite the lethal heat. Rambert showed the gendarme his pass and the man pointed him to Tarrou's office. Its door opened on the courtyard. He met Father Paneloux coming out of the office.

In a dirty little white room, smelling of disinfectant and damp sheets, Tarrou was sitting behind a black wooden desk with his shirt sleeves rolled up, dabbing the sweat in the crook of his arm with a handkerchief.

'Still here?' he asked.

'Yes, I'd like to talk to Rieux.'

'He's on the ward. But it would be better if we could fix it without him.'

'Why?'

'He's overworked. I'm sparing him as much as I can.'

Rambert looked at Tarrou. He had lost weight, and his eyes and features were blurred with fatigue. His strong shoulders were hunched. Someone knocked on the door and a male nurse came in wearing a white mask. He put down a bundle of filing cards on Tarrou's desk and, his voice muffled by the mask, just said 'six', then went out. Tarrou looked at the journalist and fanned out the cards to show him.

'Nice cards, aren't they? Well, no, actually they're the people who died last night.'

His forehead wrinkled. He gathered up the bundle of cards.

'The only thing we've got left is statistics.'

Tarrou got up, supporting himself against the table.

'Are you leaving soon?'

'Tonight at midnight.'

Tarrou said he was glad and that Rambert had better look after himself.

'Do you really mean that?'

Tarrou shrugged his shoulders.

'At my age, you've got to mean what you say. It's too tiring to lie.'

'Tarrou,' the journalist said. 'I'd like to see the doctor. Excuse me.'

'I know, he's more human than I am. Let's go.'

'That's not it,' Rambert said awkwardly. Then he stopped.

Tarrou looked at him and smiled suddenly.

They went down a little corridor, with its walls painted light green, where the light was like that in an aquarium. Just before they got to a double glass door, behind which one could see strange shadows moving, Tarrou made Rambert go into a very small room with cupboards all round the walls. He opened one and took two gauze masks out of a sterilizer, offered one to Rambert and asked him to put it on. The journalist asked if it served any purpose and Tarrou said no, but that it inspired confidence in others.

They pushed open the glass doors. The ward was a huge room with its windows hermetically sealed, despite the weather. High up on the walls there were humming machines which kept the air moving, their twisted propellers fanning the clotted, overheated air above two rows of grey beds. From all sides rose dull moans or sharp cries that merged into a single, monotonous wail. Men dressed in white were slowly walking around in the cruel light that came from the high barred windows. Rambert felt uncomfortable in the ghastly heat of the room and had difficulty recognizing Rieux standing over a groaning figure. The doctor was making incisions in the patient's groin while two women nurses on each side of the bed kept his legs apart. When Rieux got up, he dropped his implements onto the tray which an assistant was holding and stayed motionless, looking at the man whose wounds were being dressed.

'What's new?' he asked Tarrou as he came up.

'Paneloux has agreed to replace Rambert in the quarantine ward. He has done a lot already. We still have to reorganize the third exploratory group without Rambert.'

Rieux nodded.

'Castel has completed his first vaccines and suggests carrying out a trial.'

'Ah!' Rieux said. 'That's good.'

'And Rambert is here.'

Rieux turned round. His eyes narrowed above the mask when he saw the journalist.

'What are you doing here? You should be somewhere else.'

Tarrou said it was for tonight at midnight and Rambert added: 'In theory.'

Every time one of them spoke, the gauze mask puffed out and grew damp around the mouth. This made conversations slightly unreal, like a dialogue between statues.

'I'd like to talk to you,' said Rambert.

'We'll leave together, if you like. Wait for me in Tarrou's office.'

A moment later Rambert and Rieux were settling into the back of the doctor's car. Tarrou was driving.

'No more fuel,' he said, starting the engine. 'Tomorrow, we'll have to walk.'

'Doctor,' Rambert said. 'I'm not leaving and I want to stay with you.'

Tarrou did not flinch. He carried on driving. Rieux appeared incapable of escaping from his fatigue.

'What about her?' he said in a dull voice.

Rambert said that he had thought it over again. He still believed what he believed, but if he went away he would feel ashamed. It would make him uncomfortable loving the woman he had left. But Rieux sat up and said firmly that this was ridiculous and that there was no shame in choosing happiness.

'Yes,' said Rambert. 'But there may be shame in being happy all by oneself.'

Tarrou, who had said nothing up to now, remarked without turning his head that if Rambert wanted to share the misfortunes of mankind, he would never again have time for happiness. You had to choose.

'That's not it,' said Rambert. 'I always thought that I was a stranger in this town and had nothing to do with you. But now that I have seen what I have seen, I know that I come from here, whether I like it or not. This business concerns all of us.'

No one answered and Rambert seemed irritated.

'In any case, you know that as well as I do! Otherwise, what are you doing in that hospital of yours? Have you made your choice then and given up on happiness?'

Still neither Tarrou nor Rieux answered. The silence lasted a long time, until they were close to the doctor's house. Then once more Rambert asked his last question, still more emphatically. Only Rieux turned towards him, raising himself with difficulty.

'I'm sorry Rambert,' he said. 'But I don't know. Stay with us if that's what you want.'

He was silenced as the car swerved. Then he carried on, looking straight ahead:

'Nothing in the world should turn you away from what you

love. And yet I, too, am turning away, without understanding why.'

He slumped back into his seat.

'It's a fact, that's all,' he said wearily. 'Let's just acknowledge it and draw the necessary conclusions.'

'What conclusions?' Rambert asked.

'Oh,' Rieux said. 'One can't heal and know at the same time. So let's heal as fast as we can. That's the most urgent thing.'

At midnight Tarrou and Rieux were giving Rambert the plan of the district which he had to investigate, when Tarrou looked at his watch. Raising his head, he met Rambert's eyes.

'Did you let them know?'

The journalist looked away.

'I sent a note,' he said in a strained voice. 'Before I came to see you.'

It was in the last days of October that they tried out Castel's serum. In practical terms this was Rieux's last hope. In the event of a new failure the doctor was convinced that the town would have to surrender to the whims of the disease and either the epidemic would continue for many long months yet or else it would decide to call a halt for no reason.

On the eve of the day when Castel came to see Rieux, M. Othon's son fell ill and the whole family had to go into quarantine. The mother, who had only recently emerged from quarantine, was thus isolated for a second time. Obedient to the instructions he had been given, the judge had Rieux brought in as soon as he recognized the signs of the disease on the child's body. When Rieux arrived the mother and father were standing at the foot of the bed. The little girl had been sent off. The child was in the phase of exhaustion and allowed himself to be examined without fuss. When the doctor looked up he met the magistrate's eyes and also saw behind him the pale face of the mother who had put a handkerchief over her face and was following the doctor's movements with wide-open eyes.

'That's it, isn't it?' the magistrate said, in a cold voice.

'Yes,' Rieux replied, looking back to the child.

The mother's eyes widened, but still she said nothing. The magistrate was also silent; then, in a low voice, he said:

'Well, doctor, we have to do what we are required to do.'

Rieux avoided the eyes of the mother, who was still holding a handkerchief to her mouth.

'It won't take long,' he said, hesitantly, 'if I might use your phone?'

M. Othon said he would show him where it was. But the doctor turned to the magistrate's wife:

'I'm very sorry. You must get some things together. You know what's needed.'

Mme Othon seemed struck dumb. She was staring at the ground.

'Yes,' she said, nodding. 'I'll do that.'

Before he left them Rieux could not stop himself asking them if they needed anything. The woman kept looking at him in silence. But this time the magistrate looked away.

'No,' he said. Then, swallowing: 'But save my child.'

At the start, quarantine had been a simple formality; now Rieux and Rambert had organized it very strictly. In particular, they demanded that the members of a family should always be isolated from one another. If one person in a family had been infected without realizing it, they should not increase the chances of the illness spreading. Rieux explained this to the magistrate who was persuaded by the argument. However, the magistrate and his wife were looking at one another in such a way that the doctor felt how devastating this separation would be for them. Mme Othon and her young daughter could be housed in the quarantine hotel run by Rambert. But for the magistrate, there was no place any longer except in the isolation camp which the Prefecture was setting up in the municipal stadium, with the help of tents provided by the refuse collection service. Rieux apologized, but M. Othon said that there was only one law for everyone and that it was right to obey it.

As for the child, he was taken to the auxiliary hospital, to a former classroom in which ten beds had been set up. After some twenty hours, Rieux considered his case desperate. The little body was being eaten up by the infection without reacting. Tiny bubos, painful but barely formed, were obstructing the joints of his slender limbs. He was beaten from the start. This is why Rieux had the idea of trying out Dr Castel's serum on him. That evening, after dinner, they gave the long injection, without a single reaction from the child. At dawn the next day they all went to the little boy's bedside to assess the result of this decisive experiment.

The child, who had emerged from his torpor, was turning convulsively under the sheets. The doctor, Castel and Tarrou had been beside him since four o'clock in the morning, following the disease as it advanced and retreated. Tarrou's solid frame was slightly hunched at the head of the bed. Rieux was standing at the foot of the bed and beside him Castel sat and read some old book with every appearance of calm. Little by little, as daylight spread through the old schoolroom, the others arrived. First, Paneloux, who took up his position on the other side of the bed from Tarrou, with his back against the wall. His face wore a pained expression, and the exhaustion of so many days in which he had given to others at the expense of his own well-being had drawn lines across his flushed forehead. Joseph Grand arrived in his turn. It was seven o'clock and the civil servant apologized for being out of breath. He would only stay for a moment; perhaps they already knew something definite. Without a word Rieux showed him the child, whose eyes were closed in his contorted face, his teeth clenched as hard as he could clench them and his body motionless. He was turning his head back and forth, from right to left on the bolster with no sheet across it. When it was finally light enough for one to see the blackboard which had remained at the back of the room with some old equations on it, Rambert came. He leant against the back of the next bed and brought out a packet of cigarettes, but after looking at the child, put it back in his pocket.

Castel, still sitting down, looked at Rieux over his glasses:

'Any news of the father?'

'No,' Rieux said. 'He is in the isolation hospital.'

The doctor was grasping the iron bar at the foot of the bed where the child was groaning. He never took his eyes off the little patient, who stiffened suddenly and, once more clenching his teeth, arched his back a little at the waist, slowly extending his arms and legs. The small body, naked under the army blanket, gave off an acrid smell of sweat and wool. The child gradually relaxed, brought his arms and legs back towards the centre of the bed and, still blind and dumb, seemed to be breathing more rapidly. Rieux looked towards Tarrou, who turned away.

They had already seen children die: for several months the terror had not discriminated in its victims; but never before had they followed a child's suffering minute by minute as they had been doing here since early morning. Of course, the pain inflicted on these innocents had never ceased to appear to them what in truth it was, an outrage. But until then they had been outraged abstractly, in a sense, because they had never looked face-to-face for so long a time at the death throes of an innocent child.

At that moment the boy, as though bitten in the stomach, doubled up again with a high-pitched moan. He remained bent like this for several seconds, shaking and trembling convulsively, as though his frail body were bowing beneath the raging wind of the plague and cracking under the repeated blasts of fever. Once the gust had passed, he relaxed a little, the fever seemed to move away, abandoning him, gasping, on a damp and polluted shore where rest already seemed like death. When the burning tide struck him again for the third time and raised him up a little, the child, bent double and throwing back his blanket, fled to the end of the bed, wildly shaking his head from side to side, in terror of the flame that was burning him. Large tears rose beneath his swollen eyelids and began to flow down his pallid face; when the crisis was over, exhausted, tensing his bony legs and his arms from which in forty-eight hours the flesh had dropped away, the child assumed the grotesque pose of a crucified man in the ravaged bed.

Tarrou leant over and with his heavy hand wiped the small face bathed in tears and sweat. A moment earlier, Castel had closed his book and was looking at the patient. He began to say something, but had to cough in order to finish it, because his voice suddenly started to crack.

'There was no morning remission, was there, Rieux?'

Rieux said no, but that the child was holding on longer than normal. Paneloux, who seemed to have slumped somewhat against the wall, said in a dull voice:

'If he is to die, he will have suffered longer.'

Rieux turned brusquely towards him and opened his mouth to say something, then thought better of it and looked back towards the child, making a visible effort to control himself.

The light spread through the ward. On the other five beds shapes were tossing and groaning, but with what appeared to be deliberate self-restraint. The only one who was shouting, at the other end of the ward, was making little cries at regular intervals, which seemed to express astonishment rather than pain. Now there was a kind of assent in their manner of approaching the disease. Only the child was struggling with all his strength. From time to time Rieux would take his pulse (unnecessarily and rather to escape from the state of powerless inactivity in which he found himself); and when he closed his eyes he could feel this agitation mingled with the throbbing in his own veins. At such times he felt himself merge with the martyred child and tried to sustain him with all his still undiminished strength. But the beating of their two hearts, united for a minute, would cease to harmonize; the child escaped him and his efforts dissolved into nothingness. At this, he would put down the slender wrist and go back to his place.

Along the whitewashed walls the light changed from pink to yellow. Behind the glass a hot morning was starting to crackle. One could hardly hear Grand as he left saying that he would come back. They all waited. The child, his eyes still shut, seemed to be slightly calmer. His hands, now like claws, were gently working away at the sides of the bed. They climbed upwards, scratched the blanket near the knees and suddenly he bent his legs, brought his thighs up near to his belly and became still. At this point he opened his eyes for the first time and looked at Rieux who was standing in front of him. In the hollow of his face, as if fixed in grey clay, the mouth opened and almost immediately a single continuous cry came out, hardly altered by the boy's breathing, suddenly filling the room with a monotonous, discordant protest, so inhuman that it seemed to be coming from all the men at once. Rieux gritted his teeth and Tarrou turned away. Rambert went up to the bed beside Castel, who closed the book which had stayed open on his knees. Paneloux looked at this child's mouth, soiled by illness, full of that cry of all the ages. He knelt and everyone considered it natural to hear him say, in a voice that was somewhat stifled but distinct, behind the continuing, anonymous howl: 'My God, save this child.'

But the child went on crying and, all around him, the other patients were becoming restless. The one at the end of the ward, whose shouts had not stopped, stepped up the rhythm of his moan until it, too, became a genuine cry, while the others groaned louder and louder. A tide of sobs broke across the room, drowning out Paneloux's prayer and Rieux, clasping the bar at the foot of the bed, closed his eyes, drunk with tiredness and horror.

When he opened them again he found Tarrou beside him.

'I have to go,' said Rieux. 'I can't stand this any more.'

But abruptly the other patients fell silent and the doctor realized that the child's cry had weakened, that it was still weakening and that it had just stopped. Around him the moans resumed, but smothered, like a distant echo of the struggle that had just ended. For ended it had. Castel went round to the other side of the bed and said that it was all over. His mouth open, but silent, the child was resting among the rumpled blanket, suddenly grown smaller, with traces of tears on his face.

Paneloux went up to the bed and made the sign of benediction. Then he gathered up his robes and went out down the central aisle.

'Must we start all over again?' Tarrou asked Castel.

The old doctor shook his head.

'Perhaps,' he said, with a strained smile. 'After all, he did fight it for a long time.'

But Rieux was already going out of the ward, walking so quickly and with such a look on his face that when he overtook Paneloux, the priest held out his arm to restrain him.

'Come now, doctor,' he said.

Without stopping as he swept along, Rieux turned round and spat out:

'Ah, now that one, at least, was innocent, as you very well know!'

Then he turned away and, going through the doors of the ward in front of Paneloux, crossed to the back of the school courtyard. He sat down on a bench between the dusty little trees and wiped away the sweat that was already running into his eyes. He wanted to shout out again, to untie the dreadful knot crushing his heart. The heat flowed slowly down between the branches of the fig trees. The blue morning sky was quickly covered by a whitish film that made the air more stifling than ever. Rieux slumped back on the bench. He watched the branches and the sky, gradually getting back his breath and bit by bit reabsorbing his fatigue.

'Why did you speak to me with such anger just now?' said a voice behind him. 'I, too, found that unbearable to watch.'

Rieux turned round to Paneloux.

'That's true,' he said. 'Forgive me. But tiredness is a form of madness. And there are times in this town when I can only feel outrage and revolt.'

'I understand,' said Paneloux. 'It is outrageous because it is beyond us. But perhaps we should love what we cannot understand.'

Rieux sat up abruptly. He looked at Paneloux with all the strength and passion he could muster and shook his head.

'No, Father,' he said. 'I have a different notion of love; and to the day I die I shall refuse to love this creation in which children are tortured.'

A shadow of profound distress passed across Paneloux's face.

'Ah, doctor,' he said sadly. 'I have just understood what is meant by God's grace.'

But Rieux had slipped back onto his bench. From the depths of his returning exhaustion, he replied more gently:

'Which I don't have, I know. But I don't want to discuss this with you. We are working together for something that unites us at a higher level than prayer or blasphemy, and that's all that counts.'

Paneloux sat down beside Rieux. He seemed moved.

'Yes,' he said. 'Yes, you too are working for the salvation of mankind.'

Rieux tried to smile.

'Salvation is too big a word for me. I don't go that far. What interests me is man's health, his health first of all.'

Paneloux hesitated.

'Doctor . . . .' he said.

Then he stopped. The sweat was also starting to run down his forehead. He muttered 'goodbye', and his eyes shone as he got up. He was about to leave when Rieux, who had been thinking, also got up and took a step towards him.

'Forgive me again,' he said. 'That outburst will not be repeated.'

Paneloux held out his hand and said sadly:

'Yet I have not managed to convince you!'

'What does it matter?' Rieux asked. 'What I hate is death and evil, as you know. And whether you accept this or not, we are together in enduring them and fighting against them.'

Rieux took Paneloux's hand.

'You see,' he said, deliberately not meeting his eye, 'even God himself cannot separate us now.'

Since he began to work for the health teams, Paneloux had not left the hospitals and other places where the plague was to be found. He put himself among the rescuers in the position which he felt was his by right, namely in the front rank. He had seen death many times. And, though in theory he was protected by the serum, the idea of his own death was also familiar to him. To all appearances, though, he had kept calm. But from the day when he had had to watch for hours while that child died, he seemed changed. His face showed evidence of increasing stress. So when one day he told Rieux, with a smile, that he was just then preparing a short exposé on the subject 'Can a priest consult a doctor?', Rieux got the impression that something more serious was involved than Paneloux appeared to be telling him. When the doctor said he would be interested to see the work, Paneloux announced that he was to give a sermon at the men's mass and that on this occasion he would develop at least some of his ideas.

'I'd like you to come, doctor, the subject will interest you.'

The priest gave his second sermon on a day of high wind. To tell the truth, the ranks of the congregation were less tightly packed than on the previous occasion. The fact is that this kind of entertainment no longer had the appeal of novelty for our fellow-citizens. In the difficult circumstances that the town was experiencing, the very word 'novelty' had lost its meaning. Moreover, most people, when they had not entirely abandoned their religious duties or managed to reconcile them with profoundly immoral personal lives, had replaced ordinary observances by quite irrational superstitions. They were more likely to wear protective charms or medallions of Saint Roch than to go to mass.

As an example, one might point to the excessive use our townspeople made of prophecies. In the spring, indeed, they expected the illness to end at any time, so no one bothered to seek any information about the duration of the epidemic because they had all convinced themselves that it would have none. But the more time passed, the more people came to fear that this misfortune really would never end and, by the same token, the ending of the epidemic became the object of everyone's hopes. So various prophecies by wise men or saints of the Catholic Church were passed around from hand to hand. Printers in the town very rapidly realized that this interest might be turned to their advantage and published many copies of the texts that were in circulation. Finding that the public's appetite was insatiable, they had some researches made in the town libraries on all the writings of this kind that could be found in the highways and byways of history and spread them around town. When history itself proved to be short on prophecies, these were commissioned from journalists, who proved, in this respect at least, to be as competent as their counterparts in earlier centuries.

Some of their prophecies even appeared serialized in the newspapers and were read with quite as much eagerness as the love stories that were to be found there in times of good health. Some predictions were based on bizarre calculations involving the number of the year, the number of deaths and the number of months already spent under the plague. Others established comparisons with the great plagues of history, bringing out the similarities (which these prophecies called 'constants') and, by means of no less peculiar calculations, claimed to extract information relative to the present outbreak. But the ones that the public liked best were undoubtedly those which, in apocalyptic language, announced a series of events, any one of which might be the one that the town was currently enduring, their complexity allowing for any interpretation. Nostradamus and Saint Odile were thus consulted daily and never in vain. What remained common to all the prophecies was that, in the last resort, they were reassuring. The plague, however, was not.

Hence, these superstitions took the place of religion for our fellow-citizens and this is why Paneloux's sermon was given to a church that was only three-quarters full. On the evening of the event, when Rieux arrived, the wind, which was seeping in currents of air through the great swinging doors of the front entrance, circulated freely among the congregation. So it was in a cold, silent church, in the midst of a congregation exclusively made up of men, that Rieux sat down and watched the priest step up into the pulpit. He spoke in a voice that was softer and more thoughtful than on the previous occasion; and several times the listeners noticed a sort of hesitation in his delivery. Another peculiar thing: he no longer said 'you', but 'we'.

However, his voice got gradually stronger. He began by recalling that the plague had been among us for many long months and that now we knew it better for having seen it so many times seated at our table or at the bedside of those we loved, walking beside us and waiting for us to arrive at our place of work, so we might now hear what it had been ceaselessly telling us, but which it had been possible that in our first surprise we did not hear very well. What Father Paneloux had preached in this same place already remained true – at least, so he believed. But perhaps – as might happen to any one of us (and at this he beat his breast) – he may have thought it and said it without charity. However, what remained true was that always, in every circumstance, there was something to learn. The cruellest trial was still beneficial for the Christian. And precisely what the Christian should seek, as a Christian, was his own benefit, and he explained what it involved and how it was to be found.

At that moment, around Rieux, people seemed to be settling in against the arm-rests of their benches and making themselves as comfortable as they could. One of the padded doors at the entrance was flapping gently. Someone got up to fasten it. And Rieux, disturbed by this movement, was hardly listening to Paneloux as he resumed his sermon. He was saying, more or less, that one must not try to explain the phenomenon of the plague, but attempt instead to learn what one could from it. Rieux vaguely understood that, according to the priest, there was nothing to explain. Paneloux captured his full attention when he said firmly that there were some things that one could explain in the sight of God and others that one could not. Certainly, there were such things as good and evil and, broadly speaking, one could easily understand what distinguished them. But it was inside evil that the problem started. For example, there were apparently necessary evils and apparently unnecessary ones. There was Don Juan cast into Hell and there was the death of a child. While it is right that the libertine should be cast aside, one could not understand the suffering of the child. And, in truth, there was nothing on earth more important than the suffering of a child and the horror that this suffering brings with it and the explanation that had to be found for it. In other aspects of life, God made everything easy for us, so in that sense there was no merit in religion. Here, on the other hand, it put us with our backs to the wall. It would have been easy for him to say that the eternity of joy that awaited the child might compensate for his suffering, but in truth he did not know about that. Who in fact could assert that an eternity of delight could compensate for an instant of human suffering? Surely not a Christian, whose Master had endured pain in his limbs and in his soul. No, when faced with the suffering of a child the priest would remain with his back to the wall, loyal to the painful disjunction symbolized by the cross. And he would say without fear to those who were listening to him on that day: 'My brethren, the moment has come. One must believe everything or deny everything. And who among you would dare to deny everything?'

Rieux had hardly time to think that the priest was getting close to heresy before he was already speaking again, forcefully, to assert that this injunction, this pure demand, was the benefit of the Christian. It was also his virtue. The priest knew that there was something extreme about the virtue he was going to speak about which would shock many minds, used to a more traditional and indulgent morality. But religion in a time of plague could not be the religion of every day and if God could accept and even wish that the soul should rest in happier times,

He wanted it to be excessive when there was an excess of unhappiness. Today, God was doing His creatures the favour of putting them in such a misfortune that they were obliged to rediscover and take on themselves the greatest virtue, which was that of All or Nothing.

A secular writer in the last century claimed to have revealed the secret of the Church when he stated that there was no such thing as Purgatory. By that he implied that there were no half-measures, that there was either Heaven or Hell, and that one could only be saved or damned according to the choices one had made. If Paneloux was to be believed, this was a heresy of a kind that could only arise in the soul of a freethinker. Because there was a Purgatory. But it was also surely true that there were times when one should not hope too much for this Purgatory, there were times when one could not speak of venial sin. All sin was mortal and all forms of indifference criminal. It was everything or nothing.

Paneloux stopped, letting Rieux hear more clearly from beneath the doors the howls of the wind which seemed to be increasing outside. At the same moment, the priest said that the virtue of the total acceptance about which he was speaking could not be understood in the restricted sense usually given to it, that it was not a matter of plain resignation or even of much harder humility. It was a question of humiliation, but one in which the humiliated person consented. Certainly the suffering of a child was humiliating for the spirit and the body, but this is why one had to become part of it. And this is why – Paneloux assured his listeners that what he was about to say was not easy to say – you had to want it because God wanted it. Only in this way would the Christian spare nothing and, with all other outlets closed off, go to the heart of the essential choice. He would choose to believe everything so as not to be reduced to denying everything. And, like those good women who, once they had learned that bubos when they appeared were the natural means by which the body rejected infection, were in churches at this very moment saying: 'Dear God, give him bubos', so the Christian must learn to give in to the divine will, even when it was incomprehensible. One could not say: 'I understand this, but that is unacceptable.' One had to leap to the heart of this unacceptable which was offered to us precisely so that we could make our choice. The suffering of children was our bitter bread, but without this bread our souls would die of spiritual hunger.

Here, the shuffling that usually accompanied Father Paneloux's pauses was starting to be heard, when unexpectedly the preacher resumed forcefully, apparently asking on behalf of his audience what was in the end the proper way to behave. He guessed that people would mention the dreadful word 'fatalism'. Well, he would not shrink from this term, but only if he was allowed to add the adjective 'active'. Indeed, once more, they should not imitate the Christians of Abyssinia about whom he had spoken. They should not even consider following those Persian sufferers from the plague who threw their rags at the Christian sanitary pickets, appealing aloud to heaven and begging God to give the plague to these infidels who were trying to fight against the evil that He had sent. On the other hand, one should not imitate the monks of Cairo who in the epidemics of the last century would give communion picking up the host with pincers in order to avoid any contact with those moist, warm mouths in which infection might linger. The Persian sufferers and the monks were equally in the wrong. For the first, the suffering of a child did not count and for the second the very human fear of pain had become the main consideration. In both cases the problem was being avoided. Both were deaf to the voice of God. But there were other examples that Father Paneloux would like to recall. If we were to believe the chronicler of the great plague of Marseille, out of the eighty-one religious inhabitants in the Convent of Mercy, only four survived the fever; and of these four, three fled. This is what the chroniclers told us and it was not their business to say more. But when he read this, the thoughts of Father Paneloux went to the one monk who remained, alone, in spite of the seventy-seven corpses and above all in spite of the example of his three brothers. And the priest, hammering with his fist on the side of the pulpit, exclaimed: 'My brethren, you must be the one who stays!'

It was not a matter of not taking precautions, the sensible order that society introduces into the chaos of a pestilence. One should not heed those moralists who said that we should fall down on our knees and abandon everything. One should merely start to move forward, in the dark, feeling one's way and trying to do good. But for the rest, one should remain and agree to put oneself in God's hands, even concerning the death of children, without seeking any personal solution.

Here Father Paneloux recalled the towering figure of Bishop Belzunce during the plague in Marseille. He reminded his listeners that towards the end of the epidemic, after the Bishop had done everything that he thought he should do, believing that there was no further remedy, he took some supplies and shut himself up in his house which he had walled up. The inhabitants of the city, who idolized him, in a change of feeling such as one finds in excessive misfortune, became angered against him, surrounded his house with corpses to infect him and even threw bodies over the walls to ensure that he would be more certain to die. So the Bishop, in a last moment of weakness, had thought that he could isolate himself from the world of death, and the dead were falling from heaven on to his head. The same must be true of us: we must not believe that there is any island in the plague. No, there is no middle way. We must accept what is outrageous, because we have to choose to hate God or to love Him. And who would choose hatred of God?

'My brethren,' Father Paneloux said at last, announcing that he was coming to an end, 'the love of God is a difficult love. It assumes a total abandonment of oneself and contempt for one's person. But it alone can wipe away the suffering and death of children, it alone makes them necessary because it is impossible to understand such things, so we have no alternative except to desire them. This is the hard lesson that I wanted to share with you. This is the faith – cruel in the eyes of man, decisive in the eyes of God – which we must try to reach. We must try to make ourselves equal to this awful image. On this peak, everything will be confounded and made equal, and the truth will break forth from apparent injustice. This is why, in many churches in the South of France, plague victims have slept for centuries beneath the stones in the choir and priests speak above their tombs; the spirit that they proclaim rises out of these heaps of ashes even though children are among those who go to make them.'

When Rieux left the church, a sharp wind poured through the

half-open door and struck the congregation full in the face. It brought a smell of rain into the church, a scent of damp pavements which warned them of how the town would look even before they went out. Walking in front of Dr Rieux, an old priest and a young deacon who were leaving at the same time had difficulty in keeping hold of their headgear. None the less, the older man went on speaking about the sermon. He paid tribute to Paneloux's eloquence, but was worried about the audacity of the priest's ideas. He considered that this sermon betrayed more uneasiness than strength and at Paneloux's age a priest did not have the right to be uneasy. The young deacon, his head bent to protect himself against the wind, insisted that he saw a lot of Father Paneloux, that he knew about the development of his thought and that his treatise would be much more daring; it would certainly not have the official *imprimatur*.

'So what is his idea?' the old priest asked.

They had reached the space in front of the church and the wind was howling around them, making it hard for the younger man to speak. When he could do so, he said merely:

'If a priest consults a doctor, there is a contradiction.'

When Rieux told him what Paneloux had said, Tarrou remarked that he knew a priest who had lost his faith during the war when he saw the face of a young man with his eyes torn out.

'Paneloux is right,' said Tarrou. 'When innocence has its eyes gouged out, a Christian must lose his faith or accept the gouging out of eyes. Paneloux does not want to lose his faith, he will stick with it to the very end. That's what he meant.'

Does this remark of Tarrou's help a little to explain the unfortunate events that followed, in which Paneloux's behaviour seemed incomprehensible to those around him? One must judge for oneself.

Indeed, a few days after the sermon, Paneloux decided to move house. This was a time when the progress of the illness was the cause of constant removals in the town. Just as Tarrou had to leave his hotel to stay with Rieux, so the priest had to leave the apartment in which his order had placed him to take up lodgings with an old woman, a regular church-goer and so far immune to the plague. During the move itself the priest felt his anxiety and exhaustion grow. And this was how he lost the respect of his landlady. One day when she was warmly extolling the merits of the prophecies of Saint Odile, the priest made a very slight gesture of impatience, no doubt due to his tiredness. From then on, whatever effort he made to win the old lady around to at least a friendly neutrality was unsuccessful. He had made a bad impression. And every evening, before going up to his room, which was filled with yards of lacework, he had to look at her back, seated in her drawing-room, and to take away the memory of the 'good evening, father' that she addressed to him in a dry voice, without turning round. It was on such an evening, as he was going up to bed, his head aching, that he felt the tide of fever which had been brewing for several days break out at his wrists and his temples.

What followed was afterwards known only through the account of his landlady. In the morning she got up early, as usual. After a while, surprised at not seeing the priest come out of his room, she decided, after much hesitation, to knock on his door. She found him still in bed after a sleepless night. He was having difficulty breathing and seemed more flushed than usual. As she later said, she politely suggested calling a doctor, but this idea was rejected with what she found unacceptable force. She could do nothing but leave. A little later the priest rang and asked for her. He apologized for his irritation and told her that it could not be a case of plague since he had none of the symptoms; it was just a temporary fatigue. The old lady replied in a dignified manner that her suggestion did not arise from any anxiety of that sort, that she was not considering her own safety which was in the hands of God, but that she had merely been thinking of the father's health for which she felt partly responsible. But since he did not add anything, his landlady, anxious (so she said) to do her duty, again suggested calling her doctor. The priest once more refused while adding some explanation which the old lady considered very confused. The only thing she thought she had understood – which seemed incomprehensible to her – was that the father was refusing a consultation with a doctor because it was against his principles. She decided that the fever was disturbing her tenant's mind and did nothing except bring him some herb tea.

Still determined to fulfil precisely the duties that the situation imposed on her, she visited the patient regularly every two hours. What struck her most forcefully was the state of continual agitation in which the priest spent the day. He would throw off his bedclothes, then pull them back over him, constantly passing his hand across his forehead and often sitting up in an attempt to cough, with a stifled, hoarse, damp cough, as though tearing something out of himself. It was as though he could not bring up some pieces of cotton wool from the back of his throat that were choking him. After these crises he would slump back with every appearance of exhaustion. In the end, he would again sit half-upright and, for a brief moment, look directly ahead with a concentration that was more passionate than all the turmoil that had gone before. But the old lady was still uncertain whether to call a doctor and go against her patient's wishes. This might be a simple high temperature, spectacular though it may be.

However, that afternoon she tried to speak to the priest, who replied with only a few confused words. She made the suggestion once more. Then the priest sat upright and, half-suffocating, replied in a clear voice that he did not want a doctor. At this the landlady decided that she would wait until the next morning and, if the father's condition had not improved, she would telephone the number that the Infodoc agency repeated a dozen times a day on the radio. Still attentive to her duties, she thought she would visit her tenant in the night and keep watch over him. But that evening, after she had given him some fresh herb tea, she felt like lying down for a while and did not wake up until the early hours of the next day in. She ran up to the room.

The priest was stretched out, motionless. The congestion and flushing of the day before had given way to a sort of livid colour which was all the more noticeable since the features were still puffy. He was staring at the little lamp of multicoloured glass beads hanging over the bed. When the old lady came in he turned towards her. According to her account, he looked at that moment as though he had been beaten all night and had lost any strength to react. She asked him how he was. In a voice which, she said, had a strangely indifferent sound, he said that he was ill, that he did not need a doctor and that it would be enough to take him to the hospital for everything to be in order. Horrified, the old lady ran to the telephone.

Rieux arrived at noon. When the landlady told him what had happened, he said simply that Paneloux was right and that it was probably too late. The priest greeted him with the same air of indifference. Rieux examined him and was surprised not to find any of the main symptoms of bubonic or pulmonary plague, except congestion and a difficulty in breathing. In any case, the pulse was so slow and the general state of health so alarming that there was little hope.

'You have none of the main symptoms of the disease,' he told Paneloux. 'But to tell the truth, there is some doubt and I must put you in isolation.'

The priest gave an odd smile, as though out of politeness, but said nothing. Rieux left to make a telephone call and came back. He looked at the priest.

'I shall stay beside you,' he said softly.

The other man seemed to revive and turned towards the doctor with eyes to which a sort of warmth seemed to have returned. Then he pronounced the following with difficulty and in such a way that it was impossible to know if he was speaking with sadness or not:

'Thank you,' he said. 'But priests have no friends. They have given everything to God.'

He asked for the crucifix which was at the head of the bed and when he had it turned to look at it.

In the hospital Paneloux kept his teeth clenched. He gave himself up like an object to all the treatment he had to endure but did not let go of the crucifix. However, the priest's case remained ambiguous. Rieux was still not certain in his mind. It was the plague and yet it wasn't. As a matter of fact, for some time the disease had seemed to enjoy upsetting medical diagnosis. But in Paneloux's case the outcome would show that this uncertainty was without importance.

The temperature rose. The cough grew more and more hoarse and tortured the patient throughout the day. Finally, in the evening, the priest coughed up the cotton wool that had been suffocating him. It was red. In the midst of his raging fever Paneloux kept his look of indifference and when, the following day, they found him dead, half-falling out of the bed, there was nothing to be read in his expression. They wrote on his card: 'Doubtful case.'

All Soul's Day that year was different from usual. The weather was certainly appropriate. It had changed abruptly and the late heat had given way overnight to chills. As in other years, a cold wind was now blowing continuously. Large clouds sped from one end of the horizon to the other, casting shadows over the houses before the cold, golden light of November returned to them after the clouds had passed by. The first mackintoshes made their appearance, but one could also see a surprising number of shiny, rubberized materials: the newspapers had reported that two hundred years earlier, in the great plagues in the South of France, doctors used to wear oilcloth for their own protection. The shops took advantage of this to unload a supply of clothes that were no longer in fashion, and from which everyone hoped to gain immunity.

However, all these seasonal indicators could not disguise the fact that the cemeteries were deserted. In other years the trams had been full of the vapid scent of chrysanthemums and processions of women making their way to the places where their loved ones were buried, to put flowers on their graves. This had been the day when people tried to make up to the dead for leaving them alone and forgetting them for many long months. But that year no one wanted to think about the dead, for the very reason that they had already been thinking too much about them. It was no longer a matter of going back to see them, with a little remorse and lots of melancholy. They were no longer the forgotten ones whom one visited in self-justification one day a year. They were the intruders about whom one would rather forget. This is why the Feast of the Dead that year was somewhat brushed aside. Tarrou noticed that Cottard's language was becoming more and more ironic: according to him, every day was a Feast of the Dead.

Indeed, the bonfires of the plague burned ever more cheerfully in the crematorium. Admittedly the number of dead from one day to the next was not rising. But it seemed that the plague had settled comfortably into its peak and was carrying out its daily murders with the precision and regularity of a good civil servant. In theory, in the opinion of experts, this was a good sign. The graph of the progress of the plague, starting with its constant rise, followed by this long plateau, seemed quite reassuring – to Dr Richard, for example. 'Good, good, an excellent graph,' he said. He reckoned that the disease had reached what he called a ceiling. From here on, it could only decrease. He ascribed this to Castel's new serum which had, indeed, achieved some unexpected successes. Old Castel did not contradict him, but felt that one could not predict anything for certain, since the history of epidemics showed that they could flare up again unexpectedly. The Prefecture had for a long time wanted to appease public anxieties – something that the plague had not allowed it to do – and was deciding to get the medical experts together for a report on the topic, when Dr Richard too was carried off by the plague, just as the epidemic reached a plateau.

Though this case after all proved nothing, it was impressive and the authorities, confronted by it, slipped back into pessimism with as little justification as they had at first welcomed Richard's optimism. Castel for his part was content to prepare his serum as conscientiously as he could. There was only one public place that was not transformed into a hospital or an isolation facility, and if the Prefecture was still given immunity, it was because they had to keep one place where people could meet. But on the whole, because of the relative stability of the epidemic at this time, the organization that Rieux provided proved sufficient. The doctors and their assistants, who were undertaking exhausting tasks, did not have to contemplate still greater efforts. They merely had to continue this superhuman work in a regular manner, one may say. The pulmonary forms of the infection that had already appeared now multiplied in every part of the town, as though the wind were lighting and fanning flames in people's chests. The sufferers died much more quickly, vomiting blood. The degree of contagion threatened to be greater with this new form of the epidemic – though the opinions of specialists had always been contradictory on this point. Meanwhile, for maximum safety, health workers continued to breathe through masks of disinfected gauze. In any case, one would have expected the disease to spread, but since the number of cases of bubonic plague was falling, the figures stayed level.

However, there might be other reasons for anxiety because of increasing difficulties in getting food supplies. Speculators were involved and vital necessities, unobtainable on the ordinary market, were being offered at huge prices. Poor families consequently found themselves in a very difficult situation, while the rich lacked for practically nothing. Because of the efficient impartiality which it brought to its administrations, the plague should have worked for greater equality among our fellow-citizens through the normal interplay of egoism, but in fact it heightened the feeling of injustice in the hearts of men. Of course, no one could fault the equality of death, but it was not one that anybody wanted. The poor who suffered in this way from hunger thought with greater nostalgia than ever of neighbouring towns and villages where life was free and bread was cheap. Since they could not be properly nourished, they had the rather unreasonable feeling that they should have been allowed to leave. So much so that someone eventually devised a slogan that you could read sometimes on the walls or which at other times was shouted at the Prefect when he went past: 'Bread or air!' This ironic phrase was the signal for demonstrations that were rapidly suppressed, though no one doubted their seriousness.

Naturally, the newspapers followed the order that they had been given, to be optimistic at any cost. Reading them you would think that the main characteristic of the situation was 'the moving example of calm and courage' shown by the people. But in a town shut in on itself, where nothing could remain secret, no one had any illusions about the 'example' given by the population. And, to get a correct notion of the calm and courage in question, one had only to go into a place of quarantine or one of the isolation camps that the authorities had set up. As it happens, the narrator was busy elsewhere and did not have this experience, so he can only quote the evidence provided by Tarrou.

In his notebooks, Tarrou describes a visit that he made with Rambert to the camp situated in the municipal stadium. This stadium stands almost at the gates of the town, having on one side a street down which trams pass and on the other some waste ground which extends as far as the edge of the plateau on which the town is built. Normally it is surrounded by high concrete walls and it was enough to put sentries at the four entrances to make escape difficult. In the same way, the walls prevented curious people outside from causing a nuisance to those unfortunates who were placed in quarantine. On the other hand, the latter could hear the trams passing all day long and guess from the noises that they brought with them when it was time for people to go to or leave work. In this way, they were informed that the life from which they were excluded continued a few metres away from them and that the concrete walls separated two worlds as foreign to one another as if they had been on different planets.

The day that Tarrou and Rambert chose to go to the stadium was a Sunday afternoon. They were accompanied by Gonzales, the football player, whom Rambert had discovered and who eventually agreed to manage supervision of the stadium on a rota system. Rambert was to present him to the camp administrator. When they met, Gonzales had told the two men that this was the time when he used to get dressed to start his match, in the days before the plague. Now that the sports grounds had been requisitioned, it was no longer possible and Gonzales felt (and looked) entirely at a loose end. This was one of the reasons why he had accepted this job as a supervisor, as long as he only had to work at weekends. The sky was half-covered in clouds and Gonzales, sniffing the air, regretfully observed that this weather, neither rainy nor hot, was just right for a good match. He recalled as best he could the smell of embrocation in the dressing-rooms, the rickety stands, the brightly coloured jerseys on the tawny pitch and the half-time lemons or lemonade that would tickle dry throats with a thousand refreshing bubbles. Tarrou notes moreover that throughout the whole journey through the run-down streets of the working-class quarters, the player was continually kicking any pebbles that lay in his path. He tried to send them straight into drainage holes and when he succeeded, he would say 'one-nil'. When he had finished his cigarette he spat out the butt in front of him and tried to drop-kick it. Some children who were playing near the stadium kicked a ball towards the passing group and Gonzales took the trouble to send it neatly back to them.

Finally they entered the stadium. The stands were full of people, and the field was covered with several hundred red tents inside which one could see, from a distance, bedding and bundles. The stands had been retained so that the internees could take shelter if it was hot or raining. They were just obliged to go back to their tents at sunset. Under the stands were the shower-rooms which had been refurbished and the players' old dressing-rooms which had been transformed into offices and infirmaries. Most of the internees were in the stands, while some others were wandering along the touchlines. A few were crouching at the entrance to their tents and looking vaguely around them. In the stands many were slumped down, apparently waiting for something.

'What do they do all day?' Tarrou asked Rambert.

'Nothing.'

Almost all of them were empty-handed, with their arms hanging by their sides. This vast assemblage of men was curiously silent.

'In the early days, you couldn't hear yourself speak here,' said Rambert. 'But as time goes by, they talk less and less.'

If one is to believe his notes, Tarrou understood them and imagined them in the beginning piled into their tents, kicking their heels or scratching their bellies, shouting out their anger and their fear whenever they found a willing ear. But as soon as the camp became over-populated, there were fewer and fewer willing ears. There was nothing left for it but to be quiet and watchful. Indeed, there was a sort of wariness that fell out of the grey but luminous sky onto the red camp.

Yes, they all looked suspicious. Since they had been separated from the rest, this was not unreasonable, and they had the faces of those who are looking for reasons and who are afraid. Each of those Tarrou looked at had a vacant eye and all appeared to be suffering from a general separation from everything that made up their lives. Since they could not always be thinking about death, they thought about nothing. They were taking a holiday. 'But the worst thing', Tarrou wrote, 'is that these are forgotten people and they know it. Their acquaintances have forgotten them because they are thinking about other things, and that is quite understandable. As for those who love them, they have also forgotten them because they must be exhausting themselves in appeals and schemes to get them out. The more they think about getting them out, the less they think about the person to be got out. That, too, is normal. And when it comes down to it, you realize that no one is really capable of thinking of anyone else, even in the worst misfortune. Because thinking about someone really means thinking about that person minute by minute, not being distracted by anything – not housework, not a fly passing, not meals, not an urge to scratch oneself. But there are always flies and itches. This is why life is hard to live. And these people know that very well.'

The administrator, coming back towards them, told them that M. Othon was asking to see them. He led Gonzales into his office and then took them towards a corner of the stands where Othon, who was sitting apart from the rest, got up to greet them. He was still dressed in the same way and wore the same stiff collar. Tarrou only noticed that the tufts of hair at his temples were far more bristly and that one of his shoelaces was undone. The magistrate seemed tired and not once did he look his visitors directly in the face. He said he was pleased to see them and that he begged them to thank Dr Rieux for what he had done.

The others said nothing.

'I hope', the magistrate said after a while, 'that Philippe did not suffer too much.'

This was the first time that Tarrou had heard him call his son by his name and understood that something had changed. The sun was sinking behind the horizon, and between two clouds its rays shone sideways into the stands, lighting their three faces with gold.

'No,' Tarrou said. 'No, he really didn't suffer.'

When they left the magistrate went on staring in the direction of the sun.

They went to say goodbye to Gonzales, who was studying a supervision rota. The football player laughed as he shook hands with them.

'At least, I've seen the dressing-rooms again,' he said. 'That's something, anyway.'

Shortly afterwards the administrator was showing Tarrou and Rambert out when a very loud crackling sound was heard from the stands.

Then the loudspeakers, which in better times had served to introduce the teams or to declare the results of games, announced in a tinny voice that the internees should go back to their tents so that the evening meal could be distributed. Slowly the men left the stands and went back to their tents, dragging their feet. When all of them were back, two small electric cars, of the kind that you see in railway stations, travelled between the tents carrying huge pots. The men held out their hands, two ladles were plunged into two of the pots and emerged to unload their contents onto two tin plates. The car drove on and the process was repeated at the next tent.

'It's scientific,' Tarrou told the administrator.

'Yes,' he replied with satisfaction, as they shook hands. 'It's scientific.'

Dusk was falling and the sky had cleared. The camp was bathed in soft, clear light. In the quiet of the evening, sounds of spoons and plates could be heard on all sides. Bats flitted around above the tents and suddenly vanished. A tram screeched on its points on the other side of the wall.

'Poor judge,' Tarrou muttered as they went through the gates. 'Something should be done for him. But how can one help a judge?'

There were several other camps of the same kind in the town about which the narrator cannot in all honesty say more, not having any direct information about them. What he can say is that the existence of these camps, the smell of human beings that arose from them, the booming voices of the loudspeakers in the dusk, the mystery of the walls and the fear of these proscribed places weighed heavily on the morale of our fellow-citizens, adding still further to the confusion and uneasiness of us all. Incidents and conflicts with the administration grew more frequent.

However, at the end of November, the mornings became very cold. Torrential rains swept down the streets, washing the sky and leaving it empty of clouds above the shining streets. Every morning a weak sun spread a sparkling, icy light across the town. Towards evening, however, the air once again became warm. This was the moment that Tarrou chose to reveal something of himself to Dr Rieux.

One day, around ten o'clock, after a long and exhausting day, Tarrou accompanied Rieux who was going to make his evening visit to the old asthmatic. The sky was glowing gently above the houses of the old quarter. A light wind blew soundlessly past the dark crossroads. Coming out of the quiet streets the two men found themselves subjected to the old man's chattering. He told them that there were some who didn't agree, that the gravy train was always for the same people, that when the jug goes too often to the well, it eventually breaks, and that probably, whenever he rubbed his hands, trouble would follow. This commentary on events did not stop at all while the doctor examined him.

They heard footsteps overhead. The old woman, noticing that Tarrou seemed interested, explained that one of the neighbours was on the terrace. They also learned that there was a fine view from up there and that since the roof terraces of houses often joined on one side, it was possible for the women of the area to visit one another without leaving home.

'Yes,' the old man said. 'Come on up. The air is good up there.'

They found the terrace empty, with three chairs on it. On one side, as far as the eye could see, all they could make out were roof terraces, which eventually came to rest against a dark rocky mass in which they recognized the first hill. On the other side, above a few streets and the port (which was invisible), the eye was lost in a horizon where sky and sea mingled in a vague throbbing. Beyond what they knew to be the cliffs, a light reappeared regularly, though they could not see where it was coming from: since the previous spring, the lighthouse on the channel had continued to shine for ships headed for other ports. In the sky, swept clean and shining by the wind, the pure stars shone and, from time to time, the distant light of the lighthouse added its brief ember. The breeze brought scents of spices and stone. The silence was absolute.

'It feels good,' said Rieux, sitting down. 'It's as though the plague had never come up here.'

Tarrou turned his back on the doctor and looked at the sea.

'Yes,' he said, after a short pause. 'It feels good.'

He came over and sat down beside Rieux, looking closely at him. Three times the light reappeared in the sky. A sound of crockery came up to them from the depths of the street. A door slammed in the house.

'Rieux,' Tarrou said in a very natural voice. 'Have you never tried to find out who I am? Do you see me as a friend?'

'Yes,' said the doctor. 'We are friends, but until now we have had too little time.'

'Good, that's a relief. Would you like us to make this hour the hour of friendship?'

In reply, Rieux merely smiled at him.

'Well, it's like this . . .'

A few streets further off, a car seemed to skid for a long time on the wet road. It drove away while behind it confused exclamations coming from afar continued to break the silence. Then this silence fell back on the two men with all its weight of sky and stars. Tarrou had got up to prop himself against the parapet, facing Rieux, who was still sunk in the bottom of his chair. All that could be seen of him was a massive form silhouetted against the sky. Tarrou spoke for a long time; here is more or less what he said:

'To simplify things, Rieux, let's say that I was already suffering from the plague long before I knew this town and this epidemic. All that means is that I am like everybody else. But there are people who do not know this or who are happy in this state, and people who know it and would like to escape. I have always wanted to escape.

'When I was young, I lived with the idea of my own innocence, that is to say with no idea at all. I'm not the worrying type, I started off properly. Everything went well for me, I was at ease in my own mind, very successful with women, and if I did have any anxieties, they vanished as they had come. One day, I started to reflect. And now . . .

'I have to tell you that I was not poor like you were. My father was a prosecuting counsel, which is an important job. However, he did not look like a prosecutor, being a good-natured sort. My mother was ordinary and self-effacing. I have never ceased to love her, but I prefer not to speak about her. My father looked after me affectionately and I believe he even tried to understand me. I am sure now that he used to have affairs, but it really doesn't upset me. In all such things he behaved as he might have been expected to behave, without shocking anybody. In brief, there was nothing especially unusual about him and, now that he is dead, I realize that while he did not live like a saint, he was not a bad man. He steered a middle course, that's all, and was the type of person for whom one feels a reasonable degree of affection, which endures.

'Yet he did have one peculiarity: his bedside book was the large *Chaix* railway timetable. Not that he travelled, except on holiday, to go to Brittany where he had a small house. But he could tell you precisely the arrival and departure times of the Paris–Berlin express, the connecting trains that you had to catch to get from Lyon to Warsaw and the precise number of railway miles between any two capital cities you chose to mention. Can you tell me how to go from Briançon to Chamonix? Even a station-master would find it confusing. My father didn't. He would practise almost every evening to improve his knowledge of the subject and was quite proud of it. It greatly amused me and I often put questions to him, delighted to check his answers in the *Chaix* and acknowledge that he had not made a mistake. These little exercises helped to bring us closer, because I provided him with an audience whose goodwill he appreciated. As for me, I considered that this superior knowledge in the matter of railways was as good as any other.

'But I am allowing myself to be carried away, and may give too much importance to this good gentleman, because when it came down to it, he had only an indirect influence in helping me to make up my mind. At the very most, he provided me with an opportunity. When I was seventeen my father invited me to go and listen to him at work. It was an important case, in the circuit court, and he must have believed that he would appear in the best light. I think he was also counting on this ceremonial – just the sort of thing that might impress a young mind – to nudge me in the direction of the career that he himself had chosen. I accepted, to please my father and because I was curious to see and hear him in a different role from the one that he played at home. I was not thinking of anything more than that. What happened in a courtroom had always struck me as no less natural and inevitable than a Fourteenth of July parade or a prize-giving. I had a very abstract idea of it, which did not disturb me at all.

'However, I have kept only one image of that day, which is that of the guilty man. I really do believe he was guilty, though it doesn't matter of what. But this little man with his meagre red hair, some thirty years of age, seemed so determined to admit to everything, so sincerely terrified by what he had done and what they were going to do to him, that after a few minutes I had eyes only for him. He looked like an owl stricken with fear by an over-bright light. The knot of his tie was not precisely in the centre of his collar. He was chewing the nails of just one hand, the right . . . Well, I need say no more – you understand, he was alive.

'But I suddenly became aware of him, though up to then I had only thought of him in the convenient category of "the accused". I cannot say that I forgot about my father, but there was something in the pit of my stomach which distracted me from concentrating on anything except the man in the dock. I heard practically nothing. I felt that they wanted to kill this living man and an instinct as powerful as a tidal wave swept me to his side with a sort of blind obstinacy. I only properly woke up when my father began his speech for the prosecution.

'Transformed by his red robe, he was neither good-natured nor affectionate and his mouth was crammed with sonorous phrases which leapt from it constantly like serpents. I realized then that he was asking for the death of this man in the name of society and that he was even demanding that his head should be cut off. In truth, all he said was: "This head must fall." But the difference was not great in the end. In fact it came to the same thing, since he got the man's head. The only thing was that he did not do the job himself. I, who subsequently followed the matter right through to its conclusion, felt a far more terrifying intimacy with that unfortunate man than my father ever could. And yet he had to be present, according to custom, at what are euphemistically called the last moments, and which one should by rights call the most shameful of murders.

'From that day onwards I could not look at the *Chaix* timetable without the most dreadful disgust. From then onwards I took a horrified interest in justice, in death sentences and in executions. I realized with a shock that my father must have been present at these murders on several occasions and that those were the same days when he got up very early. Yes, on such occasions he set his alarm. I did not dare speak about it to my mother, but I looked more closely at her and realized that there was no longer anything between them and that she led a life of renunciation. This helped me to forgive her, as I said to myself at the time. Later, I understood that there was nothing to forgive, because she had been poor all her life until her marriage and poverty had taught her resignation.

'No doubt you are expecting me to tell you that I left home at once. No, I stayed for several months, almost a year. But I was sick at heart. One evening my father asked for his alarm clock because he had to get up early. That night I didn't sleep, and the following day, when he came home, I'd left. I must say at once that he looked for me and that I went to see him; without any explanation, I told him calmly that I'd kill myself if he forced me to come back. Eventually he accepted, because he was quite mild by nature; he gave me a speech about how silly it was to want to live one's own life (this is how he explained my actions and I did not try to persuade him otherwise), and lots of good advice, while holding back the genuine tears that came to his eyes. Subsequently, though quite a long time afterwards, I would go regularly to see my mother and then I would meet him. I think this relationship was all he needed. As for me, I had no animosity against him, just a little sadness in my heart. When he died I took my mother to live with me and she would be there still if she had not died in her turn.

'I have spent a long time on this beginning to my story, because it was in fact the start of everything. I shall go faster from now on. I suffered poverty at eighteen, having been comfortably off. I did dozens of jobs to earn a living, and made a reasonable go of it. But what interested me was the death penalty. I had an account to square with the red-headed owl. Consequently, I went into politics, as they say. I did not want to be a victim of the plague, that's all. I thought the society in which I lived rested on the death penalty and that, if I fought against it,

I should be fighting against murder. This is what I believed; other people have told me the same thing and, when it comes down to it, it was largely true. So I joined with other people I liked – and still like. I stayed with them for a long time and there is no country in Europe whose struggle I have not shared. But, to continue . . .

'Of course, I knew that we too occasionally condemn to death. But I was told that these few deaths were necessary to bring about a world in which no one would kill anyone anymore. This was to some extent true and, after all, I may not be able to live with such truths. What is sure is that I wavered; but I thought of the owl and I was able to go on. That is, until the day when I saw an execution – it was in Hungary – and felt the same horror sweep over me now I was a man as I had previously felt as a child.

'You've never seen a man shot? No, of course, it's by invitation only and the audience is handpicked in advance. Consequently, you know from pictures and books – a blindfold, a stake and, in the distance, a few soldiers. Well, no! Do you realize that, on the contrary, the firing squad stands at one and a half metres from the condemned man? Do you know that if the condemned man took two steps forward, the rifles would hit him in the chest? Do you know that at this short distance the members of the firing squad concentrate their fire on the region of the heart and that all of them with their large-calibre bullets make a hole big enough to put your fist in? No, you don't know, because these are details that people don't speak about. The sleep of men is more sacred than life for plague sufferers. One must not keep these good people awake at nights. That would be in bad taste and good taste is a matter of not harping on about it, as everyone knows. But I have not slept well since that time. The bad taste stayed in my mouth and I haven't stopped harping on about it, that is to say, thinking.

'This is when I at last realized that I had continued to be a plague victim for all those long years in which, with my heart and soul, I thought I was struggling against the plague. I learned that I had indirectly supported the deaths of thousands of men, that I had even caused their deaths by approving the actions and principles that inevitably led to them. Other people did not seem to be bothered by this, or at least they did not speak about it spontaneously. But it stuck in my throat. I was with them, yet I was alone. When I did happen to express my misgivings, they told me that I had to consider what was at stake and often gave me impressive reasons for swallowing something that I could not swallow. But I replied that the big plague sufferers, those who wear the red robes, also have excellent reasons in such cases, and that if I accepted the arguments of *force majeure* and other necessities put forward by the little plague sufferers, then I could not reject those of the big ones. They pointed out to me that the best way to prove the red robes right was to leave them a monopoly on condemnation. But I decided that if one gave way once, there was no reason to stop. It seems that history has shown that I was right; nowadays it's a free-for-all in killing. They are all carried away by a fury of killing and cannot do otherwise.

'In any case, my business was not argument. My business was the red-headed owl, that dirty occasion in which dirty, plague-ridden mouths told a man in chains that he was to die and arranged everything so that he would, indeed, die, after many long nights of agony in which he waited to be killed with his eyes open. My business was the hole in the chest. And I decided that meanwhile, at least as far as I was concerned, I would refuse ever to concede a single argument, a single one, to this disgusting butchery. Yes, I chose that obstinate blindness until I could see more clearly in the matter.

'Since then I have not changed. For a long time I have been ashamed, mortally ashamed, of having been — even at a distance, even with the best will in the world — a murderer in my turn. With time I have simply noticed that even those who are better than the rest cannot avoid killing or letting others be killed because it is in the logic of how they live and we cannot make a gesture in this world without taking the risk of bringing death. Yes, I have continued to feel ashamed, and I learned that we are all in the plague, and I have lost my peace of mind. I am still looking for it today, trying to understand all of them and not to be the mortal enemy of anybody. All I know is that one must do one's best not to be a plague victim and this is the only thing that can give us hope of peace or, failing that, a good death. This is what may give relief to men and, even if it does not save them, does them the least possible harm and even sometimes a little good. And this is why I have decided to reject everything that, directly or indirectly, makes people die or justifies others in making them die.

'That is why this epidemic has so far taught me nothing except that it must be fought at your side. I have absolute knowledge of this – yes Rieux, I know everything about life, as you can see – that everyone has inside it himself, this plague, because no one in the world, no one, is immune. And I know that we must constantly keep a watch on ourselves to avoid being distracted for a moment and find ourselves breathing in another person's face and infecting him. What is natural is the microbe. The rest – health, integrity, purity, if you like – are an effect of will and a will that must never relax. The decent man, the one who doesn't infect anybody, is the one who concentrates most. And you need will-power and nervous tension not to let your mind wander! Yes indeed, Rieux, it is very tiring to be a plague victim. But it is still more tiring not to want to be one. This is why everyone appears tired, because nowadays everyone is a little infected. But this is why a few, who want to cease to be victims, experience an extreme form of tiredness from which nothing except death will deliver them.

'From now until then, I know that I am worth nothing for this world itself and that, the moment I rejected killing, I condemned myself to a definitive exile. Other men will make history. I know too that I clearly cannot judge those others. There is a quality which is lacking in me to make a reasonable murderer. So it is not a matter of superiority. But now I accept being what I am, I have learned modesty. All I say is that on this earth there are pestilences and there are victims – and as far as possible one must refuse to be on the side of the pestilence. This may seem rather simple to you, and I don't know if it is simple, but I do know that it is true. I have heard so many arguments which nearly turned my head, and which turned enough other heads for them to consent to murder, that I understood that all the misfortunes of mankind came from not stating things in clear terms. So I decided then to speak and act clearly, to put myself on the right path. Consequently, I say that there are pestilences and victims, and nothing more. If in saying this I become a pestilence myself, at least I am not a consenting one. I am trying to be an innocent murderer. You see, it's not a high ambition.

'Of course, there should be a third category, that of true healers, but it's a fact that one does not meet many of those, because it must be hard to achieve. This is why I decided to place myself on the side of the victims, on every occasion, to limit the damage. Among them, I can at least seek how one arrives at the third category, that is to say at peace.'

When he had finished Tarrou swung his leg and gently tapped his foot against the parapet. After a pause the doctor sat up a little and asked if Tarrou had any idea of the road that one should follow to arrive at peace.

'Yes, sympathy.'

Two ambulance sirens rang out in the distance. The cries which had been confused earlier gathered on the outskirts of the town, near the rocky hill. At the same time they heard something like an explosion. Then silence returned. Rieux counted two flashes of the lighthouse. The wind seemed to gather strength and at the same time a breeze coming from the sea brought the smell of salt. Now they could distinctly hear the muffled breathing of the waves against the cliff.

'In short,' Tarrou said simply, 'what interests me is to know how one becomes a saint.'

'But you don't believe in God.'

'Precisely. Can one be a saint without God: that is the only concrete question that I know today.'

Suddenly a great flash of light came from the direction of the cries and a vague noise of shouting reached the two men along the stream of wind. The light faded at once and in the distance on the edge of the roofs there was only a reddish glow. The wind died down for a moment and one could distinctly hear men's shouts, then the noise of a shot and the roar of a crowd. Tarrou got up and listened. Nothing more was to be heard.

'They're fighting at the gates again.'

'It's over now,' said Rieux.

Tarrou muttered that it was never over and that there would be more victims, since this was the normal course of things.

'Perhaps,' the doctor said. 'But you know, I feel more solidarity with the defeated than with saints. I don't think I have any taste for heroism and sainthood. What interests me is to be a man.'

'Yes, we are looking for the same thing, but I am less ambitious.'

Rieux thought Tarrou was joking and looked at him. But in the dim light of the sky, he saw a face that was sad and serious. The wind rose again and Rieux felt that it was warm on his skin. Tarrou shook himself.

'Do you know,' he said, 'what we should do for friendship's sake?'

'Whatever you like,' said Rieux.

'Go bathing in the sea. Even for a future saint, it's a worthy pleasure.'

Rieux smiled.

'With our passes we can go to the jetty. After all, it's silly to live only in the plague. Of course a man should fight for the victims. But if he ceases to love anything else, then what is the point in fighting?'

'Yes,' said Rieux. 'Let's go.'

A moment later the car stopped near the barred gate. The moon had risen and a milky sky was casting pale shadows everywhere. The town rose up in stages behind them and a warm, sick breath was coming from it which drove them towards the sea. They showed their papers to a guard who examined them for quite a long time. At last they passed through, across concrete flooring covered in barrels and giving off a scent of wine and fish, then turned towards the jetty. Shortly before they arrived, the smell of iodine and seaweed told them that the sea was there. Only then did they hear it.

It was hissing softly at the foot of the great blocks of the jetty and as they climbed up these it appeared, thick as velvet, supple and smooth as a wild animal. They sat down on some rocks facing out to sea. The water was gently swelling and sinking back. This calm breath of the sea made oily reflections appear and disappear on the surface of the water. In front of them, the darkness was limitless. Rieux, who could feel the pitted face of the rock under his fingers, was filled with a strange happiness. Turning towards Tarrou he sensed the same happiness, which forgot nothing, not even murder, on the calm and thoughtful face of his friend.

They got undressed. Rieux was the first to dive in. The water, cold to begin with, seemed warm to him when he resurfaced. After a few strokes he realized that the sea was warm that evening with the warmth of autumn seas when they take back from the earth the heat that has been stored in it for long summer months. He swam steadily. Behind him the beating of his feet left a seething foam and the water ran the length of his arms to stick on his legs. A heavy splash told him that Tarrou had dived in. Rieux turned onto his back and stayed motionless, looking up at the bowl of the sky, full of moon and stars. He took deep breaths. Then the sound of something striking the water became more and more distinct, strangely clear in the silence and loneliness of the night. Tarrou was swimming towards him and Rieux could soon hear his breathing. He turned round, came alongside his friend and swam with the same rhythm. Tarrou was moving forward more powerfully than he was and he had to speed up. For a few minutes they swam on with equal stokes and equal strength, alone, far from the world, finally free of the town and the plague. Rieux was the first to stop swimming and they returned slowly, except at one moment when they came into an icy current. Without saying a word, they both speeded up, driven on by this surprise in the sea.

Once they had dressed again they left without saying a word. But their hearts were one, and the memory of that night was sweet for both of them. When from a distance they saw the sentry of the plague, Rieux knew that Tarrou was thinking, as was he, that the sickness had just forgotten them, that this was good, but that now they had to start again.

Yes, they had to start again: the plague forgot no one for too long. During December, it flared up in the chests of the townspeople, it lit the oven, it filled the camps of empty-handed shades, in short it continued to advance with its patient, jerky steps. The authorities had counted on the cold weather to halt its advance, but it came through the first rigours of the season without a pause. We had to wait. But the longer you wait, the longer you are able to wait, and our whole town lived without a future.

As for the doctor, the brief instant of peace and friendship that had been granted him was not repeated. They had opened a new hospital and Rieux had no further private talks except with his patients. He did note, however, that at this stage in the epidemic, when the plague was increasingly adopting the pulmonary form, the patients seemed in a way to help the doctor. Instead of giving way to the prostration and madness of the early days, they seemed to have a better idea of their own interests, and demanded of their own accord what would be most beneficial to them. They continually asked for water and all wanted heat. Although the doctor felt the same tiredness, he did feel less alone in these circumstances.

Towards the end of December Rieux received a letter from M. Othon, the examining magistrate, who was still in his camp. The letter said that his period of quarantine was over, that the camp authorities could not find the date of his first internment and that, surely, he was being kept in the camp by mistake. His wife, who had been out for some time, protested to the Prefecture, but she was given short shrift there and told that mistakes were never made. Rieux got Rambert to intervene and a few days later saw M. Othon arriving. There had indeed been a mistake and Rieux was slightly indignant about it. But M. Othon, who had grown thinner, raised a limp hand and said very deliberately that anyone could make a mistake. The doctor felt that something had changed.

'What are you going to do, Judge? Your files await you,' said Rieux.

'Well, no,' said the magistrate. 'I'd like to take a holiday.'

'Yes, certainly, you need a rest.'

'That's not it, I want to go back to the camp.'

Rieux was astonished: 'But you've just come out!'

'I haven't explained myself properly. I was told that there were volunteers from the administration in the camp.' The magistrate rolled his eyes a little and tried to flatten a tuft of hair. 'You see, it would give me something to do. And then, though it may sound stupid, I would feel less separated from my little boy.'

Rieux looked at him. It wasn't possible that some tender feeling had entered those hard, flat eyes. But they had become more misty and lost their metallic purity.

'Of course,' he said. 'I'll see to it, if that's really what you want.'

The doctor did, indeed, take care of it and the life of the plague-ridden town resumed its course until Christmas. Tarrou continued to display his efficient calm everywhere. Rambert confided in the doctor that he had managed, through the two young guards, to set up a system of clandestine correspondence with his wife. He received a letter occasion- ally. He invited Rieux to take advantage of the system and the doctor agreed. He wrote for the first time for many long months, but found it extremely difficult. There was a language that he had forgotten. The letter left. It was a long time before the reply came. For his part, Cottard prospered and his little speculations were making him rich. As for Grand, the holiday period was not to be a successful one for him.

Christmas that year was more the Feast of Hell than of the coming of Christ. Empty, unlit shops, with fake chocolates or empty boxes in the windows, and passing trams loaded with dark figures: nothing to recall Christmas in the past. At this time, when once everybody rich and poor had joined together, there was no place now except for the solitary, shameful celebrations in some dingy back-room that the privileged few bought for themselves at huge expense. The churches were filled with wailing and sobbing rather than thanksgiving. In this sombre, icy town a few children ran about, still ignorant of what awaited them. But no one dared tell them about the God of former times, laden with offerings, as old as human suffering, yet as new as the freshest hope. There was no longer a place in one's heart except for a single very old and very sad hope, the same one that prevents men from giving way to death and which is no more than a simple, obstinate determination to live.

On the previous day Grand had not come for his usual appointment. Rieux was worried and went round to his house in the middle of the morning. He was not there. Everyone was informed. At about eleven o'clock Rambert came to the hospital to tell the doctor that he had seen Grand wandering around the streets with a strange look on his face. Then he vanished from sight. The doctor and Tarrou set off by car to look for him.

At noon, in icy weather, Rieux got out of the car and saw Grand in the distance, almost glued to a shop window full of crudely sculpted wooden toys. Tears were running in a steady stream down the old civil servant's face. And these tears were devastating for Rieux because he understood them and he also felt a lump at the back of his throat. He too recalled the unfortunate man's engagement, in front of a shop, at Christmastime, and Jeanne leaning towards him to say how happy she was. From the depths of years long past, in the very heart of this madness, Jeanne's fresh voice was speaking to Grand, that was sure. Rieux knew what the old man was thinking at that moment as he wept, and he thought the same: that this world without love was like a dead world and that there always comes a time when one grows tired of prisons, work and courage, and yearns for the face of another human being and the wondering, affectionate heart.

But the other man had seen him in the window. His tears did not stop but he turned round and stood with his back to the shop as he watched the doctor approach.

'Oh, doctor, doctor!' he exclaimed.

Rieux nodded in acknowledgement, unable to speak. The man's pain was his own and what was clutching at his heart at that moment was the great rage that comes to men when confronted with the pain that all men must share.

'Yes, Grand,' he said.

'I should like to have time to write her a letter. So that she knows . . . and so that she can be happy without feeling any remorse . . .'

Rieux pushed Grand forward almost violently. The other man did not resist, allowing himself to be dragged along, stammering out a few words.

'This has gone on too long. Inevitably, one wants to let oneself go. Oh, doctor! I seem calm most of the time. But it has always been an enormous effort even to be normal. And now it's too much.'

He stopped, wild-eyed and trembling in every limb. Rieux took his hand. It was burning.

'We must go back.'

But Grand escaped from him and ran a few steps, then stopped, held his arms wide and began to sway backwards and forwards. He reeled over and fell on to the icy pavement, his face streaked with the tears that continued to run down his cheeks. People passing in the street looked on from a distance, stopping suddenly and not daring to come forward. Rieux had to take the old man in his arms.

Once in his own bed, Grand struggled for breath. The lungs were affected. Rieux thought about it. The civil servant had no family. Why move him? He would be alone, with Tarrou to look after him . . .

Grand was pressed into his pillow, his skin greenish and his eyes dull. He was staring at a paltry fire that Tarrou had lit in the grate with the remains of a packing case. 'I'm not well,' he said. And an odd crackling sound emerged from the depths of his burning lungs accompanying everything he said. Rieux advised him to keep quiet and told him he would come back. The sick man gave a strange smile and, with it, a look almost of tenderness rose to his face. 'If I get through this, hats off to you, doctor!' Immediately after saying this he fell back in a state of prostration.

A few hours later Rieux and Tarrou found him half-seated in his bed, and Rieux was horrified to see on his face the progress of the disease that was eating him up. But he seemed more lucid and at once, in a strangely hollow voice, asked them to bring him the manuscript from one of his drawers. Tarrou gave him the pages which he grasped without looking at them, then handed them to the doctor, gesturing to him to read them. It was a short manuscript of some fifty pages. The doctor leafed through it and realized that all these pages contained only the same sentence, copied out over and over, reworked to make it richer or poorer. Ceaselessly, the month of May, the elegant horsewoman and the avenues of the Bois de Boulogne were made and remade in different ways. The work also contained explanations, sometimes excessively long, and different versions. But at the end of the last page, in ink that was still fresh, a studious hand had written simply: 'My dearest Jeanne, today is Christmas . . .' Above it, meticulously inscribed, was the latest version of the sentence. 'Read it,' said Grand. And Rieux read:

'On a fine morning in the month of May, an elegant woman was riding a magnificent sorrel mare, amid the flowers, down the avenues of the Bois de Boulogne.'

'Is that it?' the old man said feverishly.

Rieux did not look up.

'Oh!' the other man said, moving agitatedly. 'I know. Beautiful, beautiful is not the right word.'

Rieux took his hand on the blanket.

'Leave it doctor. I don't have time.'

His chest was moving painfully and he suddenly cried out:

'Burn it!'

The doctor hesitated, but Grand repeated the order in such a fearful tone and with such suffering in his voice, that Rieux threw the sheets onto the almost extinguished fire. The room was briefly lit up and warmed by a short burst of heat. When the doctor came back to the patient, Grand had his back turned and his face almost touching the wall. Tarrou was looking out of the window, as though a stranger to the scene. After injecting the serum, Rieux told his friend that Grand would not survive the night and Tarrou offered to stay. The doctor accepted.

Throughout the night Rieux was haunted by the idea that Grand was dying. Yet the following morning he found him sitting up in bed talking to Tarrou. His temperature was normal. He showed only the usual symptoms of complete exhaustion.

'Oh, doctor,' said the civil servant. 'I was wrong. But I'll start again. You see: I remember everything.'

'Let's wait,' Rieux said to Tarrou.

But at noon nothing had changed. By the evening Grand could be considered saved. Rieux could not understand this resurrection.

However, at about the same time, Rieux was brought a patient whose case he considered desperate and whom he had isolated as soon as she arrived in the hospital. The young woman was delirious and presented all the symptoms of pulmonary plague. But the next morning her temperature had gone down. Again, as in Grand's case, the doctor thought he was witnessing one of those morning remissions that experience had taught him to consider a bad sign. Yet by noon the temperature had not gone up. In the evening it rose by a few tenths of a degree and the next day it was back to normal. Although the girl was weak, she was breathing freely in her bed. Rieux told Tarrou that she was saved, quite unaccountably. But during that week, four similar cases appeared in the doctor's practice.

At the end of the same week, the old asthmatic came to greet the doctor and Tarrou with every sign of great agitation.

'That's it!' he said. 'They're coming out again.'

'Who's coming out?'

'Why, the rats!'

Not a single dead rat had been found since April.

'Is it going to start again?' Tarrou asked Rieux.

The old man was rubbing his hands.

'You should see them run! It's a sight for sore eyes!'

He had seen two live rats come into his house through the street door. Neighbours had informed him that the creatures were also reappearing in their houses. Behind the walls of other houses there was a hustle and bustle that had not been heard for months. Rieux waited for the general statistics to be published, as they were at the start of each week. They showed a decline in the disease.

Part V

Although this sudden decline in the disease was unexpected, the townspeople were in no hurry to celebrate. The preceding months, though they had increased the desire for liberation, had also taught them prudence and accustomed them to count less and less on a rapid end to the epidemic. However, this new development was the subject of every conversation and, in the depths of people's hearts, there was a great, unadmitted hope. All else was secondary. The new victims of the plague counted for little beside this outstanding fact: the figures were going down. One of the signs that a return to a time of good health was secretly expected (though no one admitted the fact) was that from this moment on people readily spoke, with apparent indifference, about how life would be reorganized after the plague.

Everyone agreed that the amenities of former times would not be restored overnight and that it was easier to destroy than to rebuild. They considered merely that food supplies might be somewhat improved and that in this way people would be relieved of their most immediate worry. But in reality, behind these harmless remarks, a wild hope was also raging, to such an extent that the townspeople would sometimes become aware of it and then hastened to state that in any event deliverance would not be coming in a few days.

And, in truth, the plague did not end in a few days, but it did appear to be weakening faster than one could reasonably hope. In the first days of January, the cold set in with unaccustomed persistence and seemed to crystallize above the town. Yet the sky had never been so blue. For whole days on end, its immutable and icy splendour bathed our town with uninterrupted light. In this purified air, the plague, in successive falls over three weeks, seemed to be playing itself out in the smaller and smaller lines of corpses that it produced. In a short space of time it lost almost all the strength that it had taken months to build up. When one saw it miss clearly designated prey, such as Grand or Rieux's young woman, get worse in some districts for two or three days while it vanished entirely from others, increase the number of its victims on Monday, then on Wednesday let almost all of them escape . . . seeing it in this way slip back exhausted or rush forward, one could have thought that it was falling apart with weariness and irritation and that it was losing not only its control over itself, but the sovereign, mathematical efficiency that had been its strength. Castel's serum suddenly achieved a string of successes it had not previously achieved. All the measures taken by the doctors, which had previously produced no beneficial result, seemed suddenly to be effective. It appeared that the plague in its turn had been tricked and that its sudden weakness had given strength to the previously blunt weapons used against it. From time to time, though, the disease stiffened and, in a sort of blind thrust, carried off three or four patients who were expected to recover. These were the unfortunates of the plague, those whom it killed when hope was high. This was the case of Judge Othon, who had to be evacuated from the quarantine camp, and Tarrou said of him that he had not had any luck, though one could not tell if he was thinking there of the examining magistrate's life or his death.

But, on the whole, the infection was retreating all along the line and the communiqués from the Prefecture, which at first gave rise to some timid and secret hopes, eventually confirmed the public in the conviction that victory was won and that the disease was abandoning its position. In reality, it was hard to decide whether this was a victory or not. All one could do was to observe that the sickness seemed to be going as it had arrived. The strategy being used against it had not changed; it had been ineffective yesterday, and now it was apparently successful. One merely had the feeling that the disease had exhausted itself, or perhaps that it was retiring after achieving all its objectives. In a sense, its role was completed.

None the less, one would have said that nothing had changed in the town. The streets, still silent by day, were invaded in the evenings by the same crowd, now predominantly in overcoats and scarves. The cinemas and cafés did the same amount of business. But when one looked more closely, one saw that the faces were more relaxed and occasionally smiled. And this brought home the fact that before this no one used to smile in the street. In truth, a rent had just appeared in the opaque veil that had for many months surrounded the town; and every Monday, everybody could gather from the radio news bulletins that the gap was getting wider and that they would finally be able to breathe. The consolation was still only a negative one, with no practical consequences. But whereas previously people would have learned with some incredulity that a train had left or a boat arrived, or even that cars were once more going to be allowed to drive around, the announcement of these events in mid-January would not have caused any surprise. No doubt it was not much. But this slight difference in fact reflected the vast distance that our townspeople had moved in the direction of hope. And you could say that as soon as it became possible for people to have the tiniest scrap of hope, the effective reign of the plague was over.

The fact remains, however, that throughout the month of January our fellow-citizens reacted in contradictory ways, veering from excitement to depression. So new attempts at escape were recorded, at the very moment when the statistics were most favourable. The authorities were very surprised by this – as were the sentry posts, apparently, since most of the escapes succeeded. But in point of fact those who escaped at this moment obeyed natural feelings. In some people, the plague had embedded such deep scepticism that they could not get rid of it, so there was no longer anywhere for hope to attach itself in them. Even now, when the time of the plague had passed, they continued to live according to its rules. Events had overtaken them. With others, however – and these were to be found especially among those who had until then lived apart from those they loved – after this long period of confinement and despondency, the rising wind of hope lit a fever and an impatience which deprived them of all control over themselves. A sort of panic seized them at the idea that they might perhaps die so close to the end, that they would not see the person that they adored and that there would be no reward for their long period of suffering. For months they had persisted in waiting, with self-effacing tenacity, despite prison and exile; and now the first sign of hope was enough to destroy what fear and despair had not managed to dent. They dashed off like madmen to beat the plague, unable to follow its progress down to the final moment.

At the same time, though, spontaneous signs of optimism appeared. For one thing, there was a marked fall in prices. From a strictly economic point of view, this was impossible to explain. The same problems remained: the quarantine rules were still applied at the gates and food supplies had certainly not improved. So we were witnessing a strictly non-material phenomenon, as though the retreat of the plague had repercussions everywhere. At the same time the optimism spread to those who had previously lived in groups and who had been forced by the disease to separate. The two religious houses in the town began to re-form and communal life was able to resume. The same applied to the military who were once more gathered into barracks that had been left empty; they went back to their normal life as a garrison. These small events had great symbolic significance.

The population lived in this secret turmoil until January 25. In that week the figures fell so low that, after consulting the medical commission, the Prefecture announced that the epidemic could be considered under control. Admittedly, the communiqué added – in a spirit of caution that the population could not fail to applaud – that the gates of the town would remain closed for two more weeks and sanitary measures continued for a month. During this period, at the slightest indication that the plague might resume, 'the status quo should be maintained and the necessary measures continued for as long as necessary'. However, everyone was unanimous in considering these provisions a mere formality and, on the evening of January 25, the town was filled with joyful excitement. To contribute to the general mood of celebration the Prefect gave the order to put on the town lights as in pre-plague times. Beneath a cold, clear sky, the townspeople spilled out into the brightly lit streets in noisy, laughing groups.

Admittedly, in many houses the shutters remained closed and families spent this evening in silence while others were filling it with their noisy celebrations. However, for many of these mourners, there was also profound relief, either because the fear of seeing other relatives carried off was finally appeased, or else because the feeling of their own personal preservation was more acute. But the families which were to remain least touched by the general joy were, undoubtedly, those who at that very moment had a patient fighting against the plague in hospital and who, in the quarantine centres or in their own homes, were waiting for the pestilence to be truly done with them, as it had now finished with others. Certainly, these people had hopes, but they stored them up and kept them in reserve, refusing to draw on them before they really had the right to do so. And this waiting, this silent watch, somewhere between agony and joy, seemed to them more cruel still, in the midst of the general rejoicing.

But these exceptions did not at all detract from the satisfaction of the rest. Of course the plague was not yet over and it would prove as much. Yet in everyone's mind, weeks before the real events, trains were whistling as they left on endless tracks, and ships ploughed the shining seas. The following day, spirits would be calmed and doubts return. But for the moment the whole town shook, bursting out of those enclosed spaces, dark and motionless, in which it had put down its roots of stone and finally began to move with its load of survivors. That evening Tarrou and Rieux, Rambert and the rest, walked in the midst of the crowd, and they too felt they were treading on air. Long after leaving the boulevards Tarrou and Rieux could still hear the sounds of happiness following them, at the same time as in deserted side-streets they walked past windows with closed shutters. And precisely because of their tiredness, they could not separate this suffering, which continued behind the shutters, from the joy that filled the streets only a short distance away. The coming deliverance was two-faced, combining laughter and tears.

At a time when the noise grew louder and more joyful, Tarrou stopped. A shape was running lightly across the dark street. It was a cat, the first that had been seen since the spring. It stopped for a moment in the middle of the road, hesitated, licked its paw, quickly passed it across its right ear, then carried on its silent way and vanished into the night. Tarrou smiled. The little old man, too, would be happy.

However, at the moment when the plague seemed to be moving away to return to the unknown lair from which it had silently emerged, there was at least one person in the town who was thrown into a state of consternation by this departure, namely Cottard (if one is to believe Tarrou's notebooks).

As it happens, these notebooks become quite peculiar from the time when the figures start to fall. Perhaps because of tiredness, the writing becomes hard to read and the writer hops too often from one subject to another. Moreover, for the first time the notebooks abandon objectivity and make way for personal considerations. Consequently, in the midst of quite long passages about the case of Cottard, one finds a little report on the old man and the cats. According to Tarrou, the plague had done nothing to diminish his respect for this character, who interested him no less after the epidemic than he had done before, but unfortunately he could not continue to interest him, even though his, Tarrou's, goodwill was not in doubt. Because he had tried to see him again. A few days after the evening of January 25, he had stationed himself at the corner of the little street. The cats were there, as appointed, warming themselves in patches of sun. But at the usual time the shutters remained obstinately closed. Over the following days Tarrou never saw them open again. Oddly, he had decided that the old man was either annoyed or dead, and that if he was annoyed, then he thought he was in the right and that the plague had done him wrong; but if he was dead, then one must wonder – as one did about the old asthmatic – whether he was a saint. Tarrou did not think so, but considered that there was, in the case of the old man, a 'sign'. 'Perhaps', the notebooks observe, 'one can only conclude at some approximation to sainthood. In that case, we shall just have to be content with a form of modest and charitable Satanism.'

Still mixed in with observations about Cottard one also finds in the notebooks many remarks, often scattered, some of which concern Grand, who was now convalescent and had gone back to work as though nothing had happened, and others among them refer to Dr Rieux's mother. The few conversations that Tarrou had had with her while living under the same roof, the attitudes of the old woman, her smile and her views on the plague are scrupulously noted down. Most of all, Tarrou emphasized Mme Rieux's reticence, her habit of expressing everything in simple sentences, and the particular affection which she showed for one particular window overlooking the quiet street, behind which she would sit in the evening, quite upright, her hands at rest and her eyes alert until dusk entered the room and turned her into a black shadow in the grey light that gradually spread around her, dissolving the motionless silhouette. He noted too the lightness of her step as she went from one room to another, her goodness, of which she had never given any actual proof to Tarrou but which shone through everything she did or said, and finally on the fact that, according to him, she knew everything without thinking about it, and that with so much silence and shadow she could withstand any light, including that of the plague. Here Tarrou's writing gave peculiar signs of failing. The lines that followed were hard to read and, as though to give a new proof of this weakness, the last words were the first that were personal: 'My mother was like that, I liked the same self-effacement in her and she is the one I always wanted to be with. Eight years ago, I cannot say that she died. She simply faded away a little more than usual and, when I turned round, she was no longer there.'

But we must return to Cottard. Since the figures had started to fall he had made several visits to Rieux, on various pretexts. But when it came down to it what he wanted each time was to ask Rieux for his prediction about the development of the epidemic. 'Do you think it can stop just like that, suddenly, without warning?' He was sceptical on this point, or at least claimed to be. But the further questions that he asked seemed to indicate less solid convictions. In mid-January Rieux had answered quite optimistically and on every occasion these replies, instead of filling Cottard with joy, had produced reactions which varied from day to day, but which ranged from bad temper to depression.

Subsequently, the doctor came to say that despite the favourable signs in the statistics, it would be better not to claim victory yet.

'In other words,' Cottard said, 'we don't know anything. It might resume from one day to the next?'

'Yes, just as it is possible that the number of cures will increase.'

This uncertainty, which everyone found disturbing, had visibly been a relief to Cottard. In front of Tarrou he had engaged in conversations with the shopkeepers of his area, in which he tried to spread Rieux's opinion. Admittedly, he had no difficulty in doing so because, after the thrill of the first victories, doubt had returned to many minds and was to survive the excitement caused by the declaration from the Prefecture. Cottard was reassured by the sight of this anxiety. But, at other times, he was downcast. 'Yes,' he told Tarrou. 'They will open the gates eventually and, you'll see, they'll all drop me!'

Up to January 25, everyone noticed the instability of his character. For whole days on end, after having for so long tried to get on good terms with his acquaintances and neighbours, he openly quarrelled with them. At least in appearance he retired from the world and from one day to the next started to live like a wild animal. He no longer appeared in restaurants, at the theatre or in his favourite cafés. Yet he seemed unable to resume the sensible, obscure life that he had led before the epidemic. He lived completely shut up in his apartment and had his meals sent up from a nearby restaurant. Only in the evening did he make furtive sorties to buy what he needed, emerging from the shops to hurry down empty streets. If Tarrou should meet him on such occasions, he could only get monosyllables out of him. Then, without any period of transition, he became sociable again, talking volubly about the plague, asking everyone for their opinion and happily returning every evening into the crowd.

On the day of the declaration from the authorities, Cottard completely vanished from circulation. Two days later Tarrou met him wandering through the streets. Cottard asked him to walk as far as the outskirts of the town with him. Tarrou hesitated, feeling unusually tired after his day's work. But the other man insisted. He seemed very excited, gesticulating wildly and speaking quickly, in a loud voice. He asked his companion if he thought that the declaration from the Prefecture really marked an end to the plague. Of course, Tarrou considered that an administrative declaration was not in itself enough to halt a pestilence, but that one could now reasonably believe that the epidemic was going to end, unless something unforeseen happened.

'Yes,' said Cottard. 'Unless something unforeseen happens. And the unforeseen can always happen.'

Tarrou pointed out that in any case the Prefecture had to some extent foreseen the unforeseen, by providing for a period of two weeks before the gates were opened.

'They were right to do so,' said Cottard, still in a dark and agitated mood. 'Because with the way things are going, they might well have been wasting their breath.'

Tarrou considered this possible, but thought that it was still better to look forward to the gates being opened soon and life returning to normal.

'Perhaps,' Cottard said, 'Perhaps so. But what do you call a return to normal life?'

'New films in the cinema,' said Tarrou with a smile.

But Cottard was not smiling. He wanted to know if one could imagine that the plague might change nothing in the town and that everything would begin again as before, that is to say, as though nothing had happened. Tarrou thought that the plague would and would not change the town; that, of course, the greatest desire of our fellow-citizens was and would be to behave as though nothing had happened, and that, consequently, in a sense nothing would have changed; but that, in another sense, one cannot forget everything, with the best will in the world, so the plague would leave its mark, at least on people's hearts. The little man stated quite openly that he was not interested in the heart and indeed that the heart was the last thing he was worried about. What did interest him was to know if the whole administration would be transformed and if, for example, all departments would be operating as in the past. Tarrou had to admit that he had no idea. According to him, it must be assumed that all such departments, having been disrupted by the plague, would have trouble starting up again. One must assume, too, that a host of new problems would arise, making necessary at least a reorganization of the old administration.

'Ah!' said Cottard. 'That's possible. Everyone will have to start again.'

The two men had come close to Cottard's house. He was excited, forcing himself to be optimistic. He imagined the town starting to live again from zero and wiping out its past.

'Good,' said Tarrou. 'After all, things may work out for you too. In a sense, it's a new life starting.'

They were shaking hands at the door.

'You're right,' said Cottard, growing increasingly agitated. 'Start again from nothing, that would be good.'

But two men had sprung up from the shadows in the corridor. Tarrou hardly had time to hear his colleague ask what these customers could possibly want; and the customers, who looked like civil servants in Sunday best, were asking Cottard to confirm that he was Cottard, when, giving a sort of muffled cry, he swung round and was gone into the night before the two men or Tarrou had time to make a single movement. Tarrou asked the two men what they wanted. They assumed an air of polite reserve, saying only that it was a matter of information, then left, at a deliberate pace, in the direction that Cottard had taken.

Back home Tarrou described this scene, and immediately afterwards (the handwriting bears witness) noted that he was tired. He added that he still had a lot to do, but that this was not a reason for not keeping in readiness, and asked himself if he was, in fact, ready. Finally – or this is where Tarrou's notebooks end – he replied that there was always an hour of the day or night when a man was a coward and that he was afraid of nothing but that moment.

The day after next, a few days before the opening of the gates, Dr Rieux was coming home at lunchtime, wondering if he would find the telegram that he was expecting. Although his days were as exhausting as at the height of the plague, the expectation of being free at last had dispersed all his own tiredness. Now he had hope and he was pleased that he did. One cannot constantly tighten ones will and brace oneself, and it is a joy at last to release this bundle of forces plaited together for the struggle and to let them flow free. If the expected telegram was also favourable, then Rieux could start again. It felt to him as though everyone was starting again.

He went past the concierge's lodge. The new concierge, his face pressed to the little window, smiled at him. As he went up the stairs, Rieux saw his own face, pale with exhaustion and privation.

Yes, he would start again when the abstraction was over and with a little luck . . . But he was opening his door at the very moment when his mother came to meet him saying that M. Tarrou was unwell. He had got up that morning, but had been unable to go out so had returned to his bed. Mme Rieux was worried.

'Perhaps it's nothing serious,' her son said.

Tarrou was lying flat out, his heavy head making a dent in the bolster, his large chest outlined beneath the thick blankets. He had a temperature and a headache. He told Rieux that these were vague symptoms that could easily be those of the plague.

'No, nothing definite yet,' said Rieux after examining him.

But Tarrou had a raging thirst. In the corridor the doctor told his mother that it might be the start of the plague.

'Oh, no!' she said. 'It can't be, not now!'

And immediately afterwards:

'Let's keep him here, Bernard.'

Rieux thought about it.

'I don't have the right,' he said. 'But the gates are going to reopen. I think that this would be the first right that I would claim for myself, if you were not here.'

'Bernard,' she said. 'Keep us both. You know that I have just been revaccinated.'

The doctor said that the same was true of Tarrou, but that, perhaps because he was tired, he must have forgotten the last injection of serum and forgotten to take some precautions.

Rieux was already on his way to his consulting-room. When he got back to the bedroom Tarrou saw that he was carrying the huge ampoules of the serum.

'So that's it,' he said.

'No, this is a precaution.'

In reply Tarrou merely held out his arm and submitted to the interminable injection that he had himself given to others.

'We'll see this evening,' said Rieux, looking directly at Tarrou.

'What about isolating me, Rieux?'

'It is not at all certain that you have the plague.'

Tarrou made an effort to smile.

'This is the first time that I have seen you injecting a serum without ordering isolation at the same time.'

Rieux turned away:

'My mother and I will look after you. You will be better off here.'

Tarrou said nothing and the doctor, who was putting away the ampoules, waited for him to speak before turning round. In the end, he went over to the bed. The sick man was looking at him. His face was tired, but his grey eyes were calm. Rieux smiled.

'Sleep if you can. I'll be back shortly.'

When he got to the door he heard Tarrou's voice calling him. He turned round. But Tarrou seemed to be struggling against putting what he had to say into words:

'Rieux,' he finally managed to get out. 'You must tell me everything, I need that.'

'I promise.'

The other man twisted his face into a smile.

'Thank you. I don't want to die and I shall fight. But if the struggle is lost, I want to make a good end.'

Rieux bent down and squeezed his shoulder.

'No,' he said. 'To become a saint, you have to live. Fight it.'

During the day the cold, which had started sharp, slackened a little and gave way in the afternoon to violent downpours of rain and hail. At dusk the sky cleared a little and the cold became more penetrating. Rieux went back home in the evening. Without taking off his coat he went to his friend's room. His mother was knitting. Tarrou seemed not to have moved, but his lips, whitened by the fever, spoke of the struggle that he was having to endure.

'Well?' asked the doctor.

Tarrou raised his thick shoulders a little out of the bed.

'Well,' he said. 'I'm losing.'

The doctor leant over him. The lymph nodes were knotted under the burning skin and his chest seemed to be rumbling with all the noises of an underground forge. Unusually, Tarrou was presenting the two sets of symptoms. Rieux said, as he got up, that the serum had not yet had time to take full effect. A surge of fever in his throat drowned the few words that Tarrou tried to utter in reply.

After dinner Rieux and his mother came to sit with the patient. The night started for him with a struggle and Rieux knew that this fierce combat against the angel of the plague would last until dawn. Tarrou's wide chest and broad shoulders were not his best defence; that was the blood that Rieux had made flow just now with his needle and, in that blood, something deeper than the soul, which no science could reveal. All he could do was to watch his friend struggle. Several months of repeated failures had taught him to judge the effectiveness of the remedies he would apply, the tonics he would inject and the abscesses that he would lance. In reality, his only task was to give an opportunity to that good luck which only too often does not appear unless one provokes it. And luck was what they needed, because Rieux was confronted with an aspect of the plague that disconcerted him. Once more it was devising ways of foiling the strategies adopted against it, appearing where it was least expected and disappearing just where it seemed already well settled. Once more, it was making an effort to astound.

Tarrou was struggling, motionless. Not once in the course of the night did he become agitated by the assaults of the disease, fighting only with all his solidity and his silence. But not once, either, did he speak, thus admitting in his own way that he could not afford to lose concentration. Rieux followed the phases of the struggle only in the eyes of his friend, which were by turns open or shut, the eyelids either more tight against the globe of the eye or, on the contrary, relaxed, so that his gaze was fixed on an object or brought back to the doctor and his mother.

Every time the doctor met this look, Tarrou smiled with considerable effort.

At one time they heard hurried footsteps in the street. They seemed to be fleeing in front of a distant rumbling that gradually approached and eventually filled the street with its sound of running water: the rain had started again, soon mixed with hail that clattered on the pavements. Great awnings flapped in front of the windows. In the darkness of the room Rieux, momentarily distracted by the rain, looked back at Tarrou, who was lit by a bedside lamp. His mother was knitting, raising her head from time to time to look closely at the sick man. Now the doctor had done all there was to do. After the rain the silence thickened in the room, which was only full of the noiseless tumult of an invisible war. Agitated by insomnia, the doctor thought he could hear, beyond the silence, the soft, regular whistle that had accompanied him throughout the epidemic. He nodded to his mother to go to bed. She shook her head and her eyes lit up, then she meticulously examined a dubious stitch at the end of her needles. Rieux got up to get the patient some water and went back to his place.

Some passers-by, taking advantage of the lull in the storm, were walking quickly along the pavement. Their footsteps grew fainter and faded into the distance. For the first time the doctor realized that this night, full of late strollers and without ambulance sirens, was like those of former times. It was a night liberated from the plague. And it seemed that the sickness, driven out by cold, light and crowds, had escaped from the dark depths of the town and taken refuge in this warm room to make its final assault on the motionless form of Tarrou. The pestilence was no longer threshing the sky above the town with its flail, but whistling softly in the heavy air of the room. This is what Rieux had been hearing for hours, and he needed it to stop here, so that here too the plague would admit defeat.

Shortly before dawn Rieux leant across to his mother:

'You should get some sleep so that you can take over from me at eight o'clock. Take your drops before you go to bed.'

Mme Rieux got up, put aside her knitting and went over to the bed. For some time now Tarrou's eyes had been closed. The sweat had left the hair in curls on his hard forehead. Mme Rieux sighed and the sick man opened his eyes. He saw the kind face leaning towards him and, beneath the waves of fever, the dogged smile appeared once more. But the eyes closed again immediately. When he was alone Rieux took over the chair that his mother had just left. The street was soundless and the silence was now complete. The cold of morning had started to make itself felt in the room.

The doctor dozed off, but the first wagon of dawn roused him. He shuddered and, looking at Tarrou, realized that there had been a pause and that the sick man was also sleeping. The wood and iron wheels of the horse-drawn wagon could be heard fading into the distance. Outside the window, it was still dark. When the doctor went over to the bed Tarrou was looking at him with expressionless eyes, as though still on the side of sleep.

'You did sleep, didn't you?' Rieux asked.

'Yes.'

'Are you breathing more easily?'

'A little. Does that mean something?'

Rieux paused, then said:

'No, Tarrou, it doesn't mean anything. You know about the morning remission as well as I do.'

Tarrou nodded in approval.

'Thank you,' he said. 'Always answer me precisely.'

Rieux had sat down beside the bed. He felt the patient's legs next to him, as long and hard as the limbs of an effigy on a tombstone. Tarrou was breathing more heavily.

'The fever is going to come back, isn't it, Rieux?' he said, breathlessly.

'Yes, but by midday we should know how things stand.'

Tarrou closed his eyes and seemed to be gathering his strength. There was a look of exhaustion on his face. He was waiting for the fever to rise from where it was already stirring, somewhere deep inside him. When he reopened his eyes, his look was glazed and did not clear until he saw Rieux leaning over the bed.

'Drink,' the doctor said.

The other man drank and let his head fall back.

'It takes a long time,' he said.

Rieux took his arm, but Tarrou, looking the other way, did not react. Suddenly the fever visibly swept up through his body to his forehead as though it had broken some inner dyke. When Tarrou again turned towards the doctor, Rieux's drawn features had a look of encouragement. The smile that Tarrou again tried to form could not get beyond his clenched jaws and lips sealed with whitish foam. But in the stiffened face the eyes still shone with bright courage.

At seven o'clock Mme Rieux came back into the room. The doctor went into his consulting-room to ring the hospital and arrange a replacement. He also decided to postpone his consultations and stretched out on the couch, but got up again almost immediately and went back into the bedroom. Tarrou's head was turned towards Mme Rieux. He was looking at the little figure slumped beside him on a chair, her hands folded on her lap. He was staring at her with such intensity that Mme Rieux put a finger to her lips and got up to turn off the bedside lamp. But the daylight was rapidly increasing behind the curtains and shortly afterwards, when the sick man's face emerged from the darkness, Mme Rieux saw that he was still looking at her. She leant towards him, smoothed his pillow and, getting up, put her hand for a moment on his damp, twisted hair. It was then that she heard a dull voice, which appeared to be coming from a long way off, thank her and say that now everything was all right. When she sat down again Tarrou had closed his eyes and his exhausted face seemed, in spite of the sealed mouth, to be smiling again.

At noon the fever reached it height. A sort of gut cough shook the patient's body and he was spitting blood. The lymph nodes had stopped swelling: they were still there, hard as iron screwed into the joints, and Rieux decided it was impossible to lance them. In the intervals between the fever and the coughing, Tarrou occasionally looked at his friends. But after a short while, his eyes opened less and less frequently and the light that would then shine from his ravaged features was paler every time. The storm that was shaking his body with convulsive shudders was lit with increasingly infrequent flashes, and Tarrou was slowly drifting in the midst of this tempest. Now Rieux had in front of him just a still mask from which the smile had faded. This human form, which had been so close to him, was now pierced with spears, burnt up with a superhuman fire and twisted by all the malevolent winds of the skies; it was sinking before his eyes into the waters of the plague and he could do nothing to prevent its wreck. He had to stay on the shore, his hands empty and his heart wrenched, with no means, once more, to prevent this disaster. In the end it was tears of frustration which stopped Rieux from seeing Tarrou quickly turn towards the wall and expire with a hollow moan as though, somewhere in him, some essential cord had snapped.

The night that followed was not one of struggle but of silence. In this room, Rieux, now dressed, cut off from the world and standing over this dead body, felt the surprising calm that many nights ago he had felt on the rooftops above the plague, after the attack on the gates. Already at that time he had been thinking about the silence that rose from the beds where he had left men to die. It was always the same pause, the same solemn interval, the same lull that followed a battle, it was the silence of defeat. But in the case of the silence that enfolded his friend, it was so compact, and harmonized so closely with the silence of the streets and the town liberated from the plague, that Rieux really felt that this time it was the definitive defeat, the one that ends wars and makes of peace itself an irremediable suffering. The doctor did not know whether Tarrou in the end had found peace, but at this moment at least, he thought he knew that there would no longer be any peace possible for himself, any more than there is an armistice for the mother torn from her son or for the man who buries his friend.

Outside it was the same cold night, with frozen stars in a clear, icy sky. In the half-darkness of the room one could feel the cold weighing on the windowpanes, the great, pale breath of a polar night. Near the bed Mme Rieux was sitting in her usual attitude, her right side lit by the bedside lamp. In the centre of the room, far from the light, Rieux was waiting in his chair. He remembered his wife, but pushed the thought away each time it came.

Early in the night, the heels of passers-by had sounded clear in the chill darkness.

'Have you taken care of everything?' asked Mme Rieux.

'Yes, I phoned.'

Then they resumed their silent watch. From time to time Mme Rieux looked at her son. When he intercepted one of these looks he smiled at her. The familiar sounds of the night continued in the street. Although they were not yet authorized to do so, a lot of cars were driving around again. They quickly sucked at the roadway, disappeared, then later reappeared. There were voices, shouts, returning silence, a horse's hoofs, two trams screeching on a bend, vague noises, then once more the breathing of the night.

'Bernard?'

'Yes?'

'You're not tired?'

'No.'

He knew what his mother was thinking and that she loved him at that moment. But he also knew that it is not much to love a person – or, at least, that a love is never strong enough to find its own expression. So his mother and he would always love one another in silence. And she would die in her turn – or he would – without either of them at any time in their lives being able to go further in confessing their affection. In the same way he had lived beside Tarrou, who had died, that afternoon, without them being able to have the time really to experience their friendship. Tarrou had lost the game, as he said. But what had he, Rieux, won? All he had gained was to have known the plague and to remember it, to have known friendship and to remember it, to have known affection and to have one day to remember it. All that a man could win in the game of plague and life was knowledge and memory. Perhaps that was what Tarrou called winning the game!

Once again a car passed and Mme Rieux shuffled a little on her chair. Rieux smiled at her. She told him that she was not tired, and immediately afterwards:

'You must go and rest over there, in the mountains.'

'Of course, mother.'

Yes, he would rest over there. Why not? That too would be a pretext for memory. But if that is what it meant to win the game, how hard it must be to live only with what one knows and what one remembers, and deprived of what one hopes. This was no doubt how Tarrou had lived and he was aware of the sterility of a life without illusions. There is no peace without hope and Tarrou, who denied men the right to condemn anyone, yet who knew that no one can prevent himself from condemning and that even victims can sometimes be executioners – Tarrou had lived in a state of turmoil and contradiction, and he had never known hope. Is this why he longed for sainthood and sought peace in the service of men? In truth, Rieux did not know and it was hardly important. The only images of Tarrou that he would keep were those of a man who took the wheel of his car in both hands to drive and those of his thick body, now lying motionless. A warmth of life and an image of death: that was knowledge.

This no doubt is why Dr Rieux felt calm when the next morning he received news of the death of his wife. He was in his consulting-room. His mother had arrived almost at a run to bring him a telegram, then went back to give a tip to the messenger boy. When she returned her son was holding the telegram open in his hand. She looked at him, but he persisted in staring out of the window at a magnificent new day rising over the port.

'Bernard,' said Mme Rieux.

The doctor looked at her absent-mindedly.

'The telegram?' she asked.

'That's right,' he acknowledged. 'A week ago.'

Mme Rieux turned towards the window. The doctor said nothing. Then he told his mother not to cry, that he had been expecting it, but that it was hard. Yet even as he said this he knew that there was no surprise in his suffering. For months, for the last two days, it was a continuation of the same pain.

The gates of the town finally opened, at dawn one fine February morning, and the event was hailed by the people, the newspapers, the radio, and with communiqués from the Prefecture. It remains for the narrator to become the chronicler of the hours of happiness that followed this opening of the gates, even though he was among those who were not free to join in wholeheartedly.

Great celebrations were organized for the daytime and for the night. At the same time the trains began to let off steam in the stations, while ships from distant seas were already heading for our port, marking in their own way that this day was that of the great reunion for those who had been separated.

One may easily imagine what would become of the feeling of separation that had inhabited so many of our townspeople. The trains that came into the town during the day were no less laden than those which left. Everyone had reserved a place for that day during the two weeks of suspension, fearing that the decision of the authorities might be annulled at the last moment. Some of the travellers coming into the town were not entirely relieved of their misgivings, because although they knew broadly the fate of those who were closest to them, they knew nothing of the rest and of the town itself, which they imagined would look quite fearsome. But this was only true of those who had not been burning with passion throughout this period of time.

The passionate were taken up with their *idée fixe*. Only one thing had changed for them: this time which, during the months of their exile, they would have liked to push forward so that it would go faster and which they were still determined to speed up, even when they were already in sight of the town; then, as soon as the train began to brake, before stopping, they wanted on the contrary to slow time down and hold it in suspension. The feeling, at once vague and acute in them, of all those months of life lost to their love, made them in some confused way demand a sort of compensation through which the time of joy would have passed at only half the speed of the time of waiting. And those who were expecting them, in a room or on the platform (like Rambert, whose wife, he had been informed weeks in advance, had done whatever she could to get here), were in the same state of impatience and turmoil. Because Rambert was waiting in fear and trembling to confront this love or affection that the months of plague had reduced to an abstraction and to confront it with the flesh-and-blood being who had been his support through that time.

He would like to have again become the man who at the start of the epidemic wanted to leap in a single bound out of the town and rush to meet the one he loved. But he knew that that was not possible. He had changed, the plague had introduced into him a detachment that he tried with all his strength to deny, but which none the less endured in him like a dull pain. In a sense he had the feeling that it had ended too suddenly; he did not himself have such composure. Happiness arrived at full speed, events overtook expectations. Rambert realized that everything would be given back to him in a single moment and that joy is a searing emotion that cannot be savoured.

Moreover, everyone was – more or less consciously – like him and we must speak of everyone. On this station platform where they were resuming their personal life they still felt a sense of community as they exchanged looks and smiles between themselves. But, as soon as they saw the train smoke, their feeling of exile was suddenly extinguished beneath a downpour of confused and bewildering joy. When the train stopped, interminable separations, which had started on this same station platform, ended here in a second, in the moment when arms closed with exultant greed around bodies whose living form they had forgotten. Rambert, for his part, did not have the time to look at the shape running towards him until it was already crashing against his chest. And he held her in both arms, pressing her head to him, seeing only the familiar hair, and letting his tears flow without knowing if they came from his present happiness or from a pain too long repressed, but sure at least that they would prevent him from verifying if this face buried into the hollow of his shoulder was the one about which he had so long dreamed or rather that of a stranger. Later he would find out if his suspicion was true. For the time being, he wanted to do what all those around him were doing, apparently believing that the plague can come and go without the hearts of men being changed.

Pressed one against the other they all returned home, blind to the rest of the world, apparently triumphing over the plague, forgetful of misery and of those who had also arrived by the same train but had found no one and were preparing in their homes to have confirmation of fears already born in their hearts out of a long silence. For them, the ones who now had only their brand new sorrow for companion, and for others who were at that moment contemplating the memory of a lost loved one, things were very different and the feeling of separation had reached its peak. For such people, mothers, husbands, wives and lovers, who had lost all happiness with the being who was now buried in some anonymous pit or had dissolved into a pile of ashes, the plague was still there.

But who thought of these lonely people? At noon the sun triumphed over the cold winds that had been struggling in the air since morning, and bathed the town in uninterrupted waves of tranquil light. The daylight hung in the air and from the forts and hills cannon sounded ceaselessly beneath a still sky. The whole town rushed outside to celebrate this crowded minute when the time of suffering had ended and the time of forgetting had not yet begun.

They were dancing on every square. Traffic had increased considerably from one day to the next and the cars, of which there were now many more, had difficulty driving along the packed streets. The bells of the town pealed out continually throughout the afternoon, filling the blue and gold sky with their vibrations. In the churches, they were holding services of thanksgiving. But at the same time places of pleasure were full to bursting and the cafés were handing out their last supplies of spirits, with no thought to the future. In front of the counters a crowd of equally excited people hustled and bustled, among them several couples hugging and kissing, not bothered about appearances. Everyone was shouting or laughing. That day they expended the stock of life that they had piled up during those months when they had all put their souls on the back-burner; this was like the day of their survival. The next day life proper would resume, with its reticence and restrictions. For the time being, people of very different origins were fraternizing, elbow to elbow. The equality that the presence of death had not achieved was realized by the joy of deliverance, at least for a few hours.

But this commonplace exuberance was not the whole story. Those who filled the streets at the end of the afternoon, beside Rambert, often concealed more delicate joys behind an attitude of calm. Many couples and families seemed like nothing more than peaceful strollers. In reality most were making quiet pilgrimages to the places where they had suffered, which meant showing the new arrivals the obvious or hidden signs of the plague, the vestiges of its history. In a few cases, they were content to play guide – the person who has seen lots of things and lived with the plague – and they spoke of danger without mentioning fear. These were harmless pleasures. But in other cases, the itineraries were more highly charged, when a lover, giving way to the sweet pain of memory, could say to his loved one: 'Here, at such a time, I wanted you and you were not there.' You could recognize these passionate tourists: they formed little isles of whispers and confidences in the midst of the bustling crowd around them. And it was they who, better than the bands on the street corners, announced the true deliverance, because these enchanted couples, locked together, sparing of words, proclaimed in the midst of the throng, with all the triumph and injustice of happiness, that the plague was over and that terror had had its day. Against all evidence they calmly denied that we had ever known this senseless world in which the murder of a man was a happening as banal as the death of a fly, the well-defined savagery, the calculated delirium and the imprisonment that brought with it a terrible freedom from everything that was not the immediate present, the stench of death that stunned all those whom it did not kill. In short, they denied that we had been that benumbed people of whom some, every day, stuffed into the mouth of an oven, had evaporated in oily smoke, while the rest, weighed down by the chains of impotence and fear, had waited their turn.

This at least is what struck Dr Rieux who, making his way to the outskirts of town, was journeying alone in the midst of ringing bells, firing cannon, music and deafening shouts. His work went on: there is no holiday for the sick. In the lovely soft light that bathed Oran, you could smell the old smells of grilled meat and aniseed-flavoured aperitifs. Around him laughing faces were raised towards the sky. Men and women clung to one another, their faces lit up with excitement and a cry of desire. Yes, the plague was over and so was the terror; these arms enlaced in one another said that it had been exile and separation, in the deepest sense of the word.

For the first time Rieux could give a name to the similarity that for months he had seen on the faces of people passing in the street. Now it was enough to look around him. Now that the plague was over, with its misery and privations, all these men had eventually taken on the clothing of the role that they had been playing for a long time, that of émigrés whose faces then, and clothes now, spoke of absence and distant homelands. From the moment when the plague closed the gates of the town, they had started to live in a state of separation and been cut off from that human warmth that leads us to forget everything. To a different extent, in every corner of the town, these men and women had aspired to a reunion that was not of the same kind for each of them but which, for all of them, was equally impossible. Most had appealed with all their strength for an absent one, the warmth of a body, for tenderness or familiarity. A few, often without knowing it, had suffered from being placed beyond the friendship of men and not being able to reach them by the usual means: letters, trains, boats. Others, who were rarer still, perhaps like Tarrou, had wanted to be joined with something that they could not define, but which appeared to them the only desirable good. Failing any other name, they sometimes called it peace.

Rieux was still walking. As he went on the crowd grew around him, the din increased and it seemed to him that the outer districts he was trying to reach were moving further away. Bit by bit he melted into this great bellowing body, understanding its cry better and better because at least in some respects, it was his own. Yes, they had all suffered together, in their flesh and in their souls, from a hard separation, an irremediable exile and a never satisfied thirst. Among these heaps of dead bodies, the ambulance sirens, the warnings of what is known as fate, the obstinate stamping of fear and the terrible rebellion in their hearts, a great voice had continued to call and tell these horrified people that they had to return to their true home. And for all of them, this true home was beyond the walls of the suffocating town. It was in the sweet-smelling brushwood on the hills, in the sea, in free countries and in the heavy burden of love. And it was towards this, towards happiness, that they longed to go back, turning away in disgust from everything else.

As for whatever meaning there was in this exile and this desire for reunion, Rieux had no idea. Still walking, with people calling to him and pushing him from all sides, he gradually made his way into less crowded streets and thought that it did not matter whether these things have a meaning or not, but that one must simply see what response there was to the hopes of mankind.

Now he knew what response there was, and he perceived it better in the first streets of the outer districts, which were almost empty. Those who had confined themselves to the little that they were had merely wanted to return to the house of their loved ones and were sometimes rewarded. Of course there were those among them who continued to walk around the town alone, deprived of the one they expected. Happy, too, were those who had not been twice separated, like some people who before the epidemic had not been able to build their love in the first instance but had for years pursued the hard understanding that eventually binds together hostile lovers. Those were the ones who, like Rieux himself, had been rash enough to count on time; now they were separated for ever. But there were still others, like Rambert, whom the doctor had left that very morning with the words: 'Courage, now is the time to prove you're right'; and these had unhesitatingly reunited with the absent love whom they thought was lost. At least for a period they would be happy. They knew now that if there is one thing that one can always desire and sometimes obtain, it is human affection.

For all the people who, on the contrary, had looked beyond man to something that they could not even imagine, there had been no reply. Tarrou had appeared to reach the almost unattainable peace about which he spoke, but he found it only in death, at a moment when it could be of no use to him. By contrast, there were others whom Rieux saw on the doorsteps of their houses, in the fading light, clasped to one another with all their strength and looking at one another with enchantment: if they had found that they wanted, it was because they had asked for the only thing that depended on them. And Rieux, as he turned into Grand

and Cottard's street, thought that it was right that, from time to time, joy should reward those whose desires are circumscribed by mankind and its meagre and terrible love.

This chronicle is drawing to a close. It is time for Dr Bernard Rieux to admit that he is its author. But before describing the last events, he would like at least to justify his role and to point out that he has tried to adopt the tone of an objective witness. Throughout the period of the plague his profession put him in a position to see most of his fellow-citizens and to observe their feelings. Hence he was well placed to report what he saw and heard. But he wished to do so within the necessary constraints. In general, he has been careful not to report more than he was able to observe, not to ascribe to his companions in the plague thoughts that were not necessarily theirs and to use only the documents which chance or misfortune put in his way.

Being called upon to bear witness in the event of a sort of crime, he maintained a certain reserve, as a well-intentioned witness should. But at the same time, as every decent person should, he deliberately took the side of the victim and wanted to meet others, his fellow-citizens, on the basis of the only certainties they all have in common, which are love, suffering and exile. Thus there is not one of the anxieties of his fellows that he did not share and no situation that was not also his own.

To bear faithful witness he had to report chiefly acts, documents and hearsay. What he personally had to say, his own waiting, his trials, these he had to pass over in silence. If he has used them, it is only to understand or to make others understand his fellow-citizens and to give a form, as precise as possible, to what most of the time, they were vaguely feeling. To tell the truth, he found this effort of reasoning quite undemanding. When he felt tempted to add some confidence of his own to the thousands of voices of the victims, he was prevented by the thought that there was not one of those sufferings that was not at the same time that of others, and that in a world where pain is so often solitary, this was an advantage. Incontestably, he had to speak for all.

But there is one of our fellow men at least for whom Dr Rieux could not speak. This is the one about whom Tarrou said one day to Rieux: 'His only true crime is to have given approval in his heart to something that kills men, women and children. I understand the rest, but this is something for which I have to forgive him.' It is right that this chronicle should end with the one whose heart was ignorant, which is to say alone.

When he had left the large boulevards, noisy with celebrations, and just as he was turning into Grand and Cottard's street, Dr Rieux was halted by a line of gendarmes. This he had not expected. The distant sounds of merriment made this particular district seem silent and he imagined it as deserted as it was tranquil. He took out his card.

'Impossible, doctor,' said the gendarme. 'There's a madman firing on the crowd. But stay here, you might be needed.'

At that moment Rieux saw Grand coming towards him. Grand knew nothing either. He had been prevented from going past and had learned that the shots were coming from his house. In fact, in the distance they could see the front of the house gilded by the last, cool rays of the sun. Around it was a wide open space which extended to the pavement opposite. In the middle of the road one could clearly see a hat and a scrap of dirty material. A long way off, on the other side of the street, Rieux and Grand could see a line of gendarmes, like the one that had prevented them from going on and behind which a few inhabitants of the area were quickly passing backwards and forwards. If they looked closely they could also see gendarmes holding revolvers, concealed in the doorways of buildings across the street from the house. All its shutters were closed, but on the second floor one seemed to be half hanging off. The silence in the street was total. The only sounds one could hear were intermittent bursts of music from the centre of town.

All at once, from one of the buildings across from the house, two revolver shots rang out and splinters flew from the broken shutter. Then there was silence again. At this distance, after the uproar of the day, the whole thing seemed to Rieux slightly unreal.

'That's Cottard's window,' said Grand, suddenly very upset. 'But Cottard has disappeared.'

'Why are they firing?' Rieux asked the gendarme.

'They're keeping him distracted. We're waiting for a van with the equipment we need because he fires at anyone who tries to go in through the door of the building. A gendarme has been hit.'

'Why did he fire?'

'No one knows. People were celebrating in the street. When the first shot went off, they didn't know what it was. At the second, there were screams, someone was wounded and everyone took to their heels. He's a maniac, that's all.'

The minutes seemed to drag in the renewed silence. Suddenly on the far side of the street they saw a dog run out, the first Rieux had seen for ages, a dirty spaniel, which must have been hidden by its owners up to now, trotting along by the wall. When it reached the door it paused, sat down on its hindquarters and turned round to start eating its fleas. The gendarmes called to it, giving a succession of whistles. It looked up, then decided to cross the road slowly to have a sniff at the hat. At that moment a shot rang out from the second floor and the dog flipped over like a pancake, violently waving its paws, then finally turning over on its side, shaken by long shudders. In reply, five or six bursts of fire from the doorways opposite caused further damage to the shutter. Then silence. The sun had moved a little and the shadows were starting to reach Cottard's window. There was a soft sound of brakes from the street behind the doctor.

'Here they are,' said the gendarme.

Gendarmes appeared behind them, carrying ropes, a ladder and two oblong parcels wrapped in oilcloth. They started down a street that took them round the back of the block of houses opposite the building in which Grand lived. A moment later, there was a kind of disturbance in the doorways of these houses, which one felt rather than saw. Then they waited. The dog was not moving, but was now lying in a dark pool.

Suddenly, from the windows of the houses occupied by the gendarmes, there was a burst of sub-machine-gun fire. While the firing was going on the shutter, which was still the target, literally fell to pieces and revealed a black surface on which from where they were standing Rieux and Grand could make nothing out. When the firing stopped, another sub-machine-gun opened up from a different angle, in a house further away. The shots were surely going into the window, since one round struck off a splinter of brick. At the same moment three gendarmes ran across the road and disappeared into the front door. Almost immediately three others followed them and the automatic fire stopped. Another wait. Two distant explosions rang out inside the building. Then there was a growing noise and out of the house, carried rather than dragged along, they saw a little man in shirtsleeves, giving out a continuous wail. As though miraculously, all the closed shutters in the street opened and the windows filled with curious onlookers, while a stream of people came out of the houses and crowded behind the barriers. For a moment they could see the little man in the middle of the road, his feet at last touching the ground and his arms pinned back by the gendarmes. He was shouting. A gendarme went up to him and hit him twice, with his fist, as hard as he could, deliberately and with a kind of diligent zeal.

'It's Cottard,' Grand stammered. 'He's gone mad.'

Cottard had fallen over. They saw the gendarme launch a flying kick at the mass lying on the ground. Then a confused, agitated group began to move and make its way towards the doctor and his old friend.

'Keep moving!' said the gendarme.

Rieux looked away as the group passed beside him.

Grand and the doctor left as night was falling. As though the event had shaken the neighbourhood out of its torpor, side streets began to fill once more with the hum of celebrating crowds. As they reached the house, Grand said goodbye to the doctor. He was going to work. But just before starting up the stairs he added that he had written to Jeanne and that he was happy now. He had started his sentence again: 'I've cut out all the adjectives,' he said.

With a sly smile he raised his hat in a ceremonious gesture. But Rieux was thinking about Cottard, and the dull sound of fists thudding into his face stayed with him as he walked towards the old asthmatic's house. Perhaps it was harder to think of a guilty man than a dead one.

When Rieux reached his old patient, night had already swallowed the whole sky. From the bedroom you could hear the distant sounds of freedom and the old man went on sorting his chick-peas with equanimity.

'They're right to enjoy themselves,' he said. 'It takes all sorts. And what's happened to your colleague, doctor?'

They could hear explosions, but harmless ones, children letting off firecrackers.

'He's dead,' said the doctor, listening to the grumbling chest.

'Oh!' said the old man, somewhat lost for words.

'He died of the plague,' Rieux added.

'Yes,' the old man agreed after a pause. 'The best go. That's life. But he was a man who knew what he wanted.'

'What makes you say that?' asked the doctor, putting away his stethoscope.

'No reason. He didn't talk just for the sake of it. I liked him. But that's how it is. Other people say: "It's the plague, we've had the plague." Next thing, they'll be wanting a medal. But what does it mean, the plague? It's life, that's all.'

'Make sure you have your inhalations regularly.'

'Oh, don't worry! I've got a long time yet, I'll see the lot of them out yet. I know how to live, I do.'

Yells of joy replied to him from afar. The doctor paused in the middle of the room.

'Would you mind if I went out on the roof terrace?'

'Not at all. Do you want to see them from up there? You're welcome. But they're always the same.'

Rieux went towards the stairs.

'Tell me, doctor, is it true that they're going to put up a monument to the victims of the plague?'

'So the papers say. A pillar or a plaque.'

'I knew it! And there'll be speeches.'

The old man gave a strangled laugh.

'I can hear them already: "Our dead . . ." Then they'll go and have dinner.'

Rieux was already going up the stairs. The great cold sky was shining above the houses and, near the hills, the stars were hard as flint. This night was not so different from the one when Tarrou and he had come out on this same roof to forget the plague. The sea was louder than it had been then, at the foot of the cliffs. The air was still and light, freed from the tainted breath brought by the warm winds of autumn. The noise from the town, however, was still beating with a sound like waves around the bottom of the terraces. But this night was that of deliverance, not of rebellion. Far off, a dark reddening marked the boulevards and well-lit squares. In the now free night, desire came unbridled and this was the rumbling that Rieux could hear.

Out of the dark port rose the first rockets of the official celebrations. The town greeted them with a long, muffled exclamation. Cottard, Tarrou, the men and the woman whom Rieux had loved and lost, all, dead or guilty, were forgotten. The old man had been right, men were always the same. But this was their strength and their innocence, and it was at this point, above all suffering, that Rieux felt he was one of them. In the midst of the cries that increased in strength and duration, echoing a long way right to the foot of the building, while the many-coloured wreaths and showers of fireworks rose in ever greater numbers into the sky, Dr Rieux decided to write the account that ends here, so as not to be one of those who keep silent, to bear witness on behalf of the victims, to leave at least a memory of the violence and injustice that was done to them, and to say simply what it is that one learns in the midst of such tribulations, namely that there is more in men to admire than to despise.

However, he knew that this chronicle could not be a story of definitive victory. It could only be the record of what had to be done and what, no doubt, would have to be done again, against this terror and its indefatigable weapon, despite their own personal hardships, by all men who, while not being saints but refusing to give way to the pestilence, do their best to be doctors.

Indeed, as he listened to the cries of joy that rose above the town, Rieux recalled that this joy was always under threat. He knew that this happy crowd was unaware of something that one can read in books, which is that the plague bacillus never dies or vanishes entirely, that it can remain dormant for dozens of years in furniture or clothing, that it waits patiently in bedrooms, cellars, trunks, handkerchiefs and old papers, and that perhaps the day will come when, for the instruction or misfortune of mankind, the plague will rouse its rats and send them to die in some well-contented city.